The Swan Maiden

The Swan Maiden

Heather Tomlinson

Henry Holt and Company
New York

Writing is a solitary endeavor, but making a book takes all kinds of people. Stellar critique partners Heide Boyden, Michael Fickes, Nicole Schreiber, Greg Trine, and Gina Young make all my first drafts better. Robbie Mayes and many kind, gifted, and generous SCBWI members gave encouragement at critical points. Reka Simonsen shaped *The Swan Maiden* into a coherent story; the Holt team launched it into the world. Thanks to Erin Murphy for sage counsel and to the Sunbelt gang for adventures in the book biz. Last but never least, *merci beaucoup* to family and friends for their loving support, and for sharing my excitement when "the call" came.

Henry Holt and Company, LLC
Publishers since 1866
175 Fifth Avenue
New York, New York 10010
www.HenryHoltKids.com

Henry Holt® is a registered trademark of Henry Holt and Company, LLC.
Text copyright © 2007 by Heather Tomlinson
Illustrations copyright © 2007 Julia Breckenreid
All rights reserved.
Distributed in Canada by H. B. Fenn and Company Ltd.

Library of Congress Cataloging-in-Publication Data
Tomlinson, Heather.
The swan maiden / Heather Tomlinson.—1st ed.
p.   cm.
Summary: Raised as a chastelaine-in-training unlike her sisters who are
learning the arts of sorcery, Doucette discovers when she is sixteen years old
that she too has magic in her blood, and she must brave her mother's wrath—
and the loss of the man she loves—in order to follow her birthright.
ISBN-13: 978-0-8050-8275-3
ISBN-10: 0-8050-8275-1
[1. Fairy tales.   2. Magic—Fiction.   3. Identity—Fiction.]   I. Title.
PZ8.T536Sw 2007   [Fic]—dc22   2006033774

First Edition—2007 / Book designed by Jessica Sonkin
Printed in the United States of America on acid-free paper. ∞

1   3   5   7   9   10   8   6   4   2

For Stan
Thank you, my honey
—H. T.

The Swan Maiden

Spring

Chapter One

$\mathcal{I}$n the quiet hour before dawn, Doucette Aigleron crept from her bed. The chill air made her shiver as, mouse quiet, she finger-combed her hair into two long plaits and dressed in a shift, gown, and pair of thick wool stockings.

Dim gray light filtered through the shutters, picking out silver candlesticks, richly carved chests, the sparkle of silk ribbons, and the softer sheen of three long fur robes hanging on pegs by the canopied bed. Though velvet curtains partly veiled the bed's two remaining occupants, Doucette looked to make sure her rustling garments hadn't disturbed her older sisters. Then, shoes in hand, she tiptoed across the tower chamber and around the pair of leather bags by the door.

One had been packed and strapped closed—Azelais's orderly work, no doubt. Doucette's hand skimmed along the second bag, which overflowed with gowns, gloves, ribbons, and the neck of Cecilia's unstrung lute. A cloud of white feathers engulfed Doucette's fingers. Despite the need for haste, she knelt to caress the swan skin flung so carelessly over the top. Resentment, this day's particular gift, uncoiled within her.

If only she could claim a cloak of feathers like Cecilia's, Doucette would take better care of the precious thing. Unlike some people, she would never flaunt her powers in her sisters' faces, never use sorcery to torment others or make them the butt of her jokes. She would show the world that a swan maiden could be kind. Beloc's people would love her, the court's knights and ladies would seek out her company and treat her with respect. . . .

Cecilia stirred and muttered in her sleep.

Doucette froze, waiting and listening.

The mattress rustled as Cecilia pulled a pillow over her golden head and rolled into the spot Doucette had vacated. On the far side of the bed, Azelais lay still, her dark hair a deeper shadow against the coverlet.

Doucette dared not linger. She tore herself from Cecilia's swan skin and closed the door on her sleeping sisters. If her plan succeeded, she wouldn't have to see them again for months.

Hugging the thought close, Doucette padded down the dark stone stairs. She passed the doors leading to her parents' rooms: the comte's treasury, the comtesse's sewing room, and their grand bedchamber, then sped through the Château de l'Aire's familiar corridors. The faint scent of incense told Doucette she had reached the chapel, but no light outlined the edges of its carved wooden doors. Brother Martin had not yet risen to his prayers.

Another potential obstacle safely navigated.

Now she had only to sneak past the gate guard and run. She put on her shoes and slipped out a side door. The usual barnyard smells of horses, pigs, sawdust, and wood smoke hung in the foggy air. Dew beaded the paving stones of the castle's empty upper courtyard. Doucette stepped carefully over the slick surface, keeping close to the wall.

Outside the kitchen door, a red eye winked open.

She hesitated. If the castle baker was busy enough to fire her bread oven so early, she might have an errand that would take Doucette into town. Abroad on a chastelaine's business, Doucette wouldn't have to hide in the caves after all. Wouldn't that be a stroke of luck!

She hugged her arms to her sides and called softly. "Good morning, Na Patris."

"What? Who's there?"

By the oven's ruddy light, Doucette saw the baker reach into an apron pocket and throw a pinch of salt on the ground between them. The woman held her poker high, like a weapon. "Show yourself," she demanded.

Doucette moved closer, until she could feel the oven's warmth on her skin.

"Oh, it's only you, little lady!" The baker's fierce expression softened. Using the poker, she shut the door on the crackling flames. "With your light hair, I took you for a rock sprite out of the quarry, and I've no time for their tricks today. Come in, do." Na Patris motioned Doucette into the kitchen, which smelled of garlic and onions, yeast and mint. "Tea?"

Doucette accepted a mug and perched on a stool, her face to the mint-scented steam. Most days, she wished Na Patris would accord her the respect due a young noblewoman of sixteen. This morning, the cosseting was a comfort.

Na Patris scattered raisins over a bowl and plunged her floury hands inside. The yeasty odor strengthened as the baker punched the raisins into the dough, turned the speckled mass onto the table, and kneaded vigorously. "Now, then. What's brought that worried frown to your face already, and it not yet cock-crow?"

Doucette sipped the hot tea. "You're up early, too."

"Shearing season." Na Patris jerked her chin at the lumpy, cloth-draped planks lined up on trestles. "Started the welcome loaves rising. My husband thinks his cousins—you remember the Vent'roux boys?—will bring their flock to the pens today."

"Oh?" Doucette told herself that the little heart-leap wasn't anticipation at seeing Om Toumas's handsome cousins again but relief at finding an answer to her need. The shearing pens had been erected on the plain below the castle, a goodly distance from the Luzerna road. Someone would have to take the bread for the wool mistress to distribute. Why shouldn't it be Doucette? If she could convince the baker . . .

She lifted one of the cloths and eyed the rows of fist-sized dough balls. "Shall I mark these for you?"

"If you will, Lady Doucette. Made several batches—those boys are like to eat a dozen apiece, see if the gluttons don't."

Despite her dismissive tone, the curve of Na Patris's lips betrayed the satisfaction of a woman who knows her work is appreciated.

Doucette dipped a knife in flour and scored the first loaf with a crosshatch pattern.

"Not too close, mind," the baker instructed.

"No, Na Patris." On the next loaf, Doucette obediently widened the space between the cuts, though the first loaf had been fine, in her opinion.

Not that anyone ever asked her opinion.

The moment her older sisters twitched their jeweled fingers, courtiers leaped to serve them, Doucette thought bitterly. But she, with her light brown hair, light gray eyes, and average looks, was more often mistaken for a well-dressed attendant. The court's knights and ladies, when they troubled to notice Doucette at all, called her "little lady" or "sweetling," as they might a favored hunting hawk or clever dog. As for the castle servants, every one, from the superior steward to the humblest pig-girl, felt free to instruct their apprentice chastelaine on the smallest household matter.

And one day soon, she thought, stabbing at the dough, her parents would find her a husband. Not only would he order her about as her mother did now, but he'd install her in a new household full of servants who thought they knew best. Doucette hated being reminded of all the ways she wasn't like her sisters. Azelais and Cecilia didn't need to beg the baker for a reason to leave the castle.

Unfortunately, Doucette did. And contradicting Na Patris about the proper way to mark the loaves would lead to a lecture, instead of the escape she craved. Biting her tongue, she finished one plank, exactly as directed, and uncovered the next. "So it's welcome bread for the shepherds and—what's that you're making, Na Patris?"

"A sweet raisin couronne for Lady Sarpine's breakfast." The baker separated her dough into three parts, rolled each into a snake, pinched the tails together, and braided them into a wreath. "Then there's the day's trencher bread and a fortnight's travel biscuit for the swan maidens' party."

"Mm." Doucette thought she had controlled the sigh of envy, but Na Patris raised her head alertly.

The baker's freckled face smoothed into blandness. "Don't they leave for Luzerna this morning, little lady? I suppose you're up early to fetch your sisters' meal."

"You don't suppose any such thing," Doucette contradicted her. "Please, Na Patris, may I take the shepherds' bread down to the pens for you?"

"That's no task for a lady. Anfos will do it."

"But I can't bear to watch Azelais and Cecilia ride off to Tante Mahalt's. They get to study magic and flying while I'm stuck here under Mother's thumb, to sew, inventory the linens, and memorize orders of precedence." Doucette almost cut the next loaf in half, so deeply did her knife plunge into the dough. "If I had a good excuse, Mother might not punish me for avoiding the leave-taking. You could help me. Or I'll hide in the caves."

"The caves! That's reckless talk."

"I've been there before—and found my way out."

"Mind the blade—you'll cut yourself!" Na Patris snatched the knife from Doucette's hand and slapped it onto the table. "There'll be no bleeding on my bread, little lady."

"Your pardon, Na Patris." Doucette wiped her eyes.

The baker's gruff voice softened. "Well, if I sent a cheese and a jar of honey for the wool mistress, that'd be too much for Anfos to carry by himself. You may as well go. We'll put these breads in the oven, like so, and have you away before the sun clears the eastern hills."

"Oh, thank you!" Averting her eyes so she didn't have to see the pity in Na Patris's expression, Doucette hugged the baker's ample waist.

Lady Sarpine often said that a lady never shirked a social duty, no matter how difficult. But of all the days in the year, the one Doucette hated most was the day her older sisters left to spend the summer with their aunt Mahalt, the Queen of the Birds. The second-worst day would come soon enough, when Azelais and Cecilia returned, bursting with new spells to dazzle their father's court.

Doucette wiped flour off the table and tried to fix her mind on the one hope Na Patris had given her.

No—two. There were two reasons to be glad.

For one, Doucette wouldn't actually have to brave the caves under the castle or the fearsome spirit who guarded them. And, if Om Toumas's hunch proved correct, Doucette might soon see Jaume of Vent'roux again.

The prospect lightened her steps as she helped the baker empty the oven.

Chapter Two

*D*oucette stopped in the center of the steep, rocky road. "You take the bread, Anfos. Give me the honey jar."

"Won't, little lady," the kitchen boy said stubbornly. "Na Patris gave it to me."

"I know you can carry it." Doucette cast about for a likely argument. Anfos took his duties seriously. She couldn't insult him by saying that, between the wheel of cheese strapped to his back and the big jar clutched to his tunic, he looked like a beetle. Worse, he kept them to a beetle's pace. At their current rate of descent, a line of ants might overtake them, not to speak of Azelais and Cecilia's mounted party. "But see? This sack is leaking flour on my gown."

"Girls," the kitchen boy said under his breath.

Pretending not to hear, Doucette shoved the sack of welcome bread at him. "Thank you for trading." She slipped the honey jar out of his arms and tucked it in the crook of her elbow, then picked up her skirts with her free hand and walked on.

Though the clay jar was heavy, her spirits rose with each step. The sun had begun to burn through the morning fog, and the air smelled sweet from the herbs growing wild among the rocks:

thyme, fennel, sage, and lavender. Close by, a woodlark whistled its descending song: *titloo-eet, titloo-eet.*

The bird sounded as glad as Doucette was to have escaped from the stone confines of the castle, which perched like a brooding eagle on the steep ridge above and behind her. Though the Château de l'Aire was handsome in its way, she admitted to herself. Built of local stone, its golden walls and towers rose tall over the town that straddled the ridge between castle and quarry. Terraces of flowering almond and cherry trees, gnarled olive and cypress softened the ridge's flanks, until the sheer pitch of the castle's rear defenses merged into the cliffs that protected it from the plain below.

As the road switched direction around a large boulder, Doucette spotted a glint of moving water in the distance. The shearing pens were constructed along the riverbank, so the fleeces could be easily washed. To find the wool mistress, Doucette and Anfos had only to follow the flocks drifting like clouds across the green-and-brown land. Shepherds from all the neighboring counties brought their beasts to Beloc to be shorn before continuing north to summer pasturage in the mountains.

Doucette looked forward to the shepherds' seasonal visits. The lambs were adorable, and their keepers were men and women with merry eyes and carefree ways. Joking and teasing as they worked, few felt compelled to instruct Doucette in herding, shearing, or the finer points of animal care.

But the shepherds' greatest appeal was their music. Each one, it seemed, played an instrument or sang. When the shepherds could be persuaded to climb the long road to the castle, even Lord Pascau's troubadours listened with pleasure.

"D'you think they'll play for us, little lady?" Anfos piped up, echoing Doucette's thoughts.

"I hope so," she said.

"Om Toumas said his Vent'roux cousins were coming. I like Eri best," the kitchen boy confided. "For all he's the runt of the four, he can sing. And Jaume's not bad on the pipes, neither, though I hope Vitor practiced his drumming over the winter."

"And Tinou?" Doucette asked, amused by the kitchen boy's connoisseur air.

"Eh." Anfos waggled his chin. "Strings all sound like yowling cats to me."

Doucette would have asked Anfos's opinion of her father's harpist, lured at great expense from another county, but the sound of pounding hooves distracted her. "Oh, no."

Anfos cocked his head. "Who's mad enough to take their horses that fast down the—oh." His expression changed as he understood Doucette's dismay. "The swan maidens. Get off the road, Lady Doucette! No, there's thorns that way. Up the rock here—scramble! Or they'll run right over us."

The first rider thundered past, long golden hair and white-feathered cloak streaming behind her like a banner.

Anfos whistled under his breath.

Doucette hugged the sheltering rock. Her toes curled in her walking shoes, now wet with dew and splotched with road dust. She knew she had flour on her skirts and a big sticky spot where honey had dripped onto the front of her gown. Maybe it didn't matter. Maybe her sister would gallop on.

A shrill whinny dashed Doucette's hopes. The bay mare whirled and trotted back to the boulder.

As always, Cecilia looked magnificent, in a wild sort of way. Her blue eyes sparkled, and the golden curls tumbled riotously over her shoulders, mixing with the swan skin's disordered white feathers. "Fairer-than-a-fairy" and "Passe-lys," the troubadours called her, as they called Azelais "Dark Swan" or "Passe-rose" for her equally dramatic coloring.

Doucette felt the familiar, aching mix of admiration and envy well up inside her. She didn't share her sisters' beauty or magic, but couldn't the saints at least have gifted her with a tiny portion of the assurance Azelais and Cecilia possessed?

Cecilia's lovely mouth pursed in mock surprise. "You're out for an early stroll."

Awkwardly holding the honey jar, Doucette climbed down from the rock. She could feel the color rising in her cheeks, though she tried to hide her chagrin with a mask of calm. No sense in giving her sister another weapon to wound her with. "Good morning, Cecilia."

"Wherever are you going?"

"The shearing pens, to deliver a few things for Na Patris. Welcome bread for the shepherds. Honey to Na Soufio."

Cecilia clicked her tongue. "A shame you forgot to tell Mother about the baker's important commission. Poor Na Claro ran her old bones up and down the tower stairs, calling for you."

Doucette dug her toe into the dirt. "I'm sorry."

"It's Na Claro deserves your apology, not me." Absently smoothing her ruffled swan skin, Cecilia leaned over the saddle and turned her dazzling smile on Anfos. "And who's this?"

He ducked his head. "Anfos, Lady."

"The kitchen boy?" Cecilia drawled. "Your taste in escorts is delightfully original."

Doucette was spared from responding when, with a jingle of mail shirts and swords, several armsmen reined in behind her sister.

"Lady Cecilia." The first man tugged on his leather cap. "How can we protect you if you leave us behind?"

Cecilia smirked at him. "Ride faster, Renod."

"As you command, Lady."

Her sister's latest conquest, Doucette thought, judging from the man's foolish expression. Sorceresses weren't bound by the rules that governed an ordinary woman's conduct. Azelais managed her affairs with discretion, but Cecilia took pleasure in twisting propriety into knots and tossing it over the battlements.

"What's the delay?" Azelais called from the rear of the line.

"Come see," Cecilia said.

The armsmen shifted their horses to make way for a spotted gelding whose rider wore a feathered cloak as black as the knot of ebony hair at her neck. In contrast to Cecilia's charming dishevelment, Azelais's appearance was immaculate, as always.

"Doucette!" Elegant dark brows drew together. "You missed our leave-taking to carry that ugly jug down the hill? And walking abroad without a proper escort! Have you no scrap of dignity?"

Doucette shrank under the withering stare.

"Don't fuss, Azelais," Cecilia coaxed. "She can hardly fly, can she? Provisioning the shepherds like a good little chastelaine— I call that sweet."

"Chastelaine?" Azelais's pomegranate lips compressed. "I see a drudge dressed above her station, but that is easily remedied." She flicked the polished wooden wand from her knot of black hair, murmured a few words under her breath, of which "kitchen" and "rags" were the loudest, and reached down from her horse to tap Doucette's shoulder.

The Transformation spell fell over Doucette like a shower of icy needles. Magic stung her skin. Her woolen gown dissolved into a tattered patchwork. On her feet, the leather walking shoes hardened into wooden clogs, which found no purchase on the slippery rock. Holding desperately to the honey jar, Doucette lurched to her knees. An overstressed seam gave way and ripped loudly, exposing her white shift. Doucette's jaws clenched in humiliation.

"Cruel, Azelais." Cecilia giggled. "Apt, but ooh, so unkind."

One of the armsmen coughed. Another hissed behind his hand, spreading the word though the file of riders.

Doucette struggled to her feet. Transformed by Azelais's wand, the torn dress barely covered Doucette's shins. The material was threadbare where it wasn't patched and ugly with stains. The trick was calculated both to embarrass Doucette and infuriate their mother, who loathed sorcery and unseemliness in equal measure. Since Azelais would be gone when the spell was discovered, Doucette alone would suffer Lady Sarpine's rebukes.

"Azelais, please," Doucette said miserably. "I'm sorry you were offended."

"No, no." A smug Azelais waved away Doucette's apology. "If you're not going to act like a comte's daughter, no one should mistake you for one."

Cecilia shook her golden head. "I disagree. Dressed that way, she'll bring ridicule to the Aigleron name. No, I think our Doucette needs to remember *exactly* who she is." Blue eyes shone with sly humor as Cecilia slid her wand from her sleeve and tapped Doucette's head.

This time, Doucette's skin warmed as the spell flowed over her. A rush of magic whisked away the ragged garment and replaced it with a gown so fine that Doucette's relief changed to alarm.

Silvery green ribbons trimmed the lavender velvet, which fell away from her shoulders in soft, smoky folds. Then, so softly that she almost missed the translation, the wooden clogs Azelais had bestowed melted into delicate silken slippers. Doucette hardly dared move. The fabric felt so cobweb-fine that a deep breath might tear it.

Ceilica laughed at Doucette's expression. "Isn't that better?" she teased. "You'll think twice before mucking about in this gown."

"It's beautiful, Cecilia, but—"

"Why bother, when she'll drag it through the sheep pens?" Azelais sniffed. "You might have saved yourself the trouble."

"No trouble," Cecilia said. She rolled her shoulders, shaking out the coat of white feathers so that it gleamed in the morning light. "Some of us have magic to spare."

Azelais's black swan-skin fluffed with outrage. "What are you insinuating?"

"Why, nothing." Cecilia was all blond innocence. "Of course, you must arrive in suitable style, Doucette, though I'd rather not delay our journey to deliver you." She produced a white square of linen and stroked it with her wand. "Take a corner."

Trapped inside her glorious dress, Doucette stared at the handkerchief Cecilia had tucked into her free hand. "How much will this hurt?"

"Tcha. One would think you didn't trust me." Cecilia winked at Anfos, who had been following the spell-casting with wide eyes and a wider mouth. "Boy, this side is for you. Hold tight!"

"Yes, Lady Cecilia!" Agile as a cricket despite the cheese on his back and the sack of bread tucked under his arm, Anfos reached for the cloth's far corner. Once he took hold, the white square stretched between him and Doucette until it was large as a bed sheet.

Cecilia gestured with her wand. Wind filled the white cloth, making it billow like a sail. Her mare snorted at the flapping cloth, and Cecilia patted the bay's neck in reassurance. "Don't fret, *chère*. We'll be off in a moment."

"Yet another waste of magic," Azelais said sourly.

"Close as the poor thing will get to wings," Cecilia said, and urged her mount down the hill. "Good-bye!"

"Help!" Doucette cried out in alarm.

The giant-sized handkerchief stuck to her fingers, carrying her along as the sail belled out and lifted into the air.

The ground dropped away.

"We're flying!" Anfos shouted. "Lady Cecilia Animated us!"

Doucette's stomach lurched in protest. She swallowed hard and closed her eyes, hoping it would settle. This violent swooping was nothing like she had imagined the many times she had seen Azelais and Cecilia strip off their gowns and put on their magical swan skins. She had always held her breath as the Transformation swept over them, wondering how it felt when feathers merged with your skin, when your body shifted into another shape.

And then, to fly . . .

Once, it had been pure pleasure to watch them. When Doucette was small, she had thought she, too, would learn flying and sorcery one day. After all, she had inherited her sisters' outgrown gowns, their fat old ponies, their browbeaten tutors and exhausted dancing masters.

But on her tenth birthday, Doucette had knelt before her smiling parents to open a carved wooden chest just like the ones belonging to Azelais and Cecilia. Like theirs, Doucette's box held beautifully embroidered linens, a warm fur robe, and a ring of keys.

Unlike her sisters' boxes, it contained nothing else.

"But, Mother, where's my swan skin?" Doucette had asked, disappointment robbing her of caution.

"Your *what*?" The comtesse had flushed, then paled. She shot a vicious look at her husband. "Is this your doing, Pascau?"

"Nay, I promised her no such thing," the comte said. Stroking his dark beard, Doucette's father studied his youngest daughter with unusual interest. "What put that idea into your pretty head, Doucette?"

A horrible feeling pinched Doucette's insides as she turned from her angry mother to her intent father. "Azelais and Cecilia have them."

"Yes," Lord Pascau said. "Your sisters were born swan maidens."

"Sorceresses," Lady Sarpine hissed, twisting her elegant fingers together. "I was promised one child to raise properly, with none of that Aigleron magical nonsense."

"Softly, Wife."

The smooth menace in her father's voice had made Doucette want to curl up and hide inside the birthday chest. It had affected her mother, too; the comtesse's agitated hands went still.

Lord Pascau looked down his aquiline nose. "Aigleron 'magical nonsense' maintains your entire family in its present comfort. Surely you would not care to disturb that arrangement?"

The skin tightened along Lady Sarpine's jaw. "No, by your grace."

"I thought not," the comte said pleasantly. He cupped Doucette's chin in his hand and tilted her face to meet his gaze.

The awkward position hurt her neck, but Doucette didn't complain. She was trying to breathe. It felt as though something important within her was being ripped away.

"You will never wear a swan skin, never study the High Arts," her father said. A note of regret softened the terrible words. "I'm sorry, child. But with your mother's training, you'll make a pious and capable chastelaine whom all may admire." He let go of her chin and patted her head.

Doucette's shoulders bowed.

"Exactly so." The color had returned to Lady Sarpine's face. She eased gracefully to the floor and folded her daughter in her arms, surrounding Doucette with the scent of jasmine.

"It's not fair! They can fly!" Doucette could not contain the passionate sobs that shook her body.

"Don't cry, my treasure," her mother soothed. "Sorcery's a dangerous business. Given your advantages, you'll be a power in the realm and mistress of a splendid castle one day. Oh, sweetling, you've so much to look forward to."

Doucette disagreed, but no one asked her opinion.

Over the years, she had tried to give up her dreams and accept the path mapped out for her. Each time she heard the wild note in Cecilia's laughter or spied the glint in Azelais's dark eyes that meant imminent flight, Doucette would occupy herself with a chastelaine's duties. But always she found herself stealing up the stairs to the tower chamber. Sick with longing, she'd watch her sisters turn into swans and soar over the countryside with a freedom she would never know.

She might have envied them less if she had realized how the wind would toss her about, helpless as a leaf. At times, Cecilia's Animated sail plunged toward earth, so Anfos's kicking legs and Doucette's fragile slippers trailed above the thorn bushes. Then the capricious wind lifted them until the air felt thin and strange in Doucette's lungs. Just when her nervous stomach calmed, the sail would swing them around like two puppets, and Doucette's heart would get stuck in her throat again.

One arm ached from holding the fabric, the other from clutching the honey jar to her chest. Strands of hair came loose from her braids and whipped around her face. Doucette held her breath when she and Anfos tumbled; she gasped for air when, more slowly, they climbed.

With the small part of her mind that wasn't completely terrified, Doucette noticed that the sky smelled like spring. First, wet rock and herbs, then turned earth, new grass, and sheep. The force of the wind made her eyes water, and she closed them. The sail leveled briefly, then swooped.

Down, Doucette's stomach told her. The sheep smell got very strong.

She opened her eyes and saw the sail crumple.

Chapter Three

*D*oucette and Anfos tumbled over the white backs of wildly bleating ewes. Behind the frightened sheep, the flock's guardian saw them, too. A tan-colored dog the size of a bear charged at the airborne menace.

Doucette choked on a scream as the dog's warning growl sounded in her ear. Out of the corner of her eye she caught a flash of teeth, and thought she tasted the creature's evil breath before the invisible wind freshened and the sail pulled taut, snatching Doucette out of reach.

"Peace, Osco," a friendly voice called. "What news, travelers?"

"Ho, shepherd!" Anfos shouted back.

Doucette kept her mouth closed, afraid of what would come out if she opened it. They had almost reached the shearing pens. She could see the willow fencing marking off the enclosures, the tents and wagons, the line of trees along the river's edge.

With a final flourish, the wind deposited Anfos and Doucette on the muddy ground outside the first empty pen. When they touched the earth, Cecilia's spell unraveled. The sail shrank to its original size and fluttered to earth.

Against all expectation, Anfos still held the bread sack, and Doucette had kept the honey. As she landed, the heavy jar thudded into her middle, robbing her of breath. Feeling as though she had run for miles and wrestled the big dog after that, Doucette lay still. Despite the relief that overwhelmed her, she missed the sensation of the wind tugging at her hair.

"Lady Doucette, are you well?" Anfos scrambled to sit beside her. "Because your face looks green. Did you know magic makes your skin turn colors and your insides twist up in knots? I don't mind, though, because we flew high as falcons! Didn't we?"

Doucette sighed. "Yes, Anfos."

"Can we go again?"

Before she could answer, an eager *yip, yip, yip* exploded near Doucette's head. A wet tongue lapped her face.

"Ugh! Stop!" Rolling the honey jar away from her body, Doucette thrust out an arm to fend off her attacker.

"Come here, Fidele," Anfos ordered.

"Lady Doucette?" a cheerful voice asked.

Doucette pushed her straggling hair out of her face and tried to compose herself, a task made more difficult by the realization that a cold, wet patch was spreading over her back and legs. When she sat upright, the velvet gown pulled from the ground with an ominous sucking sound. Doucette looked up and swallowed.

It was unfair, but inevitable, that the oldest and most handsome of the Vent'roux brothers had witnessed her undignified arrival.

Like other shepherds, Jaume wore a short brown tunic and leather leggings, a wool cape and broad-brimmed hat. Also like many, he was tall and strong, and he leaned on his shepherd's crook with a deceptively sleepy air. Unlike most, he had thick dark hair that curled around his strong features and a smile whose sweetness always made Doucette forget that she was the comte's plain daughter, the boring, practical, nonmagical one.

"Good morning, Jaume. I hope you had a pleasant journey to Beloc?" Embarrassment strangled Doucette's voice.

"Less eventful than yours, Lady." He took off his hat and bowed, then extended a lean brown hand and helped Doucette to her feet as though she weighed no more than Fidele.

The small brown-and-white herding dog snuffled at the sack of welcome loaves. Jaume hoisted both sack and honey jar out of his dog's reach, then handed Doucette the white cloth. "Never seen a person flying a handkerchief before," he observed. "You've taken up magic?"

"That was Lady Cecilia's spell." Anfos rubbed Fidele's ears. "Isn't she a beauty?"

"Oh, aye," Jaume said.

Unreasonably, Doucette felt betrayed. Cecilia didn't need more admirers. She had scores.

"Has she got any new tricks?" Anfos asked.

"She will, by summer's end," Doucette said, unable to suppress her bitterness. "Cecilia told me Tante Mahalt promised to teach them the greater Transformation spells this year."

Anfos and Jaume wore identically puzzled expressions.

"I meant Fidele," Anfos said.

"Oh, aye. Watch, now," Jaume said.

Silently, Doucette folded the handkerchief and tucked it into her velvet sleeve. How ridiculous she must seem! Dressed for a ball and landing in the muck. She had better finish Na Patris's errand and run home before she could do anything else to damage Jaume's good opinion of her.

Her companions kindly ignored Doucette's preoccupation. Jaume made a pushing motion with one hand. "Fidele, down."

The little dog flattened her belly to the grass, extended her front legs, and tucked her nose between her paws.

"Oh, clever!" Anfos clapped his hands.

Fidele looked so appealing that Doucette felt a smile tug at the corner of her mouth. "Well done," she said.

"That's my girl." Jaume bent at the waist and pointed to his own face. "Fidele, kiss!"

The dog leaped twice her own height and licked the shepherd's cheek.

Anfos and Doucette both laughed. Fidele barked, pranced, and then, on command, repeated her kissing trick. This time, a chorus of jeering voices responded.

"Poor Jaume, twenty years old and can't get a sweetheart."

"Give him a good nip, Fidele."

"That's our big brother. Kiss the girls and make them bark."

Baaa. Baaaaa.

Doucette almost slipped back into the mud when the wave of sheep broke over her. Anxious-eyed ewes butted her hip, trapping her against the side of the pen and adding green and brown smears to the muddy purple velvet.

Magically, Jaume seemed to be in several places at once. "Open the gate, Vitor," he said, cuffing one brother on the ear while he caught Doucette's elbow to steady her. "You brought them in far too fast, Tinou. Do you have wool between your ears? No, don't

tell me. Make yourself useful, man." As Doucette recovered her
balance, Jaume passed the honey jar to his brother, unhooked a
lamb caught in the willow hurdles, and shouted at his youngest
brother. "Eri, hold the rear with the other dogs. Fidele, pen!"

Brown-and-white herders nipped at their charges' heels.
Fidele led the flock between the gates and stood guard, not
allowing a single lamb to escape.

Doucette's feet were wet. She shifted to pull them free of the
mud, and the slippers' fine silk uppers parted from the soles, like
roasted chestnut skins peeling from the nutmeat. To her dismay,
the shoes separated into limp pieces. Cold mud oozed between
her toes.

She'd be walking home barefoot, thanks to her clever sisters
and their clever spells. Perhaps she'd have done better to take her
chances with Lavena in the caves. At least the spirit was said to
give you something in exchange for what she took.

Woof.

A paw the size of a pony's hoof crushed the remains of
Doucette's left shoe.

A little timidly, she held out her hand for the enormous dog
to sniff. "Remember me, Osco? You know I'd never hurt one of
your lambs."

The flock's guardian yawned, showing fearsome teeth, then
butted his massive jaw under Doucette's hand.

"Faugh." Her nose wrinkled as she scratched the thick tan
fur. "What have you been eating, you great brute?"

"Trolls." Jaume's brother Vitor grinned down at Doucette.
"Wolves, ogres, evil sorceresses. Thick as fleas they were, once
we crossed the Turance into Beloc county."

The sweep of a shepherd's crook knocked Vitor's hat off his head. "Manners," Jaume said.

Vitor grimaced and bowed. "Your pardon, little lady. I didn't mean to insult your aunt. Or your sisters. I meant, um."

As if she weren't standing in a field, covered with mud, thanks to one of those very same evil sorceresses, Doucette inclined her head. "Good morning, Vitor."

Hat in one hand and honey jar in the other, Tinou came up to eye Doucette's bedraggled finery. "What, a revel, and no one told me? I would have worn my dancing shoes, Lady Doucette." Despite his burden, he managed a courtier's bow.

"Tinou." Blushing fiercely, Doucette curtsied in return. As she rose, she shook out the velvet skirts and stepped behind the big dog to hide her now-bare feet. Not that the merry shepherds would believe her attempts at decorum. They'd seen her flopping around in the air like washing on a line.

With Fidele and the other herding dogs at his heels, Eri closed the gate on the last of the ewes. "Lady." As he straightened from his bow, the young man's dreamy brown eyes narrowed in concentration. Head lifted, Eri turned to Jaume. "Is that Na Patris's bread I smell?"

"You can't have it yet," Anfos told him. "Na Patris said."

"We know, Anfos." Jaume draped the bread sack over the kitchen boy's shoulder. "It's for the wool mistress to share out. We've been here afore."

"What's this?" Gently, Tinou shook the jar.

Anfos held out his free arm. "Honey for Na Soufio."

"Cheese, too!" Vitor smacked his lips. "I'll give you a hand with that, sprout."

Anfos danced out of reach. "No."

"But what if your goods spoiled on the journey?" Tinou lifted the jar lid and sniffed. "Mm. I don't think Na Soufio will care for this at all."

"Give it back!" Anfos lunged, but Tinou held the jar out of his reach.

"Have you boys come clear from Donsatrelle county to shear or to brawl?" a new voice asked.

"Na Soufio." Tinou lowered the jar as a tall woman approached them.

She was dressed like the shepherds, in a short brown tunic and leggings. In place of their wide-brimmed hats, a white linen coif covered her hair, and an enameled guild badge shone from the center of her crimson scarf.

Triumphantly, Anfos claimed the honey jar. He turned to the wool mistress. "Na Patris's compliments, Na Soufio, here's a gift from the castle kitchen." He leaned forward and continued in a loud whisper. "And if Jaume's brothers eat all the welcome breads like they did last year, you're to send word, and she'll bake more."

Half hidden behind Osco's bulk, Doucette coughed. Jaume's brothers shuffled their feet.

"Thank you, Anfos." The woman didn't smile, exactly, but she sounded less dour as she pointed to the largest of the tents. It flew the Beloc flag, a gold eagle spreading wide wings over an azure field. "I'd appreciate you taking it to the pavilion. Please convey my gratitude to Patris."

"I will," Anfos said, and strutted toward the tent.

"I'm sure we will enjoy the baker's gift." The wool mistress pinned each of the brothers with a stern eye. "*After*"—she leaned on the word—"our work is done. You brought your own shears, I trust?"

"Aye, Na Soufio." Jaume opened a leather pouch at his belt and gave Tinou the shears. "Go to it," he said. "Fidele! Osco!"

The dogs barked, one high, one low. Jaume pointed to his brother. "Mind Tinou."

Tinou scowled. "What, while you stuff your face?"

"No," Jaume said patiently. "While I walk Lady Doucette back to the castle."

His brothers hooted. "Think you'll catch a court lady's eye?" Tinou said.

Vitor pinched his nose with his fingers and spoke in a high, squeaky voice. "What is that smell? Pray take it away!"

"Lady Doucette?" For the first time, Na Soufio appeared to notice the young woman standing behind Osco. The wool mistress curtsied. "Ah. Good day. Lady Sarpine sent you to inspect the pens? I'll show you around myself; you'll find all in order."

"I'm sure of that, Na Soufio," Doucette said. "Perhaps another time? I'm not dressed for a tour."

"Not dressed? Move, you." Na Soufio shooed the dog away from Doucette. The grooves beside the wool mistress's mouth deepened as her eyes traveled up and down the once-gorgeous gown, inventorying the windblown ribbons, the mud and slime that spotted the purple velvet.

Following the woman's frown, Doucette glanced down and winced. Osco had left giant paw prints on her hem.

"Criminal mistreatment of a fine fabric," Na Soufio pronounced. "About time Lady Sarpine assigned you a turn with the laundresses, if you ask me."

Doucette stiffened. "I am familiar with their work."

"And an insult, besides. Silk and velvet! What, honest wool's not good enough for you?" Na Soufio clicked her teeth. "A chastelaine suits her attire to the task, Lady Doucette, not to her vanity."

"It was a spell." Doucette could see Jaume's brothers grinning behind the wool mistress's back. "I was wearing a different dress before Azelais and Cecilia changed it."

The woman sniffed at Doucette's explanation. "Swan maidens are moody creatures, by all accounts. You should know better than to provoke them."

"I provoke them by living," Doucette said under her breath.

"Eh?" the woman said sharply. "Speak up, little lady. A chastelaine doesn't mutter."

"No, Na Soufio."

To Doucette's relief, Jaume eased between her and the critical Na Soufio. One look sent his mocking brothers off to the shearing pen, and then Jaume unleashed his sweet smile on the wool mistress.

She blinked. "Yes, Jaume?"

"Well, now. You're a busy woman, and a capable one, to manage this lot on your own." His nod encompassed the tent encampment and pens beyond it, where a distant yapping and bleating announced new arrivals. "A flock from Mardèche county is here, looks like. We'll not keep you."

"Mardèche?" Na Soufio turned and bunched her hands on

her hips. "None of them were expected until tomorrow, and making for Saint-Rafel pens? That'll need sorting out. A rude bunch, little lady, so it's as well you can't stay. Come back tomorrow. But"—her finger wagged in warning—"dress decent, or for your own good, I'll have a word with your mother."

Doucette bit her lip and curtsied. "Yes, Na Soufio."

"Velvet, by the saints," the woman huffed as she stalked toward the river.

"Shall we?" Jaume said.

"Thank you." In an agony of silent humiliation, Doucette put her hand on his offered arm.

How stupid she had been, trying to avoid her sisters' leave-taking. If she had just endured it, she wouldn't have let Cecilia frighten her witless, disrupted the Vent'roux flock's arrival, incurred a scolding from Na Soufio, taken Jaume from his work, or made him the target of his brothers' ridicule. How flighty the handsome shepherd must think her—not at all the impression she wanted to leave.

Not for the first time, Doucette wished she knew a spell that would make the earth open up and swallow her, ruined velvet gown and all.

Chapter Four

Unfortunately, Azelais's prediction had been correct. The beautiful gown was not suited for a country ramble. The tight bodice made it difficult for Doucette to breathe; the elaborate skirts tangled around her feet. Jaume shortened his long stride without comment, and Doucette hobbled along as quickly as she could. At least the grass was soft underfoot. The rocky road ahead would be more difficult.

Surreptitiously, Doucette unfolded Cecilia's Animated handkerchief and shook it. It fluttered limply, a flag of surrender. Doucette put the thing away, realizing that even if she knew how to make the spell work, it would have returned her and Jaume to the sheep pen, not taken them up to the castle.

When they gained the road, Doucette looked north toward Luzerna, Tante Mahalt's county and her sisters' destination. She didn't see the party of riders or even the dust of their passage. Between them, her sisters would have pushed their escort hard. Unspoken, but understood by all, was the hope that the childless Queen of the Birds would soon name her heir. Both Azelais and Cecilia must be eager to curry her favor.

Doucette kicked a dirt clod. She had never seen her aunt's castle and had only met Tante Mahalt once. Lady Sarpine permitted her two eldest daughters to visit the Château de l'Île every summer, in hopes that one of them would inherit the childless woman's estate. The comtesse's mistrust of her sister-in-law precluded more frequent visits between them.

The road climbed toward the ridge. Panting in her tight dress and having to pick her way through stones that cut her bare feet, Doucette walked ever more slowly. "Have you been to Luzerna, Jaume?" she asked.

"Oh, aye," he said. "Summer pasture's over the border."

"What's it like?"

"Green."

When she wanted to hear more, he pushed his hat back on his head and scratched his neck. "I've not been upriver quite as far as your aunt's castle. Our flocks stop at the meadows, where the Immeluse empties into a lake between the mountains. Beautiful country. Wildflowers everywhere in the grass, red anemones, rockrose, yellow cowslips and primrose, peonies and valerian. And when the lilies bloom—ah." He smiled. "Best smell in the world, field lilies."

"It sounds lovely," Doucette said. She stubbed her toe hard on a rock and closed her lips over a cry of pain. The soles of her feet felt like they were on fire.

"And hot pools on the way," Jaume continued. "Hidden-like, tucked in the rocks above the road. After a day's march, we'll take turns minding the flock and climbing up to soak. It's grand, steaming water to your neck, crushed mint for a pillow, stars overhead. . . . Why, what's the matter, little lady?" he said in quite a different tone.

"Nothing," Doucette said.

"You're limping."

"No," she lied.

"My job to notice." As if she were an errant lamb, Jaume lifted her onto a boulder.

Doucette tucked her feet under her skirts, afraid to find out whether they looked as bad as they felt. "Nothing you can do," she told him.

"Can't say for sure," he countered. "A good shepherd has ten remedies for blisters on man or beast. Let's see."

Doucette glared at him, but Jaume leaned on his crook, the soul of patience.

"I'm not showing my bare feet to a stranger," she said.

"That's plain cruel. Hardly a stranger, am I? You've seen me every spring since Cousin Toumas first carried you down on his shoulders to play with the lambs." Jaume's dark eyes narrowed. "Bare feet? What about your shoes?"

Doucette clamped her lips together. Cecilia had a lot to answer for.

Not that she would.

"Show me," Jaume said.

As his attitude made plain that she'd sit on the rock until she did, Doucette hiked her skirts and gingerly extended her legs. Jaume's hands felt warm on her ankles as he turned her feet up for inspection.

Though his face darkened with anger, his touch was gentle as he lowered her feet. "I'm a blind fool, yammering about flowers!" he said. "Why didn't you say you were hurting?"

"What could you have done?" Doucette replied with equal bluntness. "Azelais scolded me already for not riding, and as

Cecilia said, I can't f-fly." To her dismay, her voice quavered and her eyes filled with tears.

"Hush." Jaume threaded the shepherd's crook through his belt, picked up Doucette, and settled her against his chest.

"What are you doing?" Doucette rubbed her eyes.

"Carrying you."

"But—"

"You're not walking another step until we wash out those cuts." He strode up the road, much faster now that he didn't have to match her careful pace.

"I'm too heavy. Put me down."

Jaume snorted. "Got ewes that weigh more than you. They don't squirm so much, which helps."

"Oh." Doucette held herself still. "Your pardon."

"No trouble," he said, and kept walking.

His tunic smelled of wood smoke, sheep, and, faintly, of garlic. Slowly, Doucette relaxed into the homey smells. She could hear Jaume's heart beating under her ear, slow and steady. His breath ruffled her hair.

It felt strange to be carried, but it was a great relief to be off the sharp stones. Though her feet still throbbed, the pain wasn't getting worse with every step, as it had before.

Jaume climbed the steep hill and threaded his way through the town's narrow streets. As they traversed the artisans' quarter in companionable silence, Doucette heard the *tap-tap* of goldsmiths' hammers, the cheerful haggling of cobblers and tailors with patrons in street-level booths. She kept her eyes lowered so she wouldn't have to see the speculation in the shopkeepers' eyes.

When she smelled a whiff of sulfur, she knew they had almost reached their destination. The only fountain in town that tapped a hot spring was located near the castle gates.

"Could we stop here, Jaume?"

"Good idea." The shepherd set Doucette on a bench near the fountain. Above the water's flow, steam wafted out of a hole at the top of the giant, moss-covered boulder, as though the rock itself breathed.

Jaume filled cupped hands from the tiled catch-basin and bathed Doucette's feet.

She winced at the sting of mineral-laden water.

"Almost done," he said. "There."

"Thank you." Doucette glanced down the street lined with narrow stone buildings. Her hands plucked at her muddy skirts. "I wish I didn't have to go on," she surprised herself by blurting out loud. "Mother will be furious."

"Why's that?"

"Isn't it obvious?"

Jaume rocked back on his heels and frowned thoughtfully. "Gown's none too clean, I'll grant you."

"I'm hideous!" Doucette wailed.

"Hideous?" The laugh lines crinkled around Jaume's eyes. "Not hardly, with that hair the color of a dove's wing and the same soft, pretty way about you. Ask me, you look very nice."

"I do?"

"Oh, aye." The shepherd pulled the crook out of his belt and scratched the back of his neck. "I've always thought so."

"You have?" Doucette said, diverted. "You never said!"

"What cause has a shepherd to be telling a comte's daughter that he admires her?"

Abruptly, Doucette recalled who and where she was. She had been so comfortable in Jaume's company, she had forgotten the social gulf that separated them.

Jaume gave her a wry look. "You see?"

Slowly, Doucette nodded. Even if she liked him better than any of the nobles at court, the two of them had no future together. Unlike a sorceress, who loved where she pleased, a virtuous young noblewoman married as her parents directed.

"I will ask a favor, now that you know," Jaume said.

"Yes?"

"If you ever . . . if you need . . ." He turned his hat in his hands.

She found it rather endearing to see the confident shepherd tongue-tied. "Yes?"

"If you're in trouble, or one of your sisters plays a trick like today"—he frowned at Doucette's battered feet—"any reason. You know you can call on me, Lady Doucette?"

"Thank you, Jaume," Doucette said, touched by the unlikely offer. Really, no matter how strong or kind or handsome he was, how could a shepherd help a noblewoman? "I'll remember."

"Good," he said. "Best get along to the castle. No, wait." He fumbled in his belt pouch and came up with a small clay jar. "Use this salve on the cuts." He pressed the jar into her hand.

Doucette pried off the cork lid and sniffed. Mostly rosemary oil, she thought, but with a wilder smell underneath. "You're giving me sheep rub?"

"Made it for sheep, but people use it, too. There's herbs shepherds know, places we pick them. This and that. It'll help the skin heal cleanly."

Doucette sniffed again. The ointment's scent made her nose tingle in a way she almost recognized.

And then she did recognize it, despite Jaume's bland explanation. "This stuff is magic," she said. "Herb magic! You know my mother doesn't approve of the Low Arts." Or the High Arts. It was Lord Pascau who had encouraged Azelais and Cecilia to practice sorcery, which caused a certain tension in the family. Doucette was always caught in the middle. Not that it was a shepherd's concern.

Jaume straightened from his casual stance. "Low Art, High Art, it's the noble folk draw those lines in the sand." He rapped his crook on a paving stone. "Transformation, Animation, Divination—showy spells, I'll grant you. But really, compared with healing, how useful are they to most folk?"

The casual dismissal of her sisters' sorcery—the magic Doucette so longed to learn and never would—nettled her. "Father's very proud of Azelais and Cecilia," she said.

Jaume's laugh had an edge to it. "Aye, he would be. Convenient for Lord Pascau, how the swan maidens can turn iron into gold. For a little while, at least."

"What are you suggesting?" Doucette said, outraged. "An Aigleron's honor would never permit her to deceive others in such an unprincipled way."

"No?"

"No!" Doucette almost stamped her foot, before she remembered she had better not.

Jaume's gaze dropped. "Aye, well, I've no wish to quarrel about it. You'll still use the salve?"

Doucette hesitated, but the shepherd sounded so concerned that she decided her mother needn't know about the ointment's unusual properties. "Yes. I'll use it."

"Shall I carry you?"

"No," Doucette said. "It's best if I go on alone."

Jaume might have argued the point, but his broad shoulders slumped. He swatted his hat against his thighs and put it on. "Good-bye, then."

"Good-bye."

But she sat by the fountain and watched the road long after Jaume had disappeared. Thoughtfully, she turned the small clay jar between her hands. What was Jaume hinting about her family?

For the first time, Doucette wondered what price Azelais and Cecilia might have paid for their freedom.

Chapter Five

"What are you about, Daughter? Stop that at once!"

Doucette flinched from the hiss of her mother's voice at the chamber door. Although the very air smelled of spring, several days had not been long enough, it appeared, to thaw Lady Sarpine's icy disapproval.

"Yes, Mother." Wishing she had worked more quickly, Doucette slid down from her parents' bed and piled the armful of dusty hangings into the waiting servant's basket. The velvet smelled of a winter's soot and sweat, mingled with a lingering trace of her mother's jasmine perfume and the less pleasant aroma of wet wool. "That's the last of them, Na Claro."

Gnarled hands tightened on the basket as the old woman nodded her thanks.

The comtesse's skirts swished across the floor. Advancing to the center of the bedchamber, she crooked an imperious finger. "Come here."

As she had done at least five times a day since Cecilia's Transformation spell, Doucette presented herself for her mother's inspection.

Lady Sarpine frowned at the light brown hair straggling out of two long braids. Doucette's rumpled skirts earned another pointed stare before the comtesse spoke. "What is required of a chastelaine?"

"A chastelaine presents the picture of elegance and composure at all times. She directs the work required to keep her castle and its people in good order," Doucette recited. Again. The words felt engraved on her tongue, she had repeated them so often.

"What must she not do?"

Doucette stared at her feet. "A chastelaine never contradicts her husband in public, never loses her temper with children or servants. She rules both kindly, but with a firm hand. Though her knowledge is superior, she does not perform her servants' tasks for them, lest she lose their respect."

"You said the same yesterday, after I found you grubbing in the orchard with Om Toumas, and later, up to your elbows in flour with Na Patris. Now you do good Na Claro's work?"

Doucette flushed at the unfairness of the accusation. "I was just checking the spring linens for moth holes, as you directed," she said, patting the sheets stacked on a chest, "but when I saw Na Claro couldn't reach the top of the bed frame—"

The comtesse held up her hand. "Indulge your tender heart elsewhere, my treasure. Sixteen is too old to be climbing on the furniture whenever the whim strikes you."

"Yes, Mother."

"That's my obedient girl." A hint of approval softened Lady Sarpine's voice. "You'll do very well, as long as you remember your station." But when the comtesse turned to address the waiting servant, all indulgence disappeared. "I rely on you to remind my daughter of her duty, Na Claro," she said in freezing tones. "She is not to be dirtying her hands in this chamber."

"Your pardon, Lady Sarpine." The old woman bobbed a curtsy over her basket.

"Couldn't you send a maid or washerwoman to help her, Mother?" Doucette asked. "The silk panels still need to be hung, and the blankets aired."

"Very well." The comtesse surveyed the room with a distracted air. "Lady of the Seas, so much remains be done before the queen and prince arrive. Did you supervise the steward counting the gold plate?"

"Yes, Mother."

"And speak to the bee-man? Her Majesty is partial to spring honey. She must have the first he collects."

"Yes, Mother."

While Beloc's Château de l'Aire boasted its own small court of knights and nobles, never in Doucette's memory had their county hosted such exalted visitors. In anticipation of the royal family's arrival, the comtesse was celebrating the annual rite of spring cleaning with an almost religious fervor. More than once, Doucette had wished for an Animation spell to power mops and dust cloths across the castle's vast expanses of floor and woodwork.

"Oh, and the welcome gift?"

"Yes, Mother," Doucette said patiently. "When I finish with the linens, I'll go to the goldsmith's. He already showed me the wax castings for the medallions. Last week, that was, the day after Azelais and Cecilia left for Tante Mahalt's. I thought them very fine. The medallions, I mean," she clarified, though she needn't have bothered. Her sisters always looked exquisite.

Dread pinched the comtesse's features. "The girls didn't leave any of their wretched Animation spells in the guest chambers?"

"Neither said anything to me," Doucette said.

Not that they would have. Doucette tried to push down the spurt of resentment. It was a battle she lost every time she remembered Azelais and Cecilia's parting tricks. No reason to think that this day would prove any different.

Lady Sarpine frowned. "We'd be ruined if your sisters' vulgar idea of a jest caused a royal guest to spend a night flapping back and forth with the shutters. After that episode with the abbess . . . we'd best have a servant check their quarters' latches, hinges, and fire tools, to be safe." She swept out of the bed-chamber. "Anfos! Where's that boy? Anfos!"

Doucette unfolded the last two pillowcases. "No moth holes in these."

"Oughtn't be." The servant sniffed as she piled the old bed linens by the door. "You had packed them with cedar balls, like I taught you?"

"I did, Na Claro."

Retrieving a set of silk hangings from a chest, the woman cast a doleful glance at the height of the bed frame.

She might as well have said "poor old knees" out loud, Doucette thought wearily. "Give them to me. I won't tell Mother, if you don't."

"But, little lady—"

Ignoring the token protest, Doucette climbed onto the bare mattress and reached up to clip the first of the whisper-light panels to the bed frame. A gust of air swirled in through the open window, carrying the smell of flowering almond from the terraced orchards below the castle walls. The breeze flirted with Doucette's wayward hair and set the white silk panel to billowing.

After working her way around the bed, Doucette jumped down and dusted her palms on her skirts while she admired her handiwork. "Doesn't that look fine? What pleasant dreams Mother and Father must have." Wistfully, Doucette remembered soaring with Cecilia's wind-sail. "You could lie in this bed and imagine you were flying."

Na Claro said nothing.

"Haven't you ever wished for a swan skin?" Doucette asked. "To wrap yourself in feathers and leave the world behind?"

The old woman sniffed. "Can't eat magic, can you?"

"No, but—"

"A sorceress can conjure a handful of grass to look like cake and taste like cake, but grass is grass, in your belly or outside it."

"I know." By admitting it, Doucette hoped to avert the usual lecture, but the old woman was well and truly launched.

"Like your lady mother says, domestic order creates its own enchantment."

"She doesn't say it to Azelais and to Cecilia," Doucette muttered.

"Eh?"

"Nothing." Doucette freed one of the panels, which the wind had twisted around the bed frame. "Housework's not like *real* spells, Na Claro. Divination. Animation. Transformation." The litany of High Arts rolled off her tongue. "Stones into rubies, straw into gold."

For once, the idea brought with it a prick of unease. "Straw into gold. . . ."

"Hush." Na Claro gestured anxiously at the chamber door. "You know Lady Sarpine doesn't like such talk. Besides, despite their clever ways, you've got something neither of your witchy sisters can boast."

"What's that?" Doucette picked at a loose flap of skin on one finger. "Calluses?"

Na Claro's wrinkled hand patted hers. "A true heart. Worth more to your folk than false gold, believe me."

"It's kind of you to say so." Doucette blinked at the woman's unexpected compliment. "Well. Let's turn the mattress, shall we? And then I'll be off to the goldsmith's."

"You go. Lady Sarpine told me to finish."

"Don't be silly. It's too heavy to manage by yourself."

"No, no!" Clucking like a frightened partridge, the old woman interposed herself between Doucette and the bed. "You've done enough! Truly!"

Doucette put her hands on her hips. "Feathers settle over time. You know Mother will scold if the mattress is poorly aired."

"Please, little lady. Stop!"

"It's no trouble." Despite the servant's protest, Doucette heaved the mattress onto its side.

The sight that met her eyes more than explained Na Claro's anguished moans. Doucette's elbows straightened to shove the mattress away. It fell to the floor with a loud thump.

The blood ebbed from her head and retreated down her body like a cold tide, leaving her unsteady on her feet. Doucette crumpled to her knees beside the bed frame and stared at the cloud of gray-tipped white feathers that had been concealed between the mattress and its supporting webbing.

She had never seen the thing before, but she knew exactly what it was.

Chapter Six

*T*he truth stole her breath. "A swan skin!" Doucette panted, her thoughts racing wildly. "I've never seen one like it. Mine—it must be! Azelais and Cecilia wore theirs to Tante Mahalt's, and this one's a different color. Oh, how beautiful!"

She reached out with trembling hands to pull it toward her.

Soft as milk, as clouds, as snow, the dappled swan skin enveloped her in a luscious warmth. Doucette caressed the feathers before turning accusing gray eyes on Na Claro.

"Mother didn't want me to find this, did she? That's why you fussed. How long have you known and never told?"

The old woman tottered to a wooden chest and sat down on the lid. "Lady Sarpine made us promise. Said she'd turn us out of the castle—every woman attending your birth—if she heard one whisper about you being a swan maiden."

A swan maiden!

Doucette buried her face in the feathers. From the crumbs of lore she had picked up from her sisters, she knew that a swan skin was the key to Transformation, the greatest of the High Arts.

Exhilaration rushed through her, followed by a sharp stab of regret. Suddenly, Doucette wanted to weep for all the times she had watched her sisters change into bird shape and fly away without her. She could have joined them. She, too, could have danced on the wind and returned starry-eyed. Everything she needed—everything she was—she held between her two shaking hands.

The extent of her parents' betrayal dawned slowly.

Being born a swan was the clearest possible sign of magical power, but her father had denied it. He had lied to her on that fateful birthday.

Doucette cast her mind back. No, he hadn't said she didn't *have* a swan skin, only that she would never *wear* one.

Because they had hidden it.

Which meant that while her sisters pleased themselves, free as the swans they could become at will, she was trapped. Of course, her mother had acted as though she was bestowing a great privilege on Doucette, to follow always two steps behind Lady Sarpine as she glided about the castle. But instead of magic, the comtesse's youngest daughter had learned domestic arts: how to make candles and dry meat, how to supervise servants. She could direct castle workers to fix a roof, hang new shutters, or prune fruit trees. She knew how to keep accounts and could compose a tournament menu for two hundred hungry knights, their ladies, and their servants. As her mother repeatedly said, casting spells formed no part of a chastelaine's duties.

And, oh, how Doucette had envied her sisters their ability.

She raised her head, stammering in confusion. "But—but— our family's power was built on magic. Azelais and Cecilia are training to be sorceresses. Why didn't Mother and Father let me?"

"Beloc folk esteem the High Arts, little lady, but Lady Sarpine was born in western Mardèche, where they think differently. The de Brochets are a proud family without a fish bone's worth of magic to their name, and that's the plain truth." The old woman had recovered enough of her composure to give Doucette a shrewd look. "Sorcery's caused plenty of trouble between folk that have it and those that don't. Your parents' marriage keeps the peace between the two counties, but it's a delicate balance, eh?"

Doucette nodded, and the old woman continued. "With the comte's blessing, your sisters do as they please, and no one dares tell them different. Mayhap Lady Sarpine has other plans for you."

"The prince, you mean? An alliance with the Crown." Doucette thought about it. Her fingers stroked the swan skin, shaping each brilliant white feather as it shaded into gray. Plume by plume, she tenderly restored order to the crumpled mess her coat had become, squashed under the mattress. "That's why Mother wouldn't say which visitors she expected until after Azelais and Cecilia had ridden away. She didn't want them to know or interfere."

"Not my place to speak for her."

"She's hinted I'd be chastelaine of a great domain. I assumed she meant me to marry some Mardèche lord or one of Beloc's nobles. As long as it wasn't that pompous Lord Luquet." Doucette frowned. "But Father's so proud of Azelais and Cecilia's magic. Why did he allow Mother to hide mine?"

"Lady Sarpine gets her way," Na Claro said dryly. "Though Lord Pascau didn't let her destroy your swan coat outright. He said they could as well give it to your husband. What man wouldn't want such a hold on his wife?"

"Without it, she couldn't ever leave him." Doucette clutched her swan skin. "No matter what he did."

"Aye," Na Claro agreed.

The idea filled Doucette with horror. After holding her own coat of feathers, the long-hidden part of herself, she couldn't bear the thought of losing it. With sudden decision, she marched over to the tapestry bag that held the comtesse's embroidery. Doucette upended the bag and shook it, spilling colored woolen balls and skeins onto the floor.

"Lady Doucette—"

"I'm sorry, Na Claro." Doucette rolled up her swan skin and stuffed it into the empty bag. A calm certainty had wrapped itself around her. "But I'm not giving up mine ever again. Not for Mother, and not for a man I've never met, prince or no."

"But—"

"First, we're going to make up this bed." Doucette shoved the mattress back onto its frame and picked up clean linens. Sheets snapped as she shook them out.

"No good can come of disobeying your mother's wishes, little lady," Na Claro warned.

"Tuck in that side, please, Na Claro, then carry the dirty linens down to the laundry. If you're not here, you can't know that I spilled the yarn." With the toe of her shoe, Doucette nudged several of the woolen balls under the bed. "Or that in going after them, I discovered my swan skin." She fixed the older woman with a commanding look. "Come back with a few other women and Mother, too, if you can manage it. Best if she sees for herself how blameless you are."

"Lady Doucette!" Na Claro sounded caught between consternation and understanding. "I'd have expected such sly counsel from Lady Azelais or Lady Cecilia, but I never thought you'd deal in schemes."

"No?" Doucette smoothed summer-weight blankets over the sheets, plumped the bolster, and twitched the coverlet into place. "The saints only know, Na Claro, what else I'll discover before this day is done."

The servant's lined face puckered with worry. "Do take care. Magic's no substitute for good sense."

"So they say." Doucette's lips twisted. "I wouldn't know, never having had the chance to make the trade." She slung the tapestry bag over her shoulder and opened the door for the older woman. "Go ahead. I'll follow in a moment."

The door closed behind her with a soft click.

Instead of walking down the tower stairs after Na Claro, Doucette went up. At every step, the emotion rising inside her threatened to erupt in a storm of tears, or shrieking, or wild laughter. She didn't know which would be worse, so she bit her lips to keep them all back.

A maid descending with a full hamper bobbed her head as she passed. "Good afternoon, little lady."

Doucette averted her eyes and nodded, hurrying to the chamber she shared with her sisters. Once safe inside, she fell across the bed, her arms wrapped around the tapestry bag. Ragged sobs tore out of her throat.

Her life had been built on a lie.

For so long, she had envied her sisters their freedom and their powers, feeling she had little in common with them. Younger than Azelais by four years and Cecilia by two, Doucette had always felt set apart, so much less mysterious and graceful and clever and powerful and beautiful than they. Yet all along, had she known it, they shared a stronger bond even than blood: the bond of magic.

What if her parents had allowed Doucette, like her sisters, to spend the summers with Tante Mahalt? She might have flown with them over their aunt's domain. If she had mastered the High Arts, Doucette, too, might have stood a chance at inheriting the sorceress's great estate.

All the years wasted, and for what?

So her sisters could belittle her, while she trained as a chastelaine. Doucette stared at the tapestry bag through tear-blurred eyes and wiped her streaming nose on her sleeve. So her parents could marry her off to a nobleman who only prized magic that he controlled.

As Na Claro had said, few brave souls ordered Azelais and Cecilia around. But Doucette was subject to instruction by all the castle servants, many of whom had performed their appointed tasks since before her birth. Doucette hadn't realized how tired she was of doing everyone else's bidding until the moment she had seen her swan skin and known she had a choice.

She could stay home, be judged by the prince her mother had invited, behave exactly as her parents expected.

Or she could go and decide her own fate.

Doucette's hands shook as she opened the tapestry bag and unfurled her swan skin. Gray-tipped white feathers spilled over the coverlet. The breeze played over them, stirring the plumage into the semblance of life.

Doucette clenched her fists. *Sixteen years, you've waited,* her mind's voice whispered. *No longer.*

Her fingers plunged into the feathers. Soft and warm, the swan skin offered a silent promise.

Change.

Did she dare?

Doucette crossed to the window, pushed aside the embroidered curtains, and stared out of the luxurious room that suddenly seemed a prison.

Over the years, Doucette had heard her father instruct her sisters' escort. Like them, she could follow the sheep flocks to a lake in the mountains, then seek the lake's eastern shore. The river Immeluse would lead her the rest of the way to her aunt's castle, to a season of studying magic with Azelais and Cecilia. If she dared.

The wind kissed her cheek.

Doucette sat and took off her shoes. Her hose. Her gown and the soft chemise underneath. Folding each item, she set it on the bed. The breeze gusted, stirring dried rose petals in a wooden bowl and raising tiny bumps along Doucette's skin.

She took a deep breath and drew on the coat of feathers. Magic tingled the length of her body and down her spine. Her neck stretched, her legs shrank. Her skin exploded in feathers. The world spun around her as her vision took on a crystalline sharpness. The floor rose to meet her, then stopped with a jolt.

She was a swan.

Doucette slapped her webbed feet on the floor. Dappled wings opened, flexed, and closed. She honked in triumph, then curled her impossibly long neck and preened a tail feather.

She looked like a swan. Could she fly like one? There was only one way to know. If she succeeded, the pile of discarded clothing, the open window, and the missing swan skin would tell her parents what she had done. If she failed, she would die.

Azelais and Cecilia had managed it, she reminded herself. She would too. Swan-Doucette waddled to the window seat, hopped up onto the broad sill, and stepped off the edge. Flapping furiously, she fell.

Down,

down,

down.

Doucette dropped until the ragged rhythm of her wings smoothed into a steady thrum. The almond trees' reaching arms fell away; the earth receded.

She flew.

Chapter Seven

Doucette pumped her wings and soared higher, delighting in the wind that bore her up. She didn't feel sick at all, as she had when Cecilia's Animated handkerchief had carried her to the sheep pens. No wonder her sisters absented themselves so often from their father's court!

If flying was even more marvelous than she had imagined, how much better might sorcery be?

The decision was easily made.

Swan-Doucette pointed her beak northward, toward Luzerna county and her aunt's castle. At her back, the Château de l'Aire dwindled until it was the size of a villager's thatched hut, a child's mud fort, a clump of dirt. And then it was gone.

Below her, the countryside unrolled like an illustrated parchment. Threaded with streams and dotted with small villages, lowland fields alternated brown and palest green. Cypress trees poked sharp fingers into the sky; fruit trees wore frothy crowns of pink and white blossoms.

On a whim, Doucette flew straight up, leaving the ground so far behind that its contours blurred into a hazy patchwork. Then she swooped low, skimming over Beloc's fields, orchards, and vineyards. When she found the tan ribbon of the northern road, she settled into a steady pace above it.

As the day wore on, the land dimpled, then pushed up into low hills below her. Careful cultivation gave way to wilder country. Rocky, brush-covered slopes sprouted solitary oak trees. The air changed also. Doucette breathed in a sharp incense that made her feel light-headed.

Unless that was hunger.

As the setting sun gilded the left side of Doucette's airborne body with fire, she realized how many hours she had spent aloft. Her elation dissolved, and suddenly she felt weary to the burnished tips of her wings. She had better rest, and eat, before she fell out of the sky.

Some distance from the road, Doucette spied a chain of small ponds. Milky white in the twilight, they appeared from the air like a necklace of moonstones strung across the rocks. As Doucette descended toward the largest one, she noticed steam rising from its surface. Hot springs must feed the pools.

She splashed down awkwardly and paddled to the pond's edge, where the reeds grew thick. A naked girl would have trouble finding food and shelter on her journey, but neither should prove difficult for a swan.

After a few trials, Doucette found fresh vegetation that satisfied her swan body's desperate hunger. That need met, she waddled over to investigate the smaller, hotter pools. Surrounded by twisted shapes of rock, each pool nestled in its own grotto. The water felt unpleasantly warm on her webbed feet, though Doucette knew that her girl shape would find it soothing to sink up to her chin in one of the steaming baths. Jaume had mentioned these pools, or ones like them. He had talked about how delightful they were.

During her flight, Doucette had shied away from wondering how she would change back from swan to girl. The hot pools tempted her to try.

Although she hadn't heard another soul, Doucette sidled behind a tall juniper bush and into a vertical cleft in the rock where she would be hidden from view. Peering at herself first with one eye, then the other, she looked for a seam in her swan skin.

She didn't find one. Worse, she realized, she no longer had hands to pull it apart.

Panic beat in her breast. She stifled it with an effort of will. Azelais and Cecilia had changed back and forth with ease. There must be some trick to it.

Doucette closed her eyes and thought about what happened when her sisters returned to the Château de l'Aire. They would spread their wings wide for balance, then arch their necks and run their beaks down their chests.

She tried it, pressing hard. In her mind, she pictured the two sides of her swan skin separating along the center of her body, allowing her human form to slip out as neatly as it must have done when she was born.

Magic rippled over her. With a whisper of sound, her swan skin parted.

Gasping, Doucette fell out of it and sprawled on the ground. Juniper needles pricked her skin. Her arms and legs felt strange, her head too heavy, her skin too thin. She breathed hard, and the sensations passed. When she could stand, Doucette tucked her swan skin high on a ledge to keep it safe. She coiled her hair into a knot at the back of her neck and spent another long moment in hiding, listening to be sure she was alone. Then she eased out from behind the evergreen shrub, ran to the nearest warm pool, and submerged herself in its depths.

Heaven.

Big enough to measure Doucette's length twice, the pool was fringed with tendrils of a mint-smelling herb. Doucette rested her head against the fragrant carpet and closed her eyes.

When she opened them again, the sky had darkened to violet. Bats flitted through the twilight, squeaking in their high-pitched voices and snapping at insects. Doucette decided she had best change back to swan and find a sheltered place to sleep.

As she rose from the water, her hair fell out of its knot and streamed down her body. Laughing out loud at the sight of her skin, pink and steaming as baked fish, Doucette hurried to retrieve her hidden swan skin from its ledge.

Too close, a dog barked. A man's low voice answered.

Doucette pushed her way through the prickly juniper and squeezed into the rock cleft.

Had someone seen her?

In the troubadours' tales, men married swan maidens they caught unawares. Would Doucette, too, spend the rest of her days in a peasant's hut, pining for her home? Or would her family find out and ransom her? How would they know where to look?

Doucette started to reach for her swan skin, then pulled her arms down, wary of revealing her location. Perhaps if she were very quiet, she wouldn't be noticed in the fading light.

She heard footsteps, then the *click-click* of a dog's nails on rock.

"Who's there?" a low voice said.

Trapped!

Chapter Eight

She had missed her chance to change. If she tried now, he would catch her.

Doucette peered between the juniper branches at the tall man walking toward her. She was relieved to see his hooked staff. Shepherds were superstitious folk; perhaps he would avert his eyes and continue on his way, thinking her no mortal maid, but a wood nymph or rock sprite.

To Doucette's frightened, all-too-human eyes, the shepherd appeared rather spectral himself, with his face hidden by the broad-brimmed hat they all wore. A herding dog capered beside him, lively as a jester in brown-and-white motley.

The shepherd stopped several paces from Doucette's hiding place, close enough for her to smell sheep, wood smoke, and the mint-herb that grew over the rocks. His dog bounded forward, yapping. A cold nose poked through the juniper, and the dog licked Doucette's bare toes.

She yelped in surprise.

The shepherd pushed his hat back and scratched his curly head. "You see, Fidele," he said in the tone of one settling an argument. "I didn't imagine her!"

The dog yipped and returned to bounce happily at his feet. Doucette crossed her arms across her chest while her thoughts tumbled over one another like gamboling lambs.

Jaume? How was that possible? Doucette must have flown even farther than she thought, to catch up with a flock that had left Beloc several days ago. Perhaps she would overtake her sisters, too.

The shepherd touched his fist to his heart. "Good evening, Lady."

It *was* Jaume—she knew that voice! But the formality of his greeting told her he hadn't yet recognized her. Perhaps she should keep silent?

Doucette hesitated. The cold stone niche enclosed her, but she was hardly aware of the chill, since her body burned with embarrassment. Under the heat, a shimmering thread of excitement wound around her limbs. So much had changed since their last meeting. She was a swan maiden now, with a sorceress's freedom—and vulnerability.

Ice touched her spine. If Jaume took her swan skin, she would have to follow him.

She shook off the fearful thought. Jaume had never treated her with anything but kindness, even when his brothers teased him for it. And here they were, alone together in wild country, and he was waiting for her to speak.

Doucette's skin tingled with a mixture of anticipation and pure mischief she had never felt before. "Good evening, Man." She tried to make her voice sound like a rock sprite's, or like Azelais's, haughty and aloof, but an inadvertent giggle spoiled the effect.

Jaume went completely still and then one giant step brought him so close that only the evergreen bush separated them. "Doucette?" His voice was raw with surprise and alarm. "Where's your escort? What happened to——" He reached through the juniper and seized her shoulder, then jumped back, as if the touch of her bare skin had scalded him. He glanced down and raised his eyes at once, his expression horrified. "Where are your clothes? Don't tell me——you've been attacked!" He whistled, shrilly.

Fidele stopped capering. The dog's hackles rose as she planted her forefeet and growled.

"No, Jaume, stop," Doucette said, as he showed every sign of calling the rest of the shepherds to her aid. "It's nothing like that. I'm fine."

"What?" His crook raised like a weapon, Jaume had turned to survey their surroundings. After the one scandalized glance, he seemed unwilling to let his eyes rest on her barely concealed nakedness.

Not sure whether she was more exasperated with him or with herself, Doucette made a face at the shepherd's back. She was sure this kind of thing didn't happen to Azelais or Cecilia. Naked or clothed, her confident sisters would never be so clumsy in the presence of a man. And, after her first fright, the situation had seemed so promising. Romantic, even, like a scene from a tale. Destiny bringing two young lovers together . . . until she bungled it.

"I'm not harmed, Jaume."

"No?" Still, his eyes searched the rocks. "Then what——"

The sound of branches snapping brought both their heads around. Jaume stepped in front of Doucette's hiding place, his shepherd's crook ready to defend or attack.

Doucette wanted to cry with mortification. If this was one of Jaume's brothers, coming to her "rescue" . . .

Brush crackled, and a large animal leaped toward Jaume. Teeth flashed in the gloom.

Doucette screamed, only to feel woefully stupid as Jaume held up his hand.

"Osco."

The dog woofed, then sat on his haunches in front of them.

"Good boy." Jaume scratched the guardian's ruff. "Out with it, Lady Doucette," the shepherd said, his back still turned to her. "Is this your sisters' doing? Have the witches left you defenseless in the wilderness?"

He sounded, Doucette thought, as if he had caught Vitor or Eri in an ill-advised prank and somebody was about to get a big brother's cuff on the ear. But she was only four years younger than he, and not his little sister; she wouldn't be treated so. "I came by myself, for your information. I flew."

"Flew?"

Jaume's disbelief stung. The sweeping reverses of the past few moments, from terror to elation and back again, had left Doucette feeling as though she had been put in a bag and shaken. The words spilled out of her.

"Yes. My parents hid my swan skin, but I found it, and I'm going to Tante Mahalt's to study magic with my sisters. I don't care what you think about the High Arts. You can't stop me. I'm a swan maiden, after all."

"A swan maiden," Jaume said, his voice completely neutral.

"Yes."

"A sorceress."

"Yes." Doucette sniffed. "That is, I'm going to be. I can do the one Transformation spell already."

"Well, now. That changes things, doesn't it?" Jaume rubbed the back of his neck and sat down on a rock. "A sorceress."

Osco and Fidele arranged themselves on either side of him. Both dogs cocked furry heads at Doucette, as if they, too, were curious to hear her explanation.

"Yes." The light had almost gone, but if Doucette couldn't read his expression, he couldn't see her clearly, either. "So, I thought," she began, a little timidly.

"Why'd you follow me, Lady Doucette?" Jaume said, still in that calm voice.

"I didn't," Doucette said. "Weren't you listening? That is, I did follow the sheep, because that's the way to Tante Mahalt's, but I wasn't looking for you." You conceited thing, she let her tone imply.

"Then it's an accident, our meeting?"

"You told me about the hot pools, remember? It's your fault, if it's anyone's."

Jaume bowed his head. His voice came out muffled. "My fault."

"Not that I'm unhappy to see you. I mean, since I'm a swan maiden now, and you said you admired me . . ." Doucette's voice trailed away. Did she have to spell it out for him?

When Jaume didn't answer, Doucette poked her head out of the concealing juniper. The man's shoulders were shaking. "What's the matter?"

"The matter?" His head lifted. He was laughing, soundlessly, in great gulps of air.

Doucette's soul shriveled. She'd as good as offered herself, and Jaume thought it a great joke. It had all been a lie, what he had said before, she realized with terrible clarity. Soothing nonsense meant to comfort a hurt child.

Jaume was a friendly soul, after all. No blame to him that she had read more than he meant into his compliments, into his offer of help.

Shudders wracked Doucette's body. No matter how hard she clenched her hands over her arms, she couldn't stop shivering.

Stupid, stupid, stupid!

Why had she thought the swan skin would change her into someone as compelling, as desirable as her sisters? She was still the drab one, the drudge. But she would show him! She'd show them all—her parents, the court, everyone! She would study harder than Cecilia and Azelais combined and become so great a sorceress that no one would dare laugh at her again.

If they did, she'd turn them into—into sheep!

"Leave me," Doucette said. At last her voice sounded like a true sorceress's, as cold as the river Immeluse, foaming around the castle where the Queen of the Birds dwelt in splendid isolation.

Fidele yipped. Jaume shook his head, still unable to answer her for laughing.

"Go away," Doucette said, more forcefully, but he didn't.

Not caring whether he saw her or not, she reached for her swan skin. "Then I will."

"Lady . . ."

Her arms full of feathers, Doucette looked over her shoulder to see that Jaume had fallen to his knees.

"Doucette, stay." Jaume extended his hand. "Sweetheart. Will you marry me?"

"Marry you?" Doucette stiffened with outrage. "I don't care how handsome you are, Jaume of Vent'roux, you can't laugh at me, then propose. I never want to see you again. I hate you."

"Please, listen," Jaume begged.

"No!" Frantic to escape fresh humiliation, Doucette stepped out of the crevice and flung the swan skin over her shoulders. As if it were a pool of water, she fell into her swan shape.

Osco growled; Fidele barked madly.

Swan-Doucette stretched her neck and hissed at both of them. She shot a warning look at the shepherd and bobbed her head in satisfaction when Jaume called off his dogs. As swiftly as she could paddle her feet and flap her wings, Doucette regained the sky, and freedom.

She wasn't running away, she told herself, wings pumping fiercely. She was running *to* something, which made all the difference.

Didn't it?

Chapter Nine

As she labored through the pine-scented air, Doucette's wings trembled with fatigue.

Shortly after leaving Jaume the previous night, she had found an island in a larger lake and tucked her head under her wing. Sleep, however, had eluded her. She started at every unfamiliar noise, and when at last she had slipped into an uneasy doze, she dreamed of falling. Mouth open, she screamed without making a sound, until a shepherd's crook pulled her out of the sky and into an embrace that smelled of wood smoke and mint. She had woken with a jerk and not slept again.

Taking to the air at first light, Doucette had found the Immeluse, then flown above the river without stopping. Far below, the rocky scrub changed to meadow and then to forest. After many weary hours, she glimpsed her destination ahead.

Pearly gray in the morning light, the castle's stone shoulders parted the river like a lady rising from her bath. A most private lady, who disdained company. No bridge spanned the torrent that poured past the island stronghold. The closest road, hardly more than a dirt track, emerged from the forest to cross a shallow stretch downstream from the castle. Beyond the ford, the road disappeared once more into the trees.

As she neared the Château de l'Île, Doucette counted four towers encircled by a high wall. Wide balconies ringed the top portion of each tower, and she puzzled over their purpose. Defense? Decoration?

The inside courtyard was planted with fruit trees, their bare branches sporting white and pink buds. Arched windows and doorways pierced the castle's stone walls at intervals, but only, Doucette realized, on the interior sides. The outer walls turned blank faces to the river, the forest, and the sky.

"My sister will know who seeks her," Doucette's father had told the armsmen who escorted Azelais and Cecilia, but on this peaceful morning, the castle appeared deserted.

No—not quite deserted. Several white doves swirled out an open window, over the castle wall, and into the forest.

Doucette descended, listening in vain for a human voice raised in a shout or laughter or song. She didn't hear any of the Château de l'Aire's usual noises: axes chopping wood, squealing pigs, the scrape of a shovel against a stable floor. Although the sun had risen in the sky, Doucette could see no sign of a meal being prepared; no plume of smoke rose from cook fire or oven, carrying the smell of fresh bread.

Unsure of her welcome at this silent castle, she decided to stop and feed. Perhaps when she felt stronger she would know exactly what to do.

Exerting her tired muscles, Doucette searched for a quiet patch of water in which to land. A rocky gorge contained this stretch of the Immeluse, channeling it into a foaming rush. Where the steep banks gentled at the ford below the castle, several women were washing clothes in the shallows. Doucette veered away from them and spotted a break in the trees where cultivated fields surrounded a huddle of houses.

Curious, she flew closer. At the edge of a tidy-looking village, a millpond beckoned. Doucette sank gratefully out of the sky. She splashed down and paddled to the side of the pond farthest from the mill gate, then plunged her head underwater to forage among the reeds. Digging deep, she didn't see the mill door open, or the man with the net come out.

The miller hiked his white-spotted brown tunic over his knees. Bare feet silent on the muddy ground, he crept around the pond and cast his net.

"Got you," he crowed.

Doucette whipped her neck out of the reeds as the mesh settled over her.

A net?

Had she escaped from one man only to fall prey to another? She hissed in fear and bit at the mesh.

Careful to avoid her snapping beak, the miller waded into the pond, pulled the sides of the net together, and towed his catch toward the bank. "Calm yourself, my beauty," he soothed. "No neck chain, eh? So you're not one of hers. Fair game, I say. Very fair." He chortled at his own wit. "Nobody to miss you, and the four of us to welcome you at dinner."

At dinner? The man planned to roast her because she wasn't wearing a necklace?

Despair froze Doucette's blood as she considered her choices. She could change, but then she'd be a naked girl in a net and the miller would know exactly what prize he had caught. Besides, if she could get free for a moment, a swan had a better chance of escape. One blow of her powerful wings could break a man's arm. A buffet could stun him.

"Bodo! Ravioun!" The miller waved at the two flour-dusted boys who had come to gape at the spectacle. "Give me a hand, you louts. See what I've caught!"

"A swan, Father?" The smaller boy's eyes were round, dark holes in his white-speckled face. "Is it safe?"

"Unmarked!" The older boy whooped. "Last one there's a blood-sucking leech!" He ran at Doucette, shouting over his shoulder. "Leech, leech, Ravioun is a sucking leech." He splashed into the pond and tugged a corner of the net.

The younger boy had stopped to pick up a stick. He reached the melee as his brother jumped backward.

"Hey!" The taller boy let go of the net and sat down in waist-deep water, shaking his hand. "It bit me!"

Doucette barked and hissed.

"Too close, Bodo." The muscles bunched in the man's arms as he tried to regain control of the net. "Ravioun! Quickly. If we lose her—"

The net flapped.

Doucette surged toward the opening and freedom, but the younger boy shook his stick. "Get back!"

"Boy. Lay down the cudgel." The voice that spoke was as clear as snowmelt.

Ravioun dropped the stick. Both boys bowed their heads, touched their hearts with their fists, and stood shivering in the cold water. Doucette peered through the mesh.

"Lady Mahalt." The miller's face had turned as white as his flour. "She's yours?"

"You know the penalty for harming one of my swans." Mahalt Aigleron shrugged her blue cloak away from the shoulders of her gown. A slender finger tapped the key strung on a ribbon around her neck.

The man cringed. "Saint Armentarius be my witness, I didn't see your sign. . . ."

Doucette squawked at her rescuer.

Mahalt limped to the edge of the pond. Like a bird's dragging wing, the blue cloak hem brushed her fine leather shoes. Strangely, her awkward gait only intensified the elegance of her face and dress.

"As well I came," she said in the same level, terrifying voice, "and averted a costly misunderstanding."

"Yes, my lady." The miller scooped up the sopping bundle of net and bird and water weed and set it at the woman's feet. "Your pardon, Lady Mahalt. I never—"

"Go," she said.

"My lady." He bowed. Then, seizing each of the boys by an ear, he hustled them into the mill. The door banged shut.

The woman folded her arms.

Doucette shifted her weight. She arched her neck and poked her orange beak through the net.

Mahalt slipped off the blue cloak and held it open in front of her. "Change," she said.

There was no question of disobeying that voice. Doucette changed. Like the first time she returned to her human shape, she lay gasping for several moments before her skin felt the right size. When she could control her legs, she stood up and kicked the net away. Clutching her muddy swan skin, she draped the offered cloak around herself and curtsied as best she could. "Tante Mahalt. Thank you. I . . . I—" She stuttered to a halt.

Her aunt looked like an older, colder version of Azelais. Silver streaked the two long black braids that shone in the sunlight, iridescent as a magpie's feathers. Fine lines radiated from the corners of her dark eyes; the wine-red lips were set in a disapproving expression. Again, Doucette's aunt touched the key strung around her neck. "Reckless girl, flying without a sign. You're Pascau's youngest?"

"Yes. I'm Doucette."

Mahalt's eyebrows arched. "Where are Azelais and Cecilia? Did Sarpine keep them this year?"

"No, they're riding with an escort of Father's armsmen, as usual."

The dark gaze rested on Doucette with a palpable weight. "You've not come to me before."

"Mother hid my swan skin." Doucette studied her muddy feet. She felt grubby and small as she pleaded for understanding. "I have to learn magic, Tante Mahalt. Azelais and Cecilia have had all these years, and I didn't—I have to know. Please, don't send me home."

"Not until you've learned to take better care in your swan form." Her aunt frowned at the discarded net. "If my sister-in-law hoped to hide your true nature forever, she deluded herself, and Pascau was twice a fool to humor her." She fixed Doucette with a stern look. "Fortunately for you, I wondered why a lone swan hadn't the courtesy to pay her respects. Without my intervention, you'd be dead or wed. Neither of the miller's boys is a prize."

"Yes, Tante. I'm sorry." For no reason, Doucette thought of Jaume's unexpected offer. Should she have stayed and listened? He could have taken her swan skin outright, but he hadn't. And, unlike the miller's boys, Jaume was so handsome . . . kind, too. Usually, anyway. Doucette bowed her head to hide the heat creeping up her cheeks. No doubt a sorceress should have loftier matters than a shepherd to occupy her thoughts.

"Come." Mahalt's long skirt flared as she stalked away from the millpond. Despite the limp, she set a swift pace.

Doucette hurried down the muddy track after her aunt. They left the mill village and entered a stand of cedar and pine, where the air smelled of wet leaves and wood violets. Patches of granular snow still flecked the ground under the trees. Spring came later to Luzerna's mountains than it did to Beloc's lowland valleys.

Ahead, the faint sound of the washerwomen's voices rose over the chuckle of running water. Before they reached the source of either noise, Mahalt turned and picked her way through the trees to a squat stone tower. Beyond the tower, a wide stream drained a soggy meadow to the river.

Mahalt took the key from her neck and unlocked the tower's only door. Doucette would have followed her aunt inside, but Mahalt shook her head. "I flew after you in haste," she said. "The clothing remains for the next time I require it. Give me the cloak."

The breeze whipped through the pine trees behind the tower and laid cold fingers on Doucette's arms and legs. Shivering, she held tightly to her swan skin, which gave off the dank aroma of millpond, and waited until her aunt reemerged carrying a black swan skin.

Although Mahalt wore nothing more than the key around her neck and her shining hair for garment, the older woman maintained her self-possessed air. "I built several of these towers on my land to keep my swan skin safe. I advise you to do the same when you establish yourself."

"Yes, Tante Mahalt." Doucette stared at her aunt's bare feet, one of which was oddly set on her ankle. The malformed limb didn't appear to cause her pain, but Doucette felt a pang of sympathy.

Mahalt locked the tower door and draped the ribbon over the latch. She cocked her head at Doucette. "What, are you waiting for me to part the waters? We fly to the castle, Niece. Change."

"Yes, Tante." For the third time, Doucette donned her swan skin, welcoming the heat that surged the length of her body, turned her inside out, and left her standing on two webbed feet.

Oh, but she itched! Swan-Doucette unfurled her wings and preened, rooting out flakes of dirt and pond weed. Fastidiously, she nibbled each gray-tipped plume into place.

In one fluid motion, Mahalt threw her feathered coat over her shoulders. Her shape rippled and changed into that of a black swan. Like heraldic markings, two white bands barred each glossy wing.

Doucette thought her aunt's swan shape as beautiful as her human form, marred only by one damaged foot. But lameness didn't matter, Doucette reminded herself, once a swan was flying.

Swan-Mahalt thrust her head through the dangling ribbon and twisted her neck until the key dangled over her breast. She signaled to Doucette with an imperious glance.

Together, the black swan and the white waddled to the water. Feet pattering, wings beating, they leaped into the air.

Chapter Ten

"Again," Mahalt said.

"Yes, Tante." As if the magic she sought might be hiding in the maze of branches overhead, Doucette stared upward, then scratched her cheek. The feathers of her swan skin, which she wore slung over her shoulders like a cape, kept brushing against her, distracting her from the matter at hand.

Her fingers curled over the wand Tante Mahalt had given her. Dark with age, the polished oak felt slippery.

Gathering her scattered thoughts, Doucette touched the wand to a twig laid out on the gravel before her.

> *Be applewood spoon,*
> *wide-bowled,*
> *long-handled,*
> *sanded smooth and fine,*
> *until I release thee from that shape.*

The twig shimmered and changed. One end spread wide and dimpled into a bowl; the other arched up in an elegant curve.

Doucette held her breath. Unlike the overwhelming sensation she felt when she donned her swan skin, the wand tickled her fingertips with the barest echo of magic. Was it enough? Would the enchantment hold?

With a loud snapping sound, her spell came undone. The spoon shape contracted to applewood twig, its bark as knobby as before. Along the twig's length, tiny leaves drooped as if they, too, despaired of Doucette's success.

"Not quite," Mahalt said.

Doucette groaned with frustration. "I don't understand. What am I doing wrong?"

Doucette's aunt tapped her lip thoughtfully. Sunlight gleamed on her black-and-silver hair; rings glinted on her fingers. "You have the eye, Doucette," she said. "Your spoons are the right size, and their proportions are good. From Azelais's first attempts, one would think your sister had spent her life eating with her fingers."

"I've polished enough spoons to know the shape," Doucette said. "Mother's particular about her silver."

"Sarpine would be," Mahalt said.

Doucette poked the ground with her wand. "Then why don't my spells stick?"

"Three qualities are required to work magic." Mahalt ticked them off on her fingers. "An observant eye, a clear mind, and a strong will. It's no small matter, Niece, to impose your intent over the Creator's."

"Is that why clerics frown on sorcery?" Doucette asked. "Brother Martin lectured Azelais and Cecilia no end when he caught them casting spells after a service."

Mahalt's eyebrows drew together. "Depends on the spell, depends on the cleric. Like many other gifts—wealth, or beauty, or an eloquent tongue—sorcery can be corrupted. When we employ our powers without regard to our fellow creatures, we risk our immortal souls."

Doucette ran her thumb down the wand. "How do you know whether you're using your magic wisely?"

Mahalt's dark gaze held Doucette's. "How do you judge any of your actions?"

"Brother Martin says our conscience should guide us."

"The trick is to listen to it," Mahalt said. "As your powers grow, it's tempting to think you can solve every problem with magic. But does Animating your loom keep the village weaver from earning her bread? Does paying your accounts in false coin ruin your neighbors?" One elegant shoulder lifted. "Transforming twigs into spoons is a fairly harmless occupation. Try another."

"Yes, Tante."

Doucette tried again.

And again.

And again.

None of her spoons held its shape for more than a moment. She kept at it, but her eyes were scratchy with unshed tears when a dove fluttered over the castle wall and perched on Mahalt's shoulder.

The little bird stroked its beak against the sorceress's cheek and cooed.

Mahalt cocked her head at a listening angle and nodded once. "Thank you, my lovely," she said, smoothing the dove's gray feathers. "Go your way. I'll see to them."

"Who's come?" Doucette asked as the bird took wing.

"Your sisters." Leaning against an apple tree, Mahalt stood and shook out her skirts.

Worry and anticipation battled within Doucette as she tucked her wand into her sleeve and followed her limping aunt across the courtyard. Over the past few days, she had wondered whether Azelais and Cecilia knew about her swan skin. Would they be surprised? Pleased to see her? Or would they be angry that she, too, had come to stake a claim on their aunt's crown?

Mahalt stopped and rested her ringed hand against the far wall. She murmured words Doucette couldn't hear.

With the blur that heralded magic-working, a pair of tall wooden doors appeared within the stone blocks. Noiselessly, the doors swung wide. As she stepped through the opening, Mahalt flicked her niece an amused glance.

Doucette closed her open mouth. She watched Mahalt kneel on a wide lip of stone that extended past the other side of the doors, over the river. The sorceress dipped her hand into the flowing Immeluse and spoke again.

The water flashed with rainbow color, and twin waves curled away from Mahalt's hand. Majestically, like a court lady curtsying, the Immeluse drew back her foaming skirts. A glistening pathway of wet stone opened in the center of the riverbed.

"Come, Doucette."

With a whoosh of air, Doucette let go the breath she had been holding and followed her aunt downstream.

A dozen horsemen and two women awaited at the ford. Horses stamped and blew at the currents of water swirling along each bank. Their riders looked only a little less unnerved by the river's behavior.

Cecilia leaped from her mount. Tossing the mare's reins to an armsman, she danced along the riverbed. One hand held up her travel bag; the other waved wildly. At every step, a feathery white cape fluttered against her back.

"Tante Mahalt! Tante Mahalt!" she cried. "We're here at last! The road stretches longer every year, or maybe it's—Doucette?" Cecilia's voice swooped upward. She dropped her bag, seized Doucette's arms, and shook her. "Is that you?"

"Good afternoon, Cecilia." Doucette tried to keep her voice steady even as her teeth rattled from her sister's impetuous greeting. "Azelais."

"Tante Mahalt." Azelais had dismounted more sedately. Her travel gown showed few wrinkles, despite the days of riding, and the swan skin draped over her shoulders shone as glossy a black as her coiled hair. She curtsied politely to their aunt before turning on Doucette. "What business could *you* possibly have at the Château de l'Île? Why aren't you home making cheese or hemming linens?"

"And however did you get here before us?" Cecilia added.

"I flew," Doucette said.

Azelais snorted in disbelief.

Doucette turned so they could see her swan skin.

"From Beloc?" Cecila's rosebud lips made an O of surprise. "How did you manage it? An afternoon on the wing exhausts me completely."

Azelais's dark eyes narrowed with suspicion. "Where'd you come by a swan skin? And when?" Her hands curled into claws. "You sly creature! Why didn't you ever wear it? To curry favor with Mother?"

"No!" Doucette said. "She hid it from me."

Azelais sneered. "We're to believe that?"

"Perhaps explanations can wait until we've seen to your escort," Mahalt said.

"Yes, Tante." Azelais's even voice and lowered lashes failed to hide her fury. She hoisted her own leather bag over her shoulder and turned her back on Doucette.

At the head of the group, Captain Denis bowed over his horse's neck. "Lady Mahalt."

"Will you and your men take some refreshment, Captain?" she asked.

"Thank you, Lady," he replied politely, "but we'll provision ourselves in the village, by your leave. Do I understand that you have taken charge of Lady Doucette as well as Lady Azelais and Lady Cecilia?"

"Yes. You may reassure her parents on that account."

Mahalt's dry tone told Doucette that her aunt knew exactly how comforting Doucette's mother would find the news.

"As you command, Lady," Captain Denis said. "We'll return for all three at summer's end."

Mahalt nodded. "Safe journey to you," she said, then limped up the streambed. Azelais followed closely behind her.

"Good-bye!" Cecilia blew kisses at the armsmen as they urged their horses, including the two Azelais and Cecilia had ridden, through knee-high water and up the muddy bank. "Till summer's end!"

"They won't spend the night?" Doucette asked Cecilia in a low voice.

"No, never." Nonchalantly, Cecilia handed Doucette her travel bag and hiked up her divided riding skirts. "Twelve mighty warriors and every one afraid that Tante Mahalt would turn him into a toad if he presumed to spend a night under her roof."

"Would she?" Doucette said.

"Who knows?" Cecilia glanced upriver to make sure their aunt was out of earshot. "After the husband she had, the Queen of the Birds doesn't care for men."

"Did he break her foot?"

"What?"

Doucette felt stupid for asking, but she had wondered. "To keep her from running."

Cecilia hooted a laugh. "No, silly. Lavena did that."

"The spirit? Why?"

Cecilia shrugged. "A spell, what else? Tante Mahalt told us. The Rassemblement, it's called. Sounded too uncertain for my taste, frankly, what with jumping into Lavena's Cauldron and not knowing what you'll look like after your companion puts you back together. If he can find all the bits and bones." She shuddered delicately and smoothed her coat of white feathers. "I'm happy with the power I have, though of course Tante Mahalt had no choice."

"She didn't?"

Cecilia's mouth set in a straight line. "Her husband locked away her swan skin," she said, very low. "Afraid she'd leave him, so he stole her magic in the name of love."

Doucette turned her chin into her own swan skin, touching the feathers for comfort. "How did she get it back?"

"After the Rassemblement, no lock could keep her out. She recovered her swan skin and flew from Beloc to Luzerna."

"So he lost her anyway."

"Yes." Cecilia hesitated, intent on the river bottom's uneven footing. "You had better know the rest, now that you're one of us. He tried to stop her."

"And?"

"He died."

"What?" Doucette almost dropped her sister's travel bag. "She killed him?"

"It might have been an accident. Tante didn't give us the details." Cecilia faced Doucette with a challenging expression. "Have I shocked you, little sister? Until you know what you would do to regain your magic, your freedom, don't you dare judge her."

"But *murder*?"

With a toss of her golden curls, Cecilia returned to her usual levity. "Maybe the fool picked up an Animated ax and it hacked him to bits." She shot Doucette a sly smile. "Around sorceresses, a man should take care where he puts his hands, don't you think?"

Blushing at her sister's innuendo, Doucette picked her way along the wet stones. She knew very little, really, about the woman to whom she had entrusted her hopes.

But what choice had she? Tante Mahalt was the only sorceress Doucette knew who might be willing to teach her the High Arts. She must trust in her aunt's goodwill.

Summer

Chapter Eleven

*H*er head ached. Doucette leaned against the bedchamber door and rubbed her cheekbones, trying to relieve the pressure behind her eyes. Her head felt too solid, as if her skull had been packed with dough and baked. After a day spent Transforming herself with a wand instead of the swan skin, her very shape felt foreign. Her balance couldn't be trusted, and she kept expecting to see a hawk's talons at the end of her arms instead of fingers.

Aside from these odd aftereffects, working magic had proved every bit as exciting as she had hoped. With two months of intense practice behind her, Doucette had learned to Animate simple tools and Transform objects in ways limited only by her imagination and will. Though often, as today, it left her feeling very strange.

Her mind was stuffed to bursting with all the natural observations, magical theory, and dire prohibitions Tante Mahalt had instilled. Lurking below the day-to-day struggle to remember it all, fears about what her mother would do at summer's end surfaced to trouble Doucette at unguarded moments. She had flouted Lady Sarpine's wishes. What measures would her mother think suitable to answer such flagrant disobedience?

Between the work and the worry, Doucette slept fitfully. At times she dreamed of falling, or of meeting Jaume again by the lake, where events occurred quite differently. In the best dreams, he didn't scorn her, but took her hand and kissed her—oh, so sweetly. Those were nights she didn't want to end, though when she woke she felt doubly foolish for yearning after a man who had laughed at her.

Hanging her swan skin on a peg, Doucette sank onto the bed. She'd take a nap before mending the tear she had noticed in Azelais's favorite overdress. In return, perhaps her oldest sister would have the grace to mute her constant criticism.

Doucette pushed Azelais's discarded green gown and linen shift to one side and plumped the pillows into a nest. Though unadorned, the bed was comfortable, like the chamber Tante Mahalt had assigned them. It seemed much larger than the one she and her sisters shared at home. Or perhaps the impression of space came from the fact that the mistress of the Château de l'Île had a more restrained taste in furnishings than her sister-in-law.

At the Château de l'Aire, jars of flower-scented lotions and bowls of dried petals accented polished walnut-wood tables. Cushioned benches, silver candlesticks, embroidered hangings, and rugs brightened the stone chamber, and a welter of gloves, shoes, fur robes, books, and musical instruments added to the cheerful clutter.

This room had a large bed and three wooden stools.

It was austere enough to pass for a cell in the abbey of Saint-Trophime, but for the enormous weaving, taller than a man and three times as wide, that covered one wall of the tower room.

Within the tapestry's border of stars, a crowned black swan flew over a field of flowers.

As Doucette relaxed into the pillows, the door opened and Cecilia flounced in, her feathered cloak twitching.

At once, she spotted the gold chain on one of the stools. "Your work, Doucette?"

"Yes," Doucette said, yawning. "Braided straw. What do you think?"

Cecilia fingered the links. "A pleasing color, though it weighs a bit light for gold. The hammer dents are a clever touch. It might pass for true."

Offended by the suggestion, Doucette sat up. "It's meant to be pretty, not to deceive."

"No?" Cecilia pulled a hand mirror from her bag. Draping the chain against her throat, she studied her reflection. "When did you enchant it?"

"This morning."

They both glanced out the narrow western window. The sky was tinged with the apricot color heralding day's end.

Cecilia pursed her lips. "If the spell holds until dawn, it shouldn't unravel. Not bad."

"You sound surprised. Didn't you think I could learn?"

Cecilia shrugged and dropped the chain on the bed. Restless as a cat, she prowled the chamber, trailing her fingers over smooth stone walls and window ledges. She straightened the swan hanging. "We're not used to being shown up by our baby sister. Though I'll admit your domestic talents have been useful. Since Tante Mahalt doesn't keep servants, we're usually sick unto death of millet porridge and onion soup by the end of our stay.

Your cooking we like." Cecilia flashed a mischievous smile before her blue eyes sobered. "But watching you master the lore we thought our own? No."

"Why not?" Doucette said. "I've just as much right, but Azelais acts like I'm her enemy."

"Aren't you?" Cecilia took another turn around the room. "Think, Doucette. Only one of us can inherit Tante Mahalt's crown."

"True." Abandoning her plan to nap, Doucette pulled the green gown onto her lap and rolled the torn hem between her fingers. "Lend me your needle case, would you, Cecilia?"

"Forgot it," Cecilia said. "Azelais likely packed hers. Prepared for every occasion, that sister of ours." Cecilia rifled through Azelais's bag and tossed Doucette a leather case. "There. With colored thread to match each one of her gowns."

"Naturally." Doucette threaded the needle and repaired the hem with small, even stitches.

Cecilia picked up the chain again and poured it from hand to hand. Links clinked against one another with a dull, metallic sound.

"Don't mistake me. I intend to wear Tante Mahalt's crown." Cecilia wrinkled her nose. "Though I don't blame you for trying. Being any kind of sorceress is better than a chastelaine's dull life. If you'd put aside your silly scruples, you, too, could avoid the fat old duke or baron Mother's no doubt scheming to procure."

Doucette decided not to mention the prince. She set the last few stitches in the hem and knotted the thread. "If you and I are sorceresses, who'll marry and provide the Aigleron heirs?"

Cecilia tossed her head. "Azelais can do it."

The swan tapestry rippled as the bar supporting it swung away from the wall. A black head, poised on a long, graceful neck, butted open the door that had been concealed behind the wall hanging.

Doucette caught a glimpse of the balcony outside as the black swan marched from the flight court into the bedchamber.

"Did your ears burn?" Cecilia said. "We were just discussing you."

The swan hissed.

The door closed; the tapestry returned to its place.

With her beak, swan-Azelais dislodged a diamond pendant from her feathered breast, then twisted her neck. The necklace twinkled across the room.

"Temper, temper." Cecilia laughed and snatched the diamond pendant out of the air. She dropped necklace and chain in a glittering tangle on the bed.

Ebony plumage shimmered with color before the swan skin split open. Azelais stepped out, her face half hidden by the sweep of her long black hair.

Doucette admired how her sister never sprawled on the floor, gasping, when she returned from swan to human shape. "Your gown's mended."

"Give it here." Naked, Azelais stalked to the bed. She pulled her shift over her head, then snatched the gown so roughly that the needle Doucette held twisted and bit deep.

"You're welcome," Doucette said crossly and sucked her wounded finger. So much for courtesy.

Cecilia clucked. "What ill humor rides you, Sister?"

Azelais hung her black swan skin next to Doucette's dappled one. "I saw them, by the chain of lakes." Spots of color stained her cheeks. Her lips tightened as she attacked her loose hair, coiling it into a knot, then jabbed her wand through the black strands. "They're coming."

"Who?" Doucette's pulse sped. Had Azelais, too, met the brown-eyed shepherd and his little dog? Had her beautiful sister been wearing her swan skin? Or not?

None of Doucette's affair, if Jaume decided he preferred Azelais. Men were always pursuing her sisters. Or being pursued. And it wasn't as though Doucette held any illusions about her own looks. She was accustomed to walking in her sisters' shadow.

Doucette opened Azelais's leather case. Before she could tuck the needle inside, it slipped and pricked her again. Tears of vexation, she told herself, swiping her arm across her eyes. Not of disappointment. Stupid shepherds. Stupid needles.

Cecilia was counting on her fingers. "Already? Early, isn't it? We should have had another month."

"Ask her." Azelais bared her teeth at Doucette. "Mother will have made Father's life a misery, fretting over how her 'sweetling,' her 'treasure,' has fared with the godless sorceresses."

Cecilia's blond eyebrows winged upward. "You mean her other two daughters and their aunt? Those godless sorceresses?"

"You know Mother fears our magic, Cecilia. She never cared how long we stayed away while she had Doucette to follow her around like a fledgling chick." Azelais glared at her youngest sister. "We've two days, at most. It's your fault Captain Denis is fetching us so early."

"Captain Denis?" Doucette dropped the needle case, which skittered under the bed. She bent down to retrieve it.

"Why, you sound relieved," Cecilia said. "Who did you think Azelais meant?"

"She can't wait to show off her new accomplishments at court," Azelais said sourly.

"No." Doucette could hardly tell them about the man who'd been haunting her dreams. A shepherd. Her sisters would laugh in her face.

Fortunately, a swallow swooped into the room and cut short Azelais's harangue. The bird twittered at them and flitted out.

"Tante wants us," Doucette said. She left the needle case where it lay, seized her swan skin, and ran down the stairs ahead of her sisters.

Mahalt was waiting for her nieces in the great hall.

For the first time that summer, she did not wait alone.

Chapter Twelve

*D*oucette crossed the threshold and looked up in wonder. Fluttering plumage filled the raised gallery that wrapped three sides of the castle's vaulted hall. All around, birds made a restless, white-capped sea of brown and gray and black, streaked with the vivid blue of bee-eaters and the pale rose of flamingos. On the gallery's waist-high railing, flocks of little birds— warblers, sparrows, linnets, and woodlarks—had assembled. Tall white egrets and majestic herons peered over their smaller cousins' shoulders. Swallows wheeled through the stone arches that surmounted the railing. At the far end of the hall, a pair of crows quarreled with a hawk, until an owl clapped its wings and silenced both parties. Magpies scolded; a peacock screamed like a lost soul.

Closer, a seagull shrieked near Doucette's ear. She flung her arm up to protect her face, then lowered it when the gull flew by.

Cecilia skidded to a stop beside Doucette. Azelais arrived hard on her sisters' heels. Temper forgotten, her dark eyes shone with excitement. "What does it mean?"

"All the birds of the world have come," Doucette said.

Mahalt stood by the hearth, where a blackened pot hung

over a small fire. Their aunt wore a crimson gown. Rubies and diamonds flashed at her ears. She called the three young women, her voice low and calm.

Confidently, Azelais strode forward. "Yes, Tante Mahalt?"

Cecilia and Doucette trailed after her, staring at the masses of birds.

"Your escort from Beloc arrives earlier than expected," their aunt said.

The young women nodded.

"You knew? Good. Vigilance becomes you. A sorceress will always have enemies seeking to curb her power and independence." Mahalt's dark gaze traveled from one face to another. "I have not spoken of this overmuch, but I tell you now: Beware of men. Their promises are not to be trusted. If one finds your swan skin, he will make your life a misery."

"Yes, Tante," Azelais said. Cecilia murmured agreement.

Not all men were untrustworthy! Doucette wanted to say, but she held her tongue.

"You see our guests." Mahalt gestured at the gallery.

The sisters nodded.

"The birds come to witness who will be Queen after me," Mahalt said.

"Queen of the Birds?" Cecilia bounced on her toes.

Azelais licked her lips. "You're ready to choose your heir, Tante Mahalt?"

"Choose?" Mahalt drew out the word. "No. The title is not mine to give, but rather yours to earn."

"A magical contest?" Cecilia clapped her hands.

Excitement hummed inside Doucette. She, too, had a chance. If she were named Mahalt's heir, perhaps her parents would realize how wrong they had been to hide the swan skin from her.

Except I'm not ready, another part of her wailed silently. With only two months of practice, how could she equal Azelais's and Cecilia's spellcraft?

"I had hoped you would have more time to prepare," Mahalt said, her glance resting on Doucette as if reading her thoughts, "but Sarpine forces my hand. There are several parts to the trial." She pointed at a table where three river stones rested. "First, you will Transform an object. Azelais?"

"Yes, Tante." The dark-haired girl tapped one of the stones with her wand and muttered under her breath. The rock sparkled, then flattened like a lump of melting butter. Its gray color warmed to a rich green.

Thin. Thinner. Thinnest.

When elegant folds of fabric draped across the table, Azelais nodded in satisfaction. The color of the scarf matched her dress exactly.

Mahalt picked up the length of green silk. The fabric whispered over her hands. "Nicely done," she said, "though the weave is loose here"—she pointed to a section. "And here."

Azelais flushed.

"Observation," her aunt reminded her. "You must picture exactly what you want before you begin."

"Yes, Tante."

Cecilia's Transformation, a golden harp, was judged more successful.

Mahalt skimmed her fingers over the strings. Sound rippled

into the room, and nightingales trilled in response. "Lovely," Mahalt said.

Cecilia curtsied gracefully. "Thank you."

Doucette's stomach clenched. Her turn. She tapped the remaining rock with her wand and tried to fix her idea in her mind before she spoke.

> *Be thou painted image,*
> *show Azelais,*
> *Cecilia,*
> *Doucette.*
> *A memory*
> *for our aunt to hold*
> *when we have gone.*

The rock flattened into a wooden oblong the size of Doucette's clasped hands. The other women leaned closer as the board's surface streaked with patches of color, then sharpened into three faces—a portrait.

Perfectly detailed in every respect, Azelais's dark beauty, Cecilia's mirthful face, and Doucette's worried gray eyes regarded them.

"Oooh," Cecilia said.

Doucette frowned. Her eyes looked too big, and her hair—

The image wavered; the bright colors smeared. "No!" Doucette cried out in disappointment as the board lost its shape and reformed as a rock.

Her hand trembled on the wand. She was sure she had the

will to make a spell endure. She had to win this contest, to prove herself.

"It was a pretty idea," Cecilia said generously.

"While it lasted." Relief flashed under Azelais's calm.

Mahalt didn't waste breath on Doucette's failure. She held up her arm, and three doves fluttered down to perch on her sleeve. "Next, you are to Transform a living creature," she said, giving a bird to each niece. "Cecilia, will you begin?"

"Yes, Tante." With her usual exuberance, Cecilia turned her dove into an enormous brown bear.

It shook its head, as if getting its bearings. Then the bear lumbered to Mahalt and stood, putting its mighty paws to the sorceress's shoulders. Toothed jaws opened in an earsplitting growl.

Cecilia shrieked in horror. Frantically, she waved her wand, but the bear remained a bear.

Squawks and whistles and a desperate honking filled the air as the queen's subjects flew to her defense.

At the still center of a blizzard of darting, clawing, pecking birds, Mahalt smacked the bear across the chin and spoke a sharp command.

Sparks spangled the brown fur. The roar dwindled to a coo as the huge beast turned back into a dove. With a whir of wings, the little bird joined the flock circling the hall.

In the uproar, Doucette had let go of her dove. It flew to the top of a pillar. "Please," she said, "come back. Come back!" But although she coaxed and whistled, she couldn't persuade the dove to return to her hand.

Her aunt directed the birds to settle themselves. "A sorceress keeps her mind fixed on her goal, Doucette," she said, watching her niece's vain attempts to retrieve her dove. "Like Cecilia, you failed to think ahead. She made no provision to curb her beast. You lost yours to fear. You have both failed. Can you do better, Azelais?"

Doucette stepped aside, biting back her protest. How unjust, that she hadn't even had a chance to try!

A smug Azelais tapped her wand on the dove she had kept tightly clasped to her breast.

> *Be thou catling,*
> *fluffy white,*
> *spare*
> *with thy claws, but*
> *lavish*
> *with thy affections,*
> *until Mahalt releases thee*
> *from thy unaccustomed shape.*

When Azelais opened her hands, the kitten blinked, then mewed. It stretched adorably, licked one paw, and washed its whiskered face.

Doucette and Cecilia traded despairing looks.

Azelais handed the ball of white fur to the Queen of the Birds. The kitten purred and bumped its head against Mahalt's fingers, paying no attention to a goose's derisive honking.

"As you know, I am not best fond of cats," Mahalt said. "However, this one wins the second test." She brought the kitten to her lips and whispered. With an irritated fillip of wings, a dove rose from her hands.

Mahalt surveyed her nieces. "For the last trial, you will Transform yourselves and see who is the strongest. Take as many or as few forms as you like, but remember that your spell must include a means of returning your own shape."

Doucette resolved to do better. If she could only win this task, neither sister would have an advantage, and the contest might be extended another round.

The young women set down their wands.

Cecilia crouched to touch hers and changed into a long yellow serpent. In a deliberate challenge, one sweep of her tail knocked Azelais's wand across the floor.

Azelais responded instantly. Where she had stood, a black horse reared, laid back its ears, and screamed in defiance. Returning to the ground with a loud clatter, powerful hooves pounded the floor.

Snake-Cecilia coiled and struck, but the horse's well-aimed kick sent the long yellow body flying into the wall. Serpent hit stone with a wet-sounding smack.

Cecilia rolled out of the snake shape and vomited onto the floor. Panting, she wiped her mouth with her sleeve and burst into sobs.

Horse-Azelais bugled victory.

Doucette swallowed hard. With a crown for the taking, she could not afford to fail. And to beat Azelais, Doucette would have to surprise her sister. Nothing too ambitious, though—Doucette had barely mastered this spell. She pressed her foot against her wand and whispered:

I'll be wasp,
my sting

to drive
a high horse mad,
until she
or I
surrender.

Flying straight to the horse's vulnerable muzzle, wasp-Doucette arched her body.

But Azelais was too quick for her.

Before Doucette could sting, one hoof touched Azelais's wand. The black horse dissolved into a cyclone of spinning air that picked up the wasp and whirled it around the hall.

As the invisible wind whipped Doucette past a thousand snapping beaks, her mind spun with terror. Fearing each moment would be her last, she blamed herself for choosing such a helpless form.

It seemed to Doucette like an eternity before her sister tired of the cruel sport. At last, wind-Azelais dropped her dazed wasp sister to the floor and whistled around the wand. Lightning shot through the column of boiling air, then thickened into streaks of green and black.

Azelais stepped from the whirlwind, one leather slipper poised within an easy step of crushing her rival.

Doucette buzzed. "I surrender, Azelais!"

The words could be clearly heard, though her voice sounded strange coming from a wasp's small body. Obediently, her spell unraveled, leaving Doucette lying in a crumpled heap across from the still-whimpering Cecilia.

Mahalt's fathomless gaze rested on each of her nieces in turn. "Winning two of the three trials, Azelais has bested both of you," she said. "The birds of the air deserve the most powerful champion. Azelais shall be my heir."

Doucette slumped on the floor. Azelais preened, savoring her victory and the death of her sisters' hopes. Their aunt drew a thin gold fillet from behind her back (and where had that come from? Doucette wondered dully) and set it over Azelais's brow.

The birds greeted the crowning with raucous acclaim, twittering and chirping, hooting and cawing. Their beating wings obscured the ceiling of the great hall.

Azelais stood proudly next to Mahalt as birds wheeled over her head. Most contented themselves with dipping a wing in salute before flying out the open doors, but some alit for an instant on a shoulder or outstretched hand. Affectionate as a turtledove, a sea eagle slid its head under Azelais's ear and tugged loose a strand of black hair.

One of the doves landed near Doucette's hand and cooed at her, as if in apology. But when she would have stroked the white feathers, it flapped away.

Forever lost, like the chance she had squandered for a triumphant return to Beloc.

The hall emptied.

Chapter Thirteen

$\mathcal{D}$oucette ladled a supper of millet porridge into a bowl and stole up to the flight court outside her chamber. In the comforting night, perched between the Immeluse's tumbling water below and the silent stars above, she needn't hide her disappointment or her dread. She didn't have to pretend, like Cecilia, that losing a crown was a minor setback, that life would continue to unroll as merrily as it had before.

Though the coming days might be long and warm, with autumn's frost still weeks away, summer had ended for Doucette. When Captain Denis and his men reached the ford, she and her sisters would return with them to the Château de l'Aire. Without a victory to shield her, Doucette would be exposed to the full force of her mother's wrath.

An owl flew past, ghostly in the moonlight, then backwinged to a stop on the balcony railing. The sleek head swiveled. Round eyes examined Doucette from under tufted brows.

The bird seemed so intelligent that Doucette was moved to extend her spoon. "Millet?" she asked. "With cinnamon. A little scorched, but not terrible."

The bird's beak clicked. A crippled talon pushed the spoon away. Then, without a sound, the mottled brown shape stretched until Doucette's aunt leaned against the railing beside her.

"I've eaten," Mahalt said. "Your pardon for burning the porridge."

Doucette gulped in surprise at her aunt's Transformation. As she swallowed the mouthful of millet, a question occurred to her. "Why don't you use a wand?"

Her aunt sounded amused. "You think magic would improve my cooking?"

"No," Doucette said. "I meant—that's not what I'm asking."

"I know." Mahalt relented. "Sorceresses may use other magical objects, rings and such, in the place of wands."

"You don't," Doucette observed. "Well, you often wear rings, but you're not wearing one now. How did you change out of owl shape?"

"Ah." The Queen of the Birds rubbed her bare hands together. "You do have the eye for this work, Niece."

Doucette took another bite of porridge and chewed. She had failed, hadn't she? What was the point of empty compliments? Unless her aunt meant to deflect the question. "How *do* you work magic without a wand, Tante?" she persisted.

"A true Aigleron, stubborn to the core," Mahalt said. "Well, I told your sisters. It's time you knew, too." Her weight shifted to her good foot; her skirts rustled softly. "Though I pray you never find yourself desperate enough to venture it."

Doucette thought of her aunt, deprived of her magic and her freedom, and shivered. "The Rassemblement?"

"Yes," Mahalt said somberly.

"Cecilia said the spirit Lavena helped you get your swan skin back, for a price."

"My ankle bone." Mahalt's malformed foot flexed in its soft leather shoe. "There's no predicting her whim. She might take a finger joint, a rib, an ear, a mind—there's no knowing in advance and no bargaining after the fact. That is one of the risks."

Doucette's appetite vanished. She dropped the spoon into the bowl and set it down. "And the others?"

"There are a thousand ways to fail. You must surrender yourself completely, knowing Lavena will root through your mind like a sow through a midden, nosing out what to keep." Remembered pain edged Mahalt's voice. "And that is only the unmaking. What to speak of the Rassemblement itself. . . ." She sighed. "Bone by bone, your companion remakes you. If true, he or she will lay you straight. But if, through your helper's disgust or cowardice, the job is ill-done . . ."

"The magic is lost?" Doucette asked when her aunt's voice trailed away.

"No, no. Lavena's no cheat. Those who survive a bath in her Cauldron do gain power. But more than one fresh-faced maiden has returned a twisted crone and turned her family's love to fear."

"You didn't," Doucette said.

"I kept my looks." Mahalt sounded almost as if she might have preferred things otherwise.

Moonlight revealed sorrow etched into her face. Had she loved the husband who took away her freedom?

Shyly, Doucette touched her aunt's hand. "I'm sorry."

Mahalt pulled away, and her face resumed its usual impassive expression. "All power has a price. If you choose sorcery, Doucette, know that you are also choosing constant vigilance. Magic will mark your soul. You must beware the motives of others. And you must beware your own."

"What do you mean?"

"The more you work magic, the more, let us say, *delicious*, it becomes," Mahalt said. "Tempering power with wisdom—it is not an easy life. Though it has its rewards." Her fingers closed like claws over the railing, then let go. One elegant hand swept over Doucette's hair in a rare gesture of affection. "If I thought you couldn't withstand the temptation, I wouldn't have taught you. Don't be discouraged by what happened this afternoon."

Doucette scuffed her shoe against the tower wall. "Azelais was haughty enough before. I hate to think how she's going to act now, knowing she'll be a queen."

"The birds may be her saving grace," Mahalt said unexpectedly, "as they were mine. Having something to care for counters the danger."

"But winning would have meant more to me than ruling your birds," Doucette confessed. "I wanted to prove myself equal to Azelais and Cecilia, for once."

"You will. I see great promise in you, Doucette. You've mastered the underlying principles of Animation and Transformation. Honing your will, your concentration, will come with practice."

"If Mother lets me," Doucette said.

"You're an Aigleron, Niece, behind that sweet smile. Don't forget." Mahalt stretched her arms to the sky. "It's a beautiful evening. Have you flown as an owl?"

"No," Doucette admitted.

"It's not to be missed." Her aunt gave her a sidelong glance. "Shall we?"

Doucette was glad to put aside her worries and her aunt's warnings. "Yes, please, Tante Mahalt."

Mahalt touched Doucette's head and spoke. Two owls swooped from the ramparts and vanished into the soft summer night.

Chapter Fourteen

*D*ays later, Doucette had cause to wish she were a bird again. She sagged in the saddle, rubbing at the road dust that crusted her lips and caught in her eyelashes. She felt dry and hard, like a piece of bread left out too long.

It would have been more pleasant by far, she thought, to fly the remaining distance, but Azelais had insisted the three of them ride home "as befitted their status as noblewomen." Doucette and Cecilia thought that Azelais was more interested in displaying her gold circlet than maintaining propriety, but both were too dispirited to challenge her.

So Doucette's mare plodded behind two armsmen's mounts, climbing the steep road that led to the Château de l'Aire. The late-afternoon sun beat on Doucette's head, while her sore thighs reminded her of each step taken in the long journey. Longingly, she remembered the shade of Tante Mahalt's woods, the fresh scent of pines and running water.

Underneath the lowland's stale heat, a constant thread of worry tightened around her middle.

Had enough time passed to blunt the worst edge of her mother's anger?

Feathers tickled Doucette's neck for what felt like the thousandth time. Riding in the lead of the party, Azelais and Cecilia had changed their swan skins to light scarves with a tap of their wands, then draped the scarves around their necks. Doucette had preferred to keep her cloak's reassuring weight against her back.

Except that she was so hot! Perhaps their idea was better. Doucette reached for the wand that nestled against her forearm, inside her long sleeve.

Before she could cast the spell, her horse lifted its head and pranced a couple of steps. Doucette had to juggle the wand and the reins to keep her seat as she rode between the town gates and into sudden shadow.

Tall, narrow houses blocked the worst of the sun's force but also trapped the hot air in the street. Doucette wrinkled her nose at the mixture of strong smells: roasting meat and baking bread, the reek of livestock manure, the fragrance of roses that climbed over doorways.

Attracted by the jingling progress of the armed party, heads popped out of open windows above the street. Two stories up, a small boy sat on a balcony between pots of blooming pinks, bouncing a stick over his knee. At the end of his makeshift fishing rod, a wooden hook dangled from a length of cord.

As Doucette rode underneath, she reached up and tapped the hook playfully with her wand. "Good catch to you, Master Fisherman," she called.

The boy shouted as the cord jerked from the weight of the painted metal fish Doucette's spell had left in the hook's place.

He flicked the line into his lap, jumped up, and ran inside, waving his new toy.

"Ma!" she heard. "They're back to the castle. The swan maids, Ma!"

Doucette straightened in the saddle. Her mare, knowing that water and grain waited in the stables ahead, quickened her pace. The file of riders bunched together, and Doucette found herself riding at her oldest sister's side.

Although Azelais didn't touch the gold circlet that crowned her dark hair, every move betrayed her awareness of it. She glanced at Doucette and frowned. "Spending your magic on a town brat? Father won't be pleased."

"Thank you for your counsel, Azelais," Doucette said, more pertly than she once would have dared. "I'm sure you know best, O Heir."

"Jealous cat." Azelais's sneer promised retribution, but before she could loose her wand, Cecilia's mare nosed into the gap between Azelais and Doucette's mounts.

Since their mutual defeat at Azelais's hands, Cecilia had begun to take Doucette's part. Once again she played the peacemaker, fanning herself with a languid hand. "It's too hot for quarreling. What I'd give for a cool drink!"

Doucette slowed the mare and let her sisters ride ahead. Accustomed as she had grown to the isolation of the Château de l'Île, she felt a little shy to see the number of people who had come out of the tile-roofed houses and shops to greet them. Women bobbed curtsies, while children ran at the riders' stirrups, cheering, until the horses clattered past the steaming fountain and through the first set of gates, into the lower courtyard of the Château de l'Aire.

Here, too, a crowd of servants, armsmen, knights, and ladies had gathered.

Doucette knew that her party would have been spotted crossing the plain, giving the castle folk plenty of time to prepare for their arrival. It felt odd to be one of the riders making a grand return, rather than the person supervising supplies of washing water and refreshment.

"Lady Azelais, Lady Cecilia!" Na Patris bustled over to the young women in the lead. The baker's freckled face beamed over a basin of water dappled with red rose petals.

Doucette slid off her horse and almost fell into the arms of a tall, curly-haired man.

A bolt of delighted surprise struck her. In the next breath, she knew it came from confusion born of fatigue. This man's dark curls were threaded with gray, and he wore a servant's leather apron, not a shepherd's tunic and leggings. Doucette had known Na Patris's husband Om Toumas, the orchard master and beeman, since she was a tiny girl. She had no reason to mistake him for another.

"Welcome home, Lady Doucette." Om Toumas took the mare's reins. "It's a long ride from Luzerna."

In his deep voice, Doucette heard the lilt of a pleasant memory. "You've been there?"

"Oh, aye." He stroked the horse's dusty neck. "Grew up in Donsatrelle county, near Vent'roux. You remember my cousins come every year for the shearing?"

"Yes." She could hardly forget, when she kept seeing one of them in her dreams. But Om Toumas was still speaking. Doucette tried to pay attention.

"Helped herd the flocks to summer pasture in Luzerna when I was a sprout. Never seen such stars. Close enough to pluck with your hand, and the music of a night! Pipes and drums. . . ."

"Mm," Doucette said, distracted by an influx of well-dressed courtiers. Had her parents come? She didn't see them, so as the servant led her horse away, she followed her sisters to dip her hands in Na Patris's basin and wipe them on the offered towel. Perhaps she would have time to change her dirty clothes before facing her mother's displeasure.

While Azelais and Cecilia chatted with the courtiers who flocked around them, Doucette left the courtyard and sought the stairs to her bedchamber.

Na Claro met her on the first landing. "There you are, little lady! Your mother has a number of tasks for you. Best get started at once, to finish by dinner. She'll see you then."

"What?" Doucette stopped short, her swan skin fluttering around her ears. "But, Na Claro, I'm a swan maiden. A sorceress."

"I know." The woman put a wrinkled hand on Doucette's sleeve and urged her upward. "Though I'd suggest putting away your pretty coat. A headache has Lady Sarpine completely out of sorts. She even sent Brother Martin off to Mardèche to fetch the de Brochet physician, since none of the usual remedies have eased her. You'd be wise not to flaunt your magic in her face."

Staring at her feet, Doucette moved steadily up the stairs after the servant. The one thing she hadn't considered was that her parents might pretend she had never left!

It couldn't last, of course. The discovery of her swan skin had changed her. Doucette could no more resume her old life than a chick could return to the egg.

A sorceress did not give up her magic for any price.

Doucette paused at the corridor that led to her parents' chamber and steeled herself for a fight. But then she thought of how tired and hot she was, of the disadvantages to appearing before her mother in travel-stained clothes, with the swan skin's majesty dulled by road dust, and her courage failed.

The feast held to welcome the returning swan maidens was always a grand occasion. If Lady Sarpine felt too unwell to see to the details herself, it would be unkind, almost spiteful, for Doucette to refuse help she could easily give.

Slowly, she set her foot on the next step and climbed.

In her bedchamber, she hastily wiped her face, rebraided the hair to get it out of her eyes, and changed from her grimy travel clothes. She thought about wearing the swan skin openly, despite Na Claro's warning. But in the end, she tapped it with her wand and murmured a spell, Transforming it into an inconspicuous gray ribbon. She laced the ribbon through her gown's ties and tucked the free ends into her bodice. To keep it close but clean and out of her way, she told herself.

Not to hide it.

She slipped the wand into her sleeve, straightened her shoulders, and opened the door. "Lead on, Na Claro," she said.

"The dairy first, Lady Doucette, if it please you."

By the time Doucette reached the final item on Na Claro's list of tasks, she was so tired she felt as though her legs might give way beneath her. Walking alone through the almond orchard, she looked over the terrace's stone wall, toward Luzerna. How unfair that the golden, drowsy landscape should be so indifferent to her fatigue.

Another slap was passing her sisters, comfortably installed in the rose garden. As a troubadour sang for their pleasure, courtiers sipped from silver goblets and nibbled summer fruits. Secure in their position, Azelais and Cecilia didn't have to worry about how their mother would greet them.

Doucette thought she had concealed her unease from the servants' knowing eyes, but her sisters would surely remark on it. She had hurried past the garden gate, hoping to steal by unnoticed. No sooner had she formed the wish than Azelais called out, drawing everyone's attention.

Doucette banished the memory of the other ladies' condescending smiles. Outwardly, Doucette might appear the dutiful daughter, the sober chastelaine, but inside, she had changed. Soon—tonight, even—everyone else would realize it. She would tell them all: Mother, Father, everyone. She would wear her swan skin proudly.

But first she had to find the bee-man.

At the far end of the orchard, he squatted in the dirt, feeding dry twigs to a fire that burned in a large clay dish.

"Om Toumas."

Two bees alit on Doucette's outstretched hand. She had almost stuck it into one of the wall niches that housed the bee skeps. "Mother wanted me to check on the honey harvest."

"Oh, aye, Lady Doucette," the man replied in his rumbling voice. "Move slowly, if you will. They won't sting unless startled. Gently, now, little sisters."

Gold-furred bees clustered in the man's curly, gray-streaked hair and crawled on his clothing. He brushed a clump of them from his chin. Obediently, they moved to his sleeve.

"You're not afraid?" Doucette asked.

He chuckled. "We have an understanding. 'Be kind to the bees that you find on your way—'"

"'Or be stung when you come to the bees' house one day.' I know the saying." She pointed at the fire in the clay dish. "You'll burn the hives?"

"Not I! Like drowning, it's an evil, wasteful method."

"Mother recommends it."

"Oh, aye. Lady Sarpine's not best fond of bees. We won't tell her, eh, little lady?" Om Toumas winked at Doucette. "I could use help, if you're so minded. Anfos offered, but the boy's too excitable—he stirs them up worse than a bear."

"Certainly." Doucette knelt beside Om Toumas. A cloud of bees hummed around her ears. While she waited, motionless, for the creatures to get used to her presence, she studied them carefully, fixing in her mind each detail of transparent wing and faceted eye. She hadn't managed her wasp Transformation very well. If she ever wanted to become a bee, she would do better.

Om Toumas watched her stillness with approval. "Wet leaves go on the fire, like so. Push the smoke toward the hive to quiet 'em." He handed Doucette a linen rag.

"Sleep, sleep, little beauties," Om Toumas crooned as he pulled the bee skep out of the wall niche. He unlaced the strap that secured the domed straw basket to its round wooden base. After tipping the basket on its side and separating the two parts, the bee-man cut dripping slices of honeycomb from the mass inside. Drowsy bees were brushed off each piece before Om Toumas placed it into a clay jar.

"Try some?" He turned the wooden base, littered with chunks of loose comb.

Doucette popped a piece into her mouth. The honey's rich flavor warmed her tongue, its sweetness flavored with wild thyme. She chewed and chewed until she had sucked out the last drop of honey, then rolled the wax between her fingers to make a ball. She'd keep it to grease her sewing needles.

The thought stirred a pang of chagrin. Maybe she was fated to be a chastelaine, after all. Despite a summer practicing the High Arts, a goodwife's practicalities weren't far from her thoughts. Firmly, Doucette dismissed the idea.

"It's delicious," she said.

"Spring flavor's more delicate, but nothing like the late-season crop to call up a summer day," Om Toumas replied.

"You've finished already?" Doucette asked as he tapped a cork into the jar, fitted the bee skep's basket back onto its base, and laced them together. "There's still honey in the hive."

"Aye. We take only a part, since few bee plants flower after Saint Aude's Day. Got to leave enough for the bees to eat all winter, when they can't make new. Eh, little sisters?"

With a long stick, Om Toumas pushed the clay dish to the next hive and built up the fire again. After shaking a few dazed bees from her skirt, Doucette followed to wave her linen rag at the smoke.

Together, they harvested honeycomb from the other hives into the three waiting jars. When the jars were capped, Om Toumas took Doucette's rag and wiped off the honey that oozed down the sides. "Patris won't appreciate the bees following honey drips to her kitchen." With a grunt of effort, he hoisted a jar in each arm. "Many thanks for your help, Lady Doucette. I'll return shortly for the other two jars. If you'd put out the fire?"

"I will."

Stirring from their smoke stupor, bees buzzed around their disturbed homes. Several alit on a honey-drip that Om Toumas had missed. Bee tongues flickered over the jar.

Remembering the man's request, Doucette pushed the clay dish to a sandy spot well away from the hives. She flipped the dish and stirred the coals into the sand with the stick. "Careful lifting the other jars, Om Toumas," she said to the tall figure walking out from between the almond trees. "They've still got bees on them."

"Your pardon?"

Doucette's skin went cold with recognition.

The voice that had answered her did not belong to Om Toumas.

Chapter Fifteen

In her surprise, Doucette leaned so hard on her stick that it snapped in two places. She pitched forward, putting her hands out to stop herself. She would have burned them on the sand-covered embers, but, as in her dreams, a man saved her from the fall. Taking a step forward, he grabbed her waist, swung her away from the buried coals, and set her on her feet.

Enfolded in the circle of his arms, Doucette was overwhelmed by a sense of relief. At not being burned, she told herself, sniffing back ridiculous tears. Anyone would be grateful for his quick action. It had nothing to do with the fact that he smelled like she remembered, of sheep and wood smoke and the herbs that grew wild on the hills: thyme, rosemary, mint, sage. His embrace felt as she had imagined it in dreams, strong and tender both, as if she had nothing to fear while he held her. As if all would be well.

But how she must look! Sweet saints. Doucette's hands flew to her mouth. Ashes on her sleeves and her dress stained from the afternoon's forays through dairy, stable, storerooms, kitchen, cellars, and garden.

Annoyance pushed out the pleasure she had felt.

Jaume had a devilish knack for catching her at her worst! Bedraggled and barefoot in the unsuitable dress Cecilia had spelled on her, then naked at the hot pools, and now grimy as a pot boy. What evil genius caused him to appear whenever Doucette least wanted anybody seeing her?

You didn't mind Om Toumas, a voice whispered in her mind.

But this—this shepherd—

Her rescuer released her and took a step back. Doucette breathed deeply. She had learned, hadn't she? This time, she would be polite but remote, as befitted a sorceress. She turned and inclined her head. "Jaume."

"Lady Doucette!" Recognition lit the dark eyes as the shepherd dropped to one knee.

"Get up," she said, hurt despite her resolve. "No need to mock me further. I'm well aware that you find me amusing."

"Amusing?" Jaume regarded her gravely. "Oh, aye. Don't forget amazing, adorable, alluring. That's for A. Would you like to hear B? Beloved, bewitching. . . ." He stood and smiled. His hand lifted, but Doucette turned her chin before he could touch her face.

"Stop it." She would have walked away but for the crook that dropped to bar her path. She stared at it, then at him. "Let me pass."

"Please, Doucette," Jaume said, "hear me out."

The tenderness in his voice was her undoing. She collapsed onto a stone bench and twisted her hands in her skirts. She had made a fool of herself once already. This time he would have to speak first.

"I'm sorry for laughing, at the pools," Jaume said. "For the misunderstanding when we parted—I should have explained I was laughing at myself, not at you. And then you were gone. . . ."

The words came out as if they had been fermenting inside him during the months they had been apart and he must speak them or explode. "I would never hurt you."

Doucette flexed her toes in their sturdy leather shoes. She remembered Jaume's hand closing around her ankle, how carefully he had bathed her battered feet. How cherished she had felt in his arms.

Jaume took her silence for encouragement. "I saw you, you know, in your swan shape, gliding out of the sky that night, and wished, as you might wish on a falling star. I almost ruined my wish come true by calling my brothers. And then I did spoil it by offending you. Later, I was afraid that it had been a dream, or a nightmare, and that you'd fly to someone else and never speak to me again." He knelt before her, leaning on the crook. "You wouldn't be so cruel?"

Doucette looked into the brown eyes so close to hers and felt a rush of warmth. He was telling the truth. He did care for her. She was so relieved, she said the first thing that popped into her head. "Where are your dogs?"

Jaume scratched his neck, looking as if he had expected a different question. "They're at home, with the sheep."

"If your flock's in Donsatrelle, what brings you to Beloc?"

"A matter left unfinished."

"Business?"

He chuckled. "Oh, aye."

Disappointment flooded her, until Jaume's next words dispelled it.

"A most pressing matter with the comte's family," Jaume leaned forward and continued softly, as if the bees might overhear and gossip. "His youngest daughter, in fact. Last time we met, I asked for her hand. She's not answered, and I want to know."

"Oh, Jaume." Doucette sighed at the sentiment, as touching as it was impossible. "Swan maidens don't marry."

"Why not?"

"It never ends well." Doucette remembered the most recent example. "Tante Mahalt's husband died."

"Other people aren't us." Jaume's jaw set in a stubborn line. "Did I take your swan skin when I had the chance?"

"No," Doucette admitted.

"Would you leave your husband for no reason?"

"No."

"You see?" Jaume spread his hands wide. "If we married, I wouldn't give you a reason."

"My parents want me to wed a nobleman. They'll cut off my inheritance," Doucette warned.

"We're not lords and ladies, but my family lives comfortably in Vent'roux town." For the first time, Jaume's certainty faltered. "I know you were to be a chastelaine. Would you miss the court so much?"

"Miss it?" She thought of escaping from the servants' bossing, the courtiers' indifference, and a chastelaine's endless responsibilities to live cozily with Jaume. "No. But my parents would never agree."

"They can't keep a sorceress against her will." Jaume took Doucette's hands. He turned her palms up and traced the edges, his touch feather-light. "I think we would suit very well. If I'm not too selfish, wanting to be your husband, not just your country lover."

Doucette could feel herself blushing. He thought that she would use him and discard him, as her sisters did their men?

Growing up in ignorance of her swan skin, Doucette had assumed she would marry for duty, as most noblewomen did. Her own honor, at the least, would demand she remain faithful to her husband whether she liked him or not.

If she married for love, could she promise less?

Was it love, what she felt for Jaume? This breathless thrill in his presence, the longing dreams when they parted? She thought so. But had he considered all it meant, to marry a sorceress? "Magic frightens some men," she said.

"Oh, aye. Transformation, Animation—uncanny, what they do. But all these years I've known you, Doucette, I never heard an unkind word cross your lips. Has finding a pretty pair of wings changed your nature?"

Doucette thought of Tante Mahalt's warnings. "I don't know," she said honestly.

"I'll ask your parents straight out for your hand. I'm not afraid of their refusal, love. Yours is the answer that counts. What say you?"

The blood buzzed in Doucette's ears. Like magic, happiness washed through her, leaving her tongue-tied and breathless.

Patiently, Jaume waited. The afternoon light gilded his skin and hair until he, too, glowed. In the orchard's hushed silence, it seemed that the almond trees, the honeybees, even the setting sun stilled in the sky to hear her response.

"Yes," Doucette breathed.

His face alight, Jaume pulled her close and rained kisses on her lips, her cheeks, the tip of her nose, her eyelids.

Laughing, Doucette returned his embrace.

"Cousin!"

At the sound of the servant's voice, Doucette and Jaume sprang apart, grinning foolishly at each other.

"Toumas!" Jaume returned the older man's greeting. "The gate guard said I'd find you with the bees."

Doucette disciplined her expression, though she felt like dancing, like singing, like Transforming gravel into flowers and jewels and scattering them through the streets of town so everyone would be as glad as she was.

Om Toumas slapped the younger man on the shoulder. "Give me a hand, won't you? Those last two pots weighed heavier every step." He turned to Doucette. "This young fellow's not bothering you, little lady? I'm sure he meant no disrespect."

Jaume bowed elaborately. "I meant exactly what I said, Lady. How would you have me show it?"

Doucette curtsied deeply in return, teasing him. "There's no court fool at present. Perhaps you'll apply for the post."

"You want a fool?" Jaume snapped a twig from an almond tree and chewed on it thoughtfully. "Well, if playing one will get my heart's desire, I'll be proud to wear the belled cap and motley." Dropping a slow wink at Doucette, he bent and lifted the two honey-filled jars as easily as if they had been empty. Not a quirk of his eyebrow showed that he had noticed her watching the play of muscles in his tanned arms.

Fighting the rush of color that climbed the back of her neck and stained her cheeks, Doucette lifted her chin in one of Azelais's haughty poses. "See that you do."

"Ahem." Om Toumas cleared his throat. The hint of mischief in his eyes strengthened the resemblance to his younger cousin. "You'll stay with us in town, eh, Jaume?"

"Thank you, Cousin," Jaume said.

"Good, good. Well, the kitchen's this way. Patris will be pleased to see you, lad, and not only for the honey. Thank you again for your help with the bees, Lady Doucette." Om Toumas nodded, Jaume tipped his broad-brimmed hat, and the two men walked away.

When they were out of sight, Doucette leaned against the nearest almond tree and closed her eyes. She shivered; she burned.

Lady of the Seas. What had she done?

Chapter Sixteen

After a breathless run up the tower stairs and a swift change of clothes, Doucette hurried down the wide corridor to the feast hall. She had deliberated too long over her swan skin. In the end, she had fluffed it out and draped it over her shoulders. With every step, feathers fluttered bravely around her face.

She had obeyed her mother's wishes. Now she would pursue her own. With Jaume, Doucette reminded herself. Tonight they would both see the advantages her new powers had gained her.

She paused before the doors to arrange her skirts and pat the wand in her sleeve, then took a deep breath and entered.

Noise and heat struck a double blow.

Though no fire had been lit on this summer evening, candles glowed on the trestle tables, and torches burned along the walls, giving off a smoky warmth. Banners drooped overhead, their colors muted by time and soot. Unlike the silence that reigned in the Château de l'Île, the Château de l'Aire's feast hall rivaled its beehives for purposeful activity. Ladies' voices fluted over the low rumble of knights and nobles. Benches scraped across the straw-covered floor as the courtiers took their places at the long tables. Barking and whining at their masters' feet, dogs scrabbled for position.

Doucette picked her way through the crowd and ascended the three shallow steps to the high table where the comte's family and favored nobles presided above the court.

"Good evening, Doucette." Lord Pascau leaned back in his chair and patted the dog crouched at his side. Eyes as dark and keen as Mahalt's studied Doucette from above the strong nose, the impeccably trimmed salt-and-pepper beard. Her father's gaze rested longest on the swan skin. "You're looking well. My sister didn't work you to the bone?"

After the first disbelieving stare, Lady Sarpine neglected to acknowledge her youngest daughter.

It boded ill, Doucette thought, that her mother judged her conduct too outrageous to be corrected in public.

"Tante sends her greetings, Father. Good evening, Mother." Doucette curtsied to her parents, trying to maintain a serene expression. As she slipped into the empty spot between her sisters, she felt as if an invisible sword hung over her head.

"You're late," Azelais said.

Trust her sister to stick that long nose where it wasn't wanted.

Doucette draped her napkin across her lap. "While you primped, I had work to do, supervising the honey harvest."

"Honey," Azelais said scornfully.

"Try some," Doucette returned. "It might sweeten your disposition."

Azelais touched her gold circlet. "Strength trumps sweetness."

But Doucette was no longer defenseless against her sister's contempt. When Azelais turned to speak to Lord Luquet, Doucette took a handful of grapes from a server's basket. With a touch of her wand, she Transformed a grape into a lump of salt and dropped it into Azelais's goblet.

Cecilia noticed, and a spark of interest brightened her face before it set once more into a coquettish mask.

Azelais's triumph was still affecting her sister's spirits, Doucette thought, though a stranger might not perceive the effort Cecilia made to keep up her flirtatious manner.

Moments later, Azelais drank, then gargled in disgust.

Doucette smiled to herself, until Azelais summoned Anfos. "Come here, you!"

"Yes, Lady Azelais?"

When the boy approached, Azelais slapped his face and poured the tainted wine over his head. "Bring me another," she said coldly. "This isn't fit to fatten swine."

"Yes, Lady," Anfos mumbled. His tunic dripping crimson, the boy retreated into the kitchen.

Doucette almost told Azelais that she had spelled the wine, but Cecilia wagged a warning finger.

Twisting her napkin in her lap, Doucette knew her sister was right. She would have to make it up to Anfos later. After all, what would be gained by confessing? Sparking a magical tit-for-tat at the high table would hardly return Doucette to her mother's good graces.

Although her appetite had vanished, the banquet continued, course after endless course. A hearty squash soup was followed by mushrooms fried with onions, spit-roasted rabbit in black pepper sauce, and lamb studded with parsley and garlic.

When she wasn't pushing the food around on her plate to disguise how little she had eaten (an art Cecilia had already perfected), Doucette pleated her napkin between her fingers. She watched the door, her breath quickening whenever a tall, dark-haired man entered the feast hall. Each time, she recognized a courtier or armsman's familiar features.

The meal wore on. Servants took away the roasted meats and brought in sizzling cheese fritters.

A scrubbed, uncharacteristically silent Anfos carried a basin of water for the comte's family to wash the grease from their hands before dessert. Doucette wondered whether it was the demands of waiting on the high table, the episode with the wine, or something else altogether, that made the kitchen boy goggle at her when she dipped her fingers in the basin. She grimaced in belated apology.

By the time pear pies and sweet custards had given way to the salted almond wafers, dried fruit, and spiced wine that would close the meal, Doucette felt limp.

With relief, not disappointment, she told herself. After the meal, she had to confront her parents and assert her claim to independence before explaining that she was in love with a shepherd. It was tactful of Jaume to give her room to clear the air. Not his fault that, surrounded by her family, she felt so alone.

"You'll tear that napkin," Cecilia said. "How did the poor thing offend you?"

"Never mind." Doucette slid down the bench and smoothed the fabric over the lap of her green-gold gown.

"Do tell." The metal band glinted in Azelais's ebony hair as she turned to Doucette. "You've been twitchy as a sand lizard since you sat down."

Doucette was saved from answering by a commotion at the entry doors. Along with her sisters, she leaned across the table for a better view.

Cecilia snickered behind her napkin. Azelais frowned. "What mischief—" she said, but the comte's voice overrode hers.

"We'll see this sport."

Dressed in a fool's red-and-black motley, Jaume was walking on his hands through the clear space between the tables. A leather strap held a set of shepherd's pipes to his lips. His legs danced in the air to the tune that he played.

Copper coins flashed across the tables as knights bet on how far the stranger could go before he fell over.

As he progressed down the hall, the tune quickened, as did the speed of the waving legs, one black, one red.

He has excellent balance, Doucette thought. She stole a glance at her sisters. Cecilia swayed to the music, and even Azelais's stern lips had relaxed into a smile. Na Patris stood at Doucette's elbow, watching her husband's cousin over a tray of dried apricots.

Jaume's particolored garb looked familiar. Since Doucette had last seen it in a castle storeroom, he must have persuaded a servant to outfit him according to her mocking suggestion. Judging from Na Patris's fond expression, Doucette could guess who might have helped.

By the time Jaume reached the dais where the high table stood, most of the courtiers were cheering his effort. Several ladies threw him tokens. He caught the colored ribbons and tucked them into his tight-fitting sleeves.

Jaume stopped in front of the comte and comtesse and blew a final flourish on the pipes. His legs flipped behind him; he bounded upright and then sank low again in a bow. The pipes vanished into the pouch at his waist.

"Who approaches?" Lord Pascau demanded.

"Jaume of Vent'roux, Sieur, begging your indulgence."

"Indeed." The comte tented his fingers over the table. "How so, friend fool?"

Courtiers murmured, trying to guess what the jester intended. Doucette's hands tightened on the napkin in her lap.

"Lord Pascau, Lady Sarpine, I've come to ask for your daughter's hand in marriage."

The sound of Doucette's napkin ripping down the middle was loud in the sudden hush. Azelais choked on her wine. In the back of the feast hall, someone dropped a jug, which smashed into pieces on the stone floor. Below the high table, courtiers recovered their wits and exclaimed over the fool's boldness.

Lady Sarpine massaged her temples. "This jest is ill-conceived."

"My daughter's hand?" Lord Pascau repeated. At his side, the dog growled.

Silently, Doucette agonized. Would her father play along with the fool's request or have him thrown from the hall?

"I have three daughters," Lord Pascau said at last, scratching the dog's raised hackles. "Which one pleases you best? Our Dark Swan, Azelais?"

Jaume turned to Doucette's oldest sister.

Azelais glared at him. She pulled the wand from her hair and raised it in warning.

"She's a beauty," Jaume said, "but too free with that wand. I've no wish to end my days as a turnip."

A knight bellowed with laughter. Ladies tittered.

Visibly, Azelais judged it beneath her dignity to respond. She put away her wand and aimed her nose in the air, then had to straighten the gold circlet before it slid off her sleek head.

Lady Sarpine drew an incredulous breath.

The comte, however, had determined to be amused. He settled into his chair. "If not Azelais, then Cecilia?"

"A fool's bride?" Cecilia tossed her golden curls. "I think not." Her wand slid out of her sleeve, and in the next instant, Doucette's sister had Transformed herself into a white doe. To the knights' shouts of acclaim, deer-Cecilia leaped over the table. Dainty black hoofs beat a tattoo on the stone floor as she pranced just out of Jaume's reach.

"Cecilia!" Lady Sarpine gasped in horror.

"A lively lass," Jaume said as the white doe turned her back to him and trotted around the feast hall, flicking her ears, "but if she ran, I couldn't catch her."

The comte pulled on his beard. "Which leaves the youngest."

The courtiers all strained forward to hear the joke that would cap the fool's play.

Doucette clenched her hands so tightly she could feel her bones grind together. How brave Jaume was! She would never have dared to address her parents so publicly, risking ridicule before the entire court.

"Aye," Jaume said. "It's Lady Doucette has conquered my heart. I'll do what you command, Lord Pascau, to win her."

In the face of his sincerity, the courtiers fell so silent that a dog could be heard scratching in the straw under a table.

Doucette peeked through her lashes at her family. Her mother and Azelais wore their iciest expressions. Cecilia, who had circled the high table and reclaimed her own form, sat once more beside Doucette. She appeared to be stifling a laugh.

"No fool like a young fool, eh?" Lord Pascau maintained the appearance of good humor, though his voice sounded hard. "Doucette?"

"Yes, Father."

"You would allow his suit?"

Doucette met Jaume's eyes and rejoiced in the message she read there. "Yes," she said.

The outburst of held breaths made candle flames dance.

Lord Pascau surveyed the hall. A grim smile played within his black-and-white beard, as if he knew exactly how many courtiers expected to see the stranger, or the comte's daughter—or both—struck down for their audacity.

Lady Sarpine's expression made clear which course of action she favored.

Instead, Lord Pascau grunted. "Well, now. Tradition requires a low-born suitor to complete three impossible tasks if he would court a nobleman's daughter."

Jaume stood quietly under the lash of scorn that edged the comte's words, though Doucette felt the sting on his behalf.

"As you will, Sieur," the shepherd said.

"Present yourself in the lower courtyard at dawn tomorrow, and we shall measure a fool's mettle."

"Thank you, Sieur." Jaume put his fist to his heart and bowed.

Lord Pascau dismissed Jaume with a curt nod. "More wine," he said, and servants leaped to attend him.

The spell that had fallen on the hall was broken. A buzz of excited talk filled the air as Jaume bowed to Doucette and her sisters. Although courtiers would have detained him in conversation, he looked neither to the right nor to the left as he walked out through the great doors.

Doucette's sisters pounced. "Who is that person?" Azelais demanded, her eyes bright with anger and curiosity. "Where did he come from?"

Cecilia's voice was a low, mocking purr. "Mm, mm. It seems our sister has been keeping secrets."

Doucette pressed her lips together and shook her head. She couldn't explain the situation while their mother stared, speechless with rage.

"It's romantic as an old ballad!" Cecilia said. "'The Shepherd and the Sorceress.' Perhaps Lord Luquet will compose us a tune."

"Would you really go with him?" Azelais lowered her voice, but the comtesse had heard the question.

"Doucette will go nowhere with that—that—gaudy jester!" Lady Sarpine said in freezing tones. "Cecilia's display of magic was vulgar enough. Completing three tasks for Doucette's hand, the idea's nonsense. Gross effrontery. I'm astonished you let it go so far, Husband."

"On the contrary." The comte stroked his beard. "This simple fellow should prove amusing."

"But, but—" his wife sputtered. "The low-born villain dared—" her voice rose in a shriek.

"Calm yourself, Sarpine, lest *you* provide the court with an unseemly display."

The comtesse quieted, though rage smoldered in her eyes.

Unconcerned, the comte sipped his wine. "If the weather's fine, we'll hunt tomorrow. That should provide entertainment, if the other palls. Eh, Doucette?"

"Yes, Father," Doucette said absently. Her mother's outburst echoed in her head. Why hadn't her father dismissed Jaume and forbid the match outright? Why give a low-born countryman the hint of a chance to win her hand?

Unless . . . unless Lord Pascau saw the trial as a way to get around the promise he had made to his wife, to deny their youngest daughter her Aigleron birthright. Indirectly, he might be honoring a sorceress's freedom to choose her companion.

Hope kindled within her, though Doucette knew better than to rely on her father's support. A chastelaine didn't contradict her husband in public, but if the comtesse thought her husband was encouraging Jaume's suit behind her back, her anger would encompass them all.

Lady Sarpine had been born a de Brochet. And, like the razor-toothed fish her family was named for, she relied on the surprise attack. Pikes waited to dart from ambush and fasten sharp teeth in an opponent's most vulnerable spot, ripping and tearing until their foe was too weak to resist. Words, not teeth, were Lady Sarpine's potent weapon, wounding where blows could not.

Doucette had often suffered her mother's criticism and seen

the comtesse reduce her serving women to tears. Lord Pascau, too, knew the damage his wife's sharp tongue could inflict. And he had sacrificed his daughter's sorcery once already on the altar of domestic tranquility. Doucette had no assurance that her father would make a different choice, if his wife pressed him.

At the time, Doucette had been a small child, ignorant of her powers. Now, she had a swan skin, a wand, Tante Mahalt's instruction, and Jaume's love. So armed, she might prevail.

But when she looked at her mother's face, Doucette's resolutions felt hollow.

How far would Lady Sarpine go to have her way?

Chapter Seventeen

The next morning, castle folk began gathering in the lower courtyard while it was still dark. Servants moved through the crowd, offering cups of hot mint tea, baskets of pears or pomegranates, and fresh bread slathered with honey. Ladies yawned behind well-kept hands, their sleepy eyelids veiling the anticipation of cats at a mouse hole. Knights and nobles crushed pomegranate seeds between their teeth and licked the scarlet juice from their fingers.

Doucette had descended the tower stairs before her sisters finished dressing. Inconspicuous in a hooded cloak over her swan skin, she leaned against the wall and listened to the conversations that swirled around her.

A richly dressed woman nibbled a pear slice. "Why'd he want the youngest?"

"A shepherd, can you imagine? I thought the comtesse would have him stripped and whipped before our eyes." Lord Luquet's fleshy lips stretched in a sneer. "A gold piece says the lout runs away before midday, the trouble he's fallen into."

"Done."

Sighing, Doucette backed away from the wagering courtiers and into her oldest sister.

"There you are," Azelais said. "Father sent us to fetch you."

"Good morning, Sieur." Cecilia fluttered her eyelashes at Lord Luquet and fell in on Doucette's other side as Azelais led them to the courtyard gate. "What will Father make the fool do?"

"Great feats, no doubt." Azelais arched an eyebrow. "A peasant!"

"But such a good-looking one," Cecilia cooed. The prospect of scandal seemed to have restored her spirits completely.

Doucette bit her lip and said nothing.

"Here are my beautiful daughters! The raven, the lark, the gentle dove." Lord Pascau drained his cup and handed it to a servant while Azelais, Cecilia, and Doucette curtsied to their parents.

The comte wore close-fitting leathers and carried a game bag slung over his shoulder. Despite the early hour, Lady Sarpine made a picture of equal elegance. She had coiled her fair hair tightly at the back of her neck and pinned a linen coif over it. Split riding skirts fell in correct folds under a crisp tunic; a pair of gloves were draped at a precise angle on her belt.

Lady Sarpine acknowledged her elder daughters with a nod, then frowned at Doucette.

Guiltily, Doucette reached up to straighten the braids that had tangled under her cloak hood. "Good morning, Mother."

"That's better, my treasure." Lady Sarpine smiled, serene as if the brief exchange had returned their relations to a more usual footing.

As if, Doucette thought, her inconvenient magic could be dealt with as easily as her wayward hair.

The comtesse toyed with a glove. "How long must we wait for this yokel?"

Lord Pascau lifted his wife's hand and kissed it. "When the sun rises, I promise the finest sport your huntress heart could desire."

Azelais, Cecilia, and the courtiers standing nearby all laughed. Doucette felt cold. Lady Sarpine nodded toward the gate. "Then let us begin," she said.

"He is prompt," Cecilia murmured. "Care to share his other virtues?"

"Stop it." Doucette tried to step away from her sisters, but Azelais caught her sleeve.

"You're not running, Doucette." Azelais exchanged a meaningful look with Cecilia. "Father has cast us all in his little entertainment."

Tall and broad as a tree, a giant walked through the gate.

Doucette blinked into the sudden brightness. The sun had risen. When she looked again, the menacing shadow had gone, and she saw only Jaume. He had given up the jester's black-and-red garb for his shepherd's hat, brown tunic, and leggings. In the crowd of colorfully dressed knights and ladies, his clothes looked plain and poor, though he wore them with the confidence of a man who knows his work and does it well.

Doucette could tell the moment he spotted her, tucked between her sisters. When she read relief in the quick sweep of his eyes over her face, she straightened proudly. She intended to stand by Jaume's side, no matter what trials her father had devised or how her sisters tormented her.

Jaume took off his hat and bowed.

Lady Sarpine stared over his head. The comte smiled. "Ready for your first test, Jaume of Vent'roux?"

"Oh, aye, Sieur."

"Follow me." Lord Pascau took his wife's arm and strode through the gate.

Nose in the air, Azelais sailed forward. Towed along in her sisters' wake, Doucette couldn't think of a word to say. She smiled helplessly at Jaume, who motioned the three young women to precede him.

"What pretty manners your friend has," Cecilia said. "I do like that in a man."

Azelais coughed repressively. Doucette gritted her teeth and wished Cecilia would find another target for her barbs.

Outside the castle gate, the comte did not continue straight into town, but turned hard to the left and skirted the castle wall. Scrubby brush and brambles covered this side of the ridge, making walking difficult.

The comtesse struggled to keep her flowing skirts clear of thorns. "What is the meaning of this excursion?"

"Just a little farther," Doucette heard her father say. When the comte stopped, the rest of the courtiers trooped up to stand as close as they could manage.

The rising sun brought a blush to the tangled weeds and gilded the brambles' red-bronze leaves. Under a thick carpet of thorns, dotted with oak trees and hardy purple wildflowers, the hill sloped toward cliffs overlooking the river valley, with its shearing pens and wheat fields beyond.

Lord Pascau gestured broadly. "A fine view, don't you think?"

"Aye, Sieur," Jaume said.

Doucette glanced at her mother, but Lady Sarpine did not appear to share the comte's enthusiasm for the vista. Someone would pay, Doucette thought, for the many tears in her mother's riding skirts.

"A pity the thorns prevent us from enjoying it," the comte said. "Since you're an able-bodied lad, I've decided your first task will be to clear this entire hillside so that a lady—our Doucette, for example—might stroll from the castle wall down to the cliff edge, barefoot, without bruising her delicate skin. Finish by sunset, or the trial is forfeit."

The courtiers whispered.

Doucette swallowed. It would take a company of laborers many days to clear the whole hillside.

Jaume bowed his head. "As you command, Lord Pascau."

"You'll need a suitable implement." Doucette's father opened the game bag on his shoulder and pulled out a child-sized tool, which he held high.

The sight of the little mattock's red-painted handle made Doucette's palms sweat with remembered terror. "Is that the one you Animated years ago?" she hissed at Azelais.

"I told Father you'd recognize it," her sister replied. "I'd completely forgotten. Father took it away after—"

"I remember." Doucette shuddered.

With a ceremonial air, Lord Pascau gave the tool to Jaume.

Jaume clasped his fingers around the handle and ran his thumb over the tool's flat edge. "Thank you, Sieur."

The comte slapped Jaume's shoulder. "No time to waste, young man," he said cheerfully. "Wield it to good effect."

But instead of using the mattock's blade to hack at the brambles, Jaume set the tool gently on a rock. He reached down for the nearest thorn bush, closed his bare hands around its spiky branches, and jerked it out of the earth.

The courtiers murmured in disappointment. "We got up for this?" one muttered to another.

"Where's the sport, if he won't use the mattock?"

Lord Pascau's genial expression didn't change. "We'll leave the man to his labors. Until sunset, Jaume of Vent'roux."

Jaume bowed. "Until sunset, Lord Pascau. Lady Sarpine."

The comtesse pulled her torn skirts close and stalked back along the wall toward the gate. Courtiers parted before her and the comte, then followed, casting disappointed looks over their shoulders.

Cecilia pouted. "Not very adventuresome, is he?"

"Not stupid, you mean," Doucette said.

Azelais rolled her eyes. "Time will tell."

"So." Doucette tucked up her skirts and planted herself on a flat rock. "I'm staying."

Azelais waved a dismissive hand at the children who had come running from town. "You prefer brats and yokels to civilized company?"

"Na Claro's sitting under that oak tree," Doucette retorted. "She'll want someone to wind her yarn."

Cecilia peered at the servant, pulling a spindle from her wool sack. "What's the old bag doing here?"

"Mother likely sent her." Azelais pinched a thorn from her shoe and let it fall to the ground. "She'll make sure the shepherd doesn't cheat."

"Cheat?" Doucette said hotly. "This isn't a true test of Jaume's worth. It's a mean trick, and you know it."

"I think your devotion is sadly misplaced." Cecilia poked Doucette in the ribs. "What good is a man who won't use his tool?"

"Cecilia," Azelais said, "that's enough."

"Just because *you* can't think of anything amusing to say. . . ."

As her sisters walked away, bickering, Doucette set aside her hooded cloak and folded her hands in her lap.

Clump by clump, Jaume yanked the brambles from the rocky soil and stacked them together. She didn't like to imagine what the thorns must be doing to his hands.

A thin scrim of clouds filtered the rising sun. The air heated, intensifying the sharp scents of low-growing herbs, the acid smell of bruised bramble canes. The patch of cleared ground grew, slowly.

At this pace, alone, Jaume couldn't possibly finish before winter set in. Doucette picked wild lavender and ran it through her fingers until the stalks came apart in sticky, aromatic threads. She wiped her hands on her skirt and picked more.

Jaume labored on.

Boys dared one another to leap over the piles of brambles. Under a bush, a bird whistled in warning, and high in the hazy sky a falcon soared, waiting for some unwary creature to show itself.

Doucette shifted on the rock. Her stomach growled. She hadn't been hungry at dawn, but now the hard knot of apprehension inside her was fraying into tendrils of worry. She picked her way over to the oak tree and sat beside the old servant.

Na Claro's wrinkled hand rose and fell with the rhythm of her spinning. "Hard worker, that young man. Might surprise us all, come sundown."

"Lady Doucette!"

Anfos ran up to them and slung a sack half his own size to the ground. The contents rattled. "Na Patris sent a jug of water and some food."

"Thoughtful of her," Na Claro said approvingly.

"Please do convey our thanks," Doucette added.

"I will." The boy ran along the castle wall, turned the corner, and disappeared from sight.

Doucette poured a cup of water and walked through the cleared patch to Jaume. Bushes had been pulled up, but loose thorns caught at her shoes. The ground would never pass the "barefoot" part of her father's impossible demand.

Up close, it was clear Jaume had been working hard. His tunic stuck to his body in big sweaty patches, and his face was flushed.

"Lady Doucette." He took off his wide-brimmed hat and saluted her. Brown hair curled damply at his ears.

She offered the cup, wishing she could soothe the angry red scratches that covered his muscular arms.

"Thank you."

Doucette surveyed the expanse of hillside as he drank. Town children straggled home for their own midday meals. Insects buzzed undisturbed among the brambles. "You can't do this."

"No?"

She folded her arms across her chest. "It's impossible."

"Maybe."

Worry—mixed with shame that he was suffering on her behalf—spilled out into words. "Why didn't you take my swan skin that night? You could have married me without my parents' blessing or a hillside of thorns to clear. Those leggings will be rags, and your arms are scratched bloody!"

"I told you already." Jaume sounded insulted. "I won't live in fear that my wife finds her coat and flies away, leaving me worse off than before. Sorceress or not, you deserve to be wooed properly." A callused finger stroked one of the gray-tipped feathers that curled over her neck.

Doucette shivered, feeling the caress the length of her body. "Why don't I Transform us both into birds? I don't care whether Father's tests are finished. They're not fair."

"I asked for your hand like an honest man. I'll face the consequences." Jaume studied her over the cup's rim. "Unless you think a shepherd's honor of no account?"

Caught by that dark gaze, Doucette couldn't speak.

He smiled, as if her silence were answer enough. "Besides, winning a woman like you should be impossible."

"Me?" The word came out in a squeak. "Why?"

"You know why. We're for each other." Jaume drained the cup and closed her fingers around it.

Doucette's hands tightened on his. "Yes," she said urgently. "But if your honor won't let you marry me without clearing this field, you'll have to use that mattock. And it's cursed."

Chapter Eighteen

rue," Jaume said.

Doucette blinked. "You knew?"

"Oh, aye. Besides herb lore, my countrymen don't hold much with sorcery. More honor in a job done by your own hand than by waving a little stick, that's our feeling." He dusted his hat on his thighs and settled it on his head. "Plenty in Vent'roux town live happy without magic of any kind, but we can recognize it, if need be."

"Wish I had," Doucette said. "Azelais made the thing and Animated it years ago. Promised it would finish weeding the herb garden."

"And?"

"It did. She just neglected to mention that it would drag me along like a cat shakes a rat. The courtiers thought it hugely funny." Doucette kicked a knot of brambles. "Azelais and Cecilia were always giving me toys that wouldn't stop playing."

"And you wonder why Donsatrelle folk don't meddle with sorceresses?"

"Jaume." Doucette seized his arm, though she could as easily have shaken sense into an oak. "Listen to me! There's no other way to complete Father's task. But if that mattock drags you over the whole hillside as it dragged me through the garden, it will kill you!"

"Your father shares your sisters' sense of humor, I take it." Jaume dropped a kiss on her head. "Let's see the thing."

They left the cup by Na Claro, who was dozing in the oak's circle of shade. The mattock lay on the rock where Jaume had set it long hours ago.

Doucette pulled her swan skin close to keep the trailing feathers from touching the nasty thing. "Once you swing it, the mattock won't stop until the task is done."

Jaume squatted by the rock. "Will it work without you hanging on?"

"By changing the Animation spell, you mean?" Doucette thought hard. "We can try. Pick up the mattock, but don't swing it."

Jaume took the tool.

Doucette laced her fingers through his, aware of each bit of skin where their hands touched, his, scratched and work-roughened; hers, sticky with lavender. With an effort, she cleared her mind of distraction and, as Tante Mahalt had taught her, pictured what she wanted the mattock to do.

Mattock, good mattock,
touch not the useful plants,
but clear weeds and thorns and brambles:
root and branch
spine and seed
from wall to cliff-top.
And when the task is done,

return
with our thanks.

The painted tool quivered, then leaped from their hands.

Doucette muffled a shriek of surprise as the mattock took flight. Jaume jumped in front of her, his hands spread protectively. Startled birds whirred away. Doucette craned her neck. "Look at it go!"

The mattock flashed through the air, diving and swooping like a demented dragonfly.

No match for the tool's relentless attack, bramble bushes were torn by their roots from the ground and rolled into heaps. Flurries of loose leaves and thorns drifted over them. Without warning, the piled vegetation sparked into flame, burned with a fierce, smokeless heat, and dissolved into gray ash.

Doucette danced behind Jaume. "It's working!"

He mustered a smile for her. "Without you to command it, yon mattock would have led me a deadly ride indeed."

"Your idea," she said.

Jaume spat in the dirt. "I'm no sorcerer."

"Maybe not to Animate the tool in the first place." Doucette remembered what Tante Mahalt had said about magic. "But to change the spell required an observant eye, a clear mind, and a strong will."

"If you say so."

The mattock raced up and down the hillside. Avoiding the wild herbs, flowers, and oak trees, it ranged back and forth until the last prickly bush and bramble root had been scoured from the ground and consumed by flame. Then it flew straight to the rock where it had started and landed with a satisfied little wriggle.

Doucette let out a deep breath of relief. Jaume knelt and sifted a handful of dirt through his fingers. "Soft as sand," he marveled.

"Not a thorn left," Doucette agreed.

They grinned at each other.

"Well done," Jaume said. Doucette favored him with her deepest curtsy. Arm in arm, they returned to Na Claro, still napping under the oak tree.

The servant rubbed her eyes and yawned. With a start of surprise, she beheld the altered landscape. "Good job, lad. Expect you've worked up an appetite, eh? How about some roast chicken?" She rummaged in the sack Anfos had brought. "There's Patris's excellent bread, and pears, and cheese. Then perhaps you'd give us a tune?" She winked at Doucette. "Never yet met a shepherd without a flute or a drum by him."

"My pleasure," Jaume said.

"Yes, please." Doucette unfolded a napkin's careful wrapping. "Ooh, honey cakes!"

They heard the children's excited shrieks over the music dancing through Jaume's pipes, then the low tones of knights and their ladies' silvery laughter. But even when the exclaiming crowd enveloped them, Doucette kept her mouth closed and her eyes on the wool she was combing for Na Claro.

Her sisters pushed the courtiers aside. Azelais gripped Doucette's shoulder. "You did this." She shook Doucette, hard.

"I should have stayed and watched you myself, you devious—"
Abruptly, she let go.

"What?" Doucette said.

Azelais was backing away. Whatever she had glimpsed in
Jaume's eyes had caused her to think better of the scolding. She
fluffed her black swan skin and vented her displeasure on
Cecilia. "Stop laughing!"

"Your face, Azelais!" Cecilia chortled. "And little Doucette,
demure as pudding. We mistook the shepherd, evidently. Wait
until Father sees!"

Doucette's stomach tightened.

The sun's disk descended to the rim of the western hills. As if
they had awaited its signal, her parents walked around the castle
wall.

Lady Sarpine must have heard that the thorns had been
cleared. She had put aside the torn riding skirts and dressed in
queenly splendor, from the gold net edging her headdress to her
silk gown and soft leather dancing slippers. Lord Pascau, too,
looked very fine in a velvet robe trimmed with fur.

As they made their regal way to the oak tree, Doucette stood
and ordered her lavender-sticky skirts. As usual, her hair had
escaped from its braids. It probably resembled the hanks of Na
Claro's matted wool, but there was no help for it.

Jaume, too, stood. He put away his pipes and collected the
enchanted mattock. Despite his dirty face and thorn-shredded
clothing, he waited next to Doucette as calmly as a man at home
by his own fireside.

"Well, Jaume of Vent'roux?" Lord Pascau said.

Jaume handed the mattock to the comte. "As you commanded, Sieur, the ground is clear."

"Let us put your work to the test." The comte raised an eyebrow. "Doucette?"

"Yes, Father." She stepped forward and curtsied.

"Take off your shoes, my dear, and walk to the cliff's edge. Barefoot, that's it."

It seemed a long, long walk.

Doucette hiked her skirts above her ankles and paced slowly. The ground was pleasantly warm under her bare feet, the rock outcroppings solid, the earth powdery in places with ash from the burned brambles. Wild herbs tickled her toes; she felt the furry softness of lavender, the gentle prick of rosemary twigs.

No thorns, she reminded herself. That was the key thing.

When she returned, her father's expression was inscrutable; her mother and Azelais looked sour. Engaged in flirting with an attentive knight, Cecilia paid her no attention. The other courtiers seemed curious, the castle servants and townsfolk plainly glad that one of their own had done so well.

Doucette met Jaume's eyes last, and his expression enabled her to curtsy gracefully to her parents. "I felt no thorns." Dipping one foot, then the other, into the pail of water that had appeared in front of Lord Pascau, she displayed each sole. The clean skin showed pink and unbroken.

"The first task is successfully completed," Lord Pascau pronounced.

Servants and townsfolk cheered. Some of the courtiers applauded; others looked stunned.

Doucette assumed the latter included those who had lost their dawn wagers against Jaume. She was pleased to note cod-faced Lord Luquet among their number.

"Meet us here at dawn tomorrow for your second task." The comte dismissed Jaume with a twitch of his fingers.

"Thank you, Sieur." Jaume bowed to the assembled company and walked in the direction of the town.

Without giving Doucette a chance to put on her shoes, her sisters pushed her after the departing comte and comtesse. When they reached the castle, Lady Sarpine accompanied her daughters to their bedchamber and sent away the servant who had brought warm water for washing.

"Your father will speak to you before dinner," Doucette's mother told her. "Change that dirty gown immediately. Cecilia and Azelais, you girls attend me." The three of them swept from the room.

Doucette stripped off the offending garment and sank into the waiting tub. She washed, combed her hair, and hurried into the clean clothing laid out for her. Then she sat.

Not long.

When she heard the heavy step outside the door, Doucette clasped her hands in her lap to still their trembling.

The bedchamber door opened and the comte entered. "Little Doucette. How did you get to be such a clever girl?"

His fond smile unsettled her. "What do you mean, Father?" she asked cautiously.

"Tch, tch. No need for false modesty between us, child." He closed the door and stood in front of the fire, arms cocked behind his back and hands spread to its warmth, the picture of lordly ease. "Your magic helped that boy."

"Was the task completed to your satisfaction?"

A shadow crossed her father's face in the instant before a hearty laugh dispelled it. "Certainly. The Château de l'Aire now boasts the finest parkland in the realm. Offered the man a reward, in fact."

"Did he take it?" Doucette asked.

"No. The fool turned down a minor title and a good income, in return for the smallest consideration!"

"What consideration, Father? That he forfeit the other trials? Mother's idea, I imagine, to buy him off before he could succeed." Doucette was guessing, but she knew she had hit the mark when her father coughed into his hand.

"Ahem. Too keen for these old wits, my girl."

"Whatever I know of subtlety, I must have learned from you," Doucette returned, rather surprised at her own daring. Although the saints knew she needed to be bold. And vigilant.

Jaume hadn't taken their bribe, but Lady Sarpine was used to getting her way. What she couldn't buy or wheedle, she might secure by force.

"My child, the jest has been amusing, but it must end." Lord Pascau stroked his beard, then sat down beside Doucette. "I know you're unhappy we hid your swan skin. Unfair, you thought, to be denied the privileges your sisters enjoy. Though your mother had her reasons." His arm curled around her shoulders and squeezed. "You haven't helped this shepherd just to spite her?"

"The tasks are Jaume's to complete," Doucette said evenly.

Her father chuckled, a strained sound. "And whose aid allowed him to get this far? Peasants don't work magic."

Doucette clamped her lips together.

"Don't purse that pretty mouth at me," the comte said sharply. "You're no longer a child, whose misdeeds affect only yourself. I'll give you three reasons, Daughter, to rethink this disastrous course of action."

He held up one ringed finger. "First, such a misalliance stains your noble name. An Aigleron, married to a nobody? How would your mother, your sisters, face the court?"

"Their affair," Doucette said curtly.

The heavy arm tightened around her shoulders. "If you care not for honor, think of your comfort. Dwelling in a barren country hut, eating gruel for day upon day—what a wretched future for a gently bred girl!"

"A sorceress chooses her life," Doucette challenged him. "Didn't Tante Mahalt leave this place with only her swan skin?"

"Bold words, young miss. But what of the young man who professes to love you? How kind is it to encourage his unseemly ambition?" Lord Pascau shook his head sadly. "Mismatched as fish and fowl. The common folk won't trust you; the nobility won't accept him. Over time, the two of you can only wear into misery. Unless, of course, you breed. To what kind of future would you condemn your unfortunate children? Expectations beyond their station and no means to satisfy them, nothing but failed hopes and bitterness—"

"Stop." Doucette wrenched herself away from the vise that circled her shoulders, the persuasive voice that dripped poison into her ears. "What do you want, Father?"

"Why, only that the young man win by his own merit," the comte said smoothly. "That's just, isn't it?"

Before Doucette could respond, Lord Pascau stood. "It's settled. I have your word that you'll remain in your chamber from dawn to dusk tomorrow, while the lad proves himself?"

Doucette bit her lip. The tests weren't fair! Without her help, Jaume might fail and be sent away in disgrace. And if she followed after him, would the shepherd's precious honor let them marry after all?

The thought of losing him pierced her heart. She opened her mouth to protest, then closed it. Her father's expression forbade further argument. Though perhaps a humble request . . .

Doucette forced herself to speak meekly. "Please, Father, couldn't I watch from a distance?"

"No," her father said. "After you've reflected on the matter, you'll understand." As if he had not just crushed her hopes, he crooked his arm in invitation. "Come, Daughter. Let us go down to dinner in charity with one another."

Though she could hardly bring herself to do it, Doucette bowed to the inevitable. Her cold fingers brushed his velvet sleeve as she allowed her father to escort her from the room.

Chapter Nineteen

"Hurry, Cecilia. We're late." Azelais lit a candle from one already burning on a table and shielded the flame with her hand. Under the hood of her cloak, dark brows knit with annoyance. "It's your fault, Doucette, that we must rise before dawn and tramp out into the wet."

"Father, not I, set the time for the trial." Doucette abandoned the pretense of sleeping. She sat up in bed and draped her swan skin over her shift for warmth. "Besides, I don't hear rain."

"You will," Azelais insisted. "The clouds came in last night."

"I can't find my cloak," Cecilia said.

"Make one," Azelais snapped. "Your wardrobe is a shambles."

Cecilia laughed. "Good advice, if sourly given." She tapped her swan skin with her wand and swirled the resulting hooded garment over her shoulders before pushing past Azelais. "Good-bye, Doucette."

Azelais's candle flickered. "Clumsy featherhead," she muttered.

"Don't tempt me, Sister."

The door swung shut. The quarreling voices receded down the stairs.

Doucette slumped against the bolster. Everyone would be gathering without her. Jaume would wonder where she was and worry. She got out of bed and stood at the window overlooking the upper courtyard's dim expanse of wet stone.

Around her, the castle felt quieter than usual. Even the roosters in the lower courtyard seemed unwilling to disturb the expectant hush. Doucette pulled her coat of feathers close.

The previous day's hazy warmth had vanished. In the gray sky, clouds hung low, trailing ghostly pennants that blurred the outline of wall and tower.

By slow, sullen degrees, the light brightened. Doucette knew when her father had finished announcing Jaume's second task. Headed by Lord Pascau and Lady Sarpine, a stream of people entered the courtyard from the direction of the new parkland. As servants returned to their tasks, they talked in low voices, carefully avoiding the vicinity of Doucette's window.

Her absence must have been noted. News of her disgrace would spread, and everyone know that the comte had forbidden his daughter to see or speak to the shepherd, lest she help him as she must have done the day before.

But they didn't have to tell her what the second task was.

Azelais had said it pleased their father to cast them all in his little entertainment. Since Azelais's mattock hadn't thrashed Jaume to pieces, Cecilia's Animated spade would be next.

With it, Jaume might be asked to trench a new channel for the river, or terrace the entire hillside he had cleared the day before. Whatever the task, Jaume would have to use the tool to finish the task in the allotted time. Like the mattock, the enchanted spade was dangerous.

And Vent'roux folk didn't care for magic.

Doucette tucked her chin into the swan skin's dappled feathers and brooded. She couldn't even warn Jaume about the spade. There'd be more eyes than old Na Claro's on him today.

Though not, perhaps, as many as she would have supposed, Doucette decided, as courtiers straggled back to the castle in ones and twos. Wet weather and boredom would drive the watchers back inside, unless Jaume actually touched the spade to earth and awoke the Animation spell laid on it.

The chamber door banged open, and Cecilia danced into the bedchamber, her face alight with amusement. Her cloak hood was thrown back; droplets beaded her fair hair like diamonds. With a tap of her wand, she turned the wet cloak back into a swan skin and shook it smartly before resettling its white perfection over her shoulders. "Someone missed you-you-you," she caroled.

Doucette turned to the window to hide the flare of pleasure. "What was the test?"

"Spade, dear spade." Cecilia chuckled. "You guessed, eh? More wits than we thought, under that mare's nest." She sidled up to Doucette and tweaked her tangled hair. "Father told your charming suitor to dig a pond in the middle of the hillside by sundown and fill it with water."

"Then what happened?"

Cecilia considered her. "What price the news?"

"I'll give you my pearl earrings," Doucette said impulsively. "Tell me."

"Done!" Cecilia clapped her hands. "Father was wise indeed to keep his little lamb penned inside. You're besotted with that young shepherd, aren't you? Oh, it's too delicious! Makes all my unsuitable men seem positively respectable."

"Cecilia, please." Doucette went to the box where she kept her treasures and pulled out the earrings. "Take them. Only tell me what Jaume did."

"Thank you, I will." Cecilia fastened the pearls to her ears and winked at Doucette. "But I would have done so for nothing, because that is the answer."

"Nothing?"

"Yes." Cecilia giggled. "It's the cream of the jest. He wandered over the hillside, mournful as a lost pup. No idea where to begin, without you to tell him. I was yawning at once. Azelais and the rest won't last much longer. Why stand in the fog, when we can sip warmed wine and amuse ourselves in perfect comfort indoors?" Cecilia picked up a mirror and admired the pearl earrings. "None of Father's new knights are quite as good looking as your shepherd, but they're sure to be better armed."

"You'd know," Doucette said rudely.

"Someone should." Cecilia smirked at her reflection. "Time I inspected their blades for myself." With an airy wave, she flitted out of the room.

Doucette sat on the window seat and leaned her head against the frame. The mist had gotten thicker. Cold drops condensed out of the clouds and ran down the castle's stone walls.

Jaume didn't act aimlessly. He must be searching for something. What could it be?

Water. Doucette heard the word as clearly as if he had spoken it in her ear.

Of course. Springs arose in the caverns under the castle's foundation, supplying its inexhaustible wells. Tante Mahalt had explained to Doucette that long ago, each county's noble family had built a fortress to protect the source of its power. For the Aiglerons, that stronghold was the Château de l'Aire, and the power twofold: enough fresh water to outlast any siege and a magical source as well. Lavena's Cauldron.

Doucette closed her eyes. With a spring and an enchanted spade, Jaume could make a pond in the hillside. She curled her legs underneath her and hugged her knees, trying to contain her rising excitement.

Wouldn't they be surprised! Azelais and Cecilia, especially, would see that Jaume was braver, stronger, smarter than a hundred knights. If he remembered how they had commanded the mattock, and his will proved strong enough to alter Cecilia's Animating spell, Jaume could complete the second task!

Unless he tried to dig in the usual way. Doucette groaned out loud and buried her head in her arms. If Jaume touched the blade to the earth, the spade would cleave to his hands until it had finished its task. By then, he might have been shaken to his death!

She hoped Jaume wasn't so stubborn that he would try to do the task without magic. She had to trust him to remember that the trial would require sorcery, because Doucette's father didn't believe a shepherd—a peasant—capable of mastering an enchanted tool by himself.

It was torture, not knowing, but none of the bedchamber windows overlooked the hillside. The day stretched endlessly ahead of her, and she had nothing to do with it but wait and worry.

Her parents' displeasure with Jaume's first success had been clear enough. What would they do if the shepherd triumphed again? And, while Jaume's quest for her hand had overshadowed all else, Doucette had still to face the consequences of her flight to Tante Mahalt's.

How long would Lady Sarpine make her disobedient daughter wait?

When Na Patris came up the stairs in the late afternoon, she found Doucette huddled on the window seat, heedless of the raindrops that dripped from the window frame and into her hair.

The baker set her tray down on a table and closed the shutters firmly. "A hot drink, little lady, to counter the weather? You don't want to catch a chill. That'll do your young man no good."

"My young man?" Doucette said warily. She knew her parents didn't approve, but she hadn't considered what the servants might think about Jaume's proposal.

"Isn't he?" the woman said. "Not a noble, our Jaume. No title, no riches compared with the courtiers' estates. Not saying I'm impartial, but he's a fine man, little lady. If you don't want him, it wasn't kind to put him through this."

"I didn't!" Doucette said, indignant at the woman's insinuation. "Asking Father was his idea."

Na Patris's surprise was almost comical. "Oh?"

"Yes. He said I deserved a proper wooing, went on about his honor. Men," Doucette said.

"Hm." The woman handed Doucette a mug of mint tea, then bustled around the room, collecting dirty dishes onto her tray and tidying the bedclothes.

The clay mug warmed Doucette's cold hands. She blew on the steaming tea, then gulped it down.

Na Patris found a drying cloth and passed it over Doucette's damp head. "So you do favor the lad."

"Why else would I help him?"

"To prove you've a swan maiden's powers?"

"No!" Doucette said.

Na Patris gave her a shrewd look.

"Well, partly," Doucette confessed. "But I wouldn't have encouraged Jaume if I hated him."

"You don't hate him. Do you love him?"

In her own way, Na Patris could be as relentless as Lady Sarpine.

"Yes," Doucette blurted. To hide her confusion, she picked up the drying cloth and rubbed her head, but the truth could not be wiped away.

She did love Jaume. When he had asked her in the orchard, she had thought so. Now, chafing at the order that barred her from her rightful place beside him, she was sure of it. As patiently as he would track a lost sheep, Jaume had called Doucette's lonely heart to him. She couldn't imagine living without the light in his eyes, the tenderness in his voice. Whether he finished the three tasks or not, she would follow him.

"That's all right, then," Na Patris said comfortably. "He's already built a wall clear across the hillside to hold in the pond, had you heard?"

"Jaume?"

"Who else?" Na Patris chuckled. "Rock on rock with his bare hands, not a chink of mortar between the stones. Lovely dry-stone work they do in Donsatrelle county. It'll hold strong."

"I suppose." Doucette tilted the cup and found it empty.

"Don't you worry, little lady." Na Patris took the cup and stacked it with the other dishes on her tray. "After he finishes the wall, Jaume'll figure how to dig the pond deep."

"You think so?" Doucette said.

"Aye. Trust the lad."

At the door, Na Patris propped the tray on her hip. "Hope I'm not speaking too far out of turn, but comes a time a body has to make her own decisions. I was a lass, my ma wanted me to join the holy sisters."

"At Saint-Trophime?" Doucette tried to imagine the lively baker swathed in a cleric's gray robe and sitting for hours in quiet contemplation.

"Unlikely, eh?" Na Patris chuckled. "Instead, I married a Donsatrelle man, hired on with the ungodly Aiglerons, and wouldn't change for the world. Without love, marriage can be a hard sentence. You think on that."

Doucette cleared her throat. "I will, Na Patris," she said.

"There's a good girl." The door closed behind the baker.

Doucette jumped to her feet. The day was swiftly ending, and she wasn't dressed for dinner.

She combed out her hair with her fingers until it crackled into a wiry cloud, then plaited it into two braids. She washed her face and dressed in her best gown and dancing slippers. Defiantly, she arrayed the dappled swan skin over her shoulders.

Strangely, wonderfully, she and Jaume belonged to one another. Whatever her parents did, she must believe her beloved could master the spade and finish the second of the tasks that would bring them together.

Chapter Twenty

*J*ust after sunset, Doucette opened the door to Na Claro's knock. The old woman's face was creased in anxious lines. "Lady Sarpine bids you wait on her."

"I will," Doucette replied.

The reckoning had come.

Despite her brave words, Doucette's steps slowed as the old woman led her down the stairs to the comtesse's sewing room.

She tried to draw courage from the feathers that caressed the nape of her neck. She had been born a swan maiden; she had become a sorceress. Jaume loved her. If he had completed the second task without her help, her parents would realize that the shepherd, too, was a person of consequence.

No matter how angry the situation made her, Lady Sarpine respected power. Doucette must show her mother that she had grown too strong in her magic to be forced into marrying against her will. Or, for that matter, to be shut in her room like a child.

Outside the chamber, Doucette settled her shoulders and straightened her skirts.

Na Claro tapped on the door.

"Enter," said a voice inside.

Na Claro waited for Doucette to step into the room before closing the door and leaving Doucette alone with the comtesse.

"So, Daughter," Lady Sarpine said without inflection.

"Good evening, Mother." Doucette curtsied deeply. Rising, she sneezed at the cloying smell of jasmine, her mother's preferred scent, mixed with the humbler odors of beeswax and wool. A partly strung tapestry frame leaned against the far wall. Otherwise, the room had been cleared of its usual clutter of shuttles, yarn, and chattering women.

A large fire burned on the hearth, and with the shutters closed against the rain, the chamber was stifling.

Was her mother ill?

She seemed composed enough, sitting in a grand carved chair by the fire and hemming a silken sash. Her eyes narrowed slightly at Doucette's swan skin, but she made no other sign of displeasure.

"I haven't asked about your visit to Luzerna," the comtesse said.

The mild remark took Doucette by surprise. She hesitated, pushing down the dread that had been building since her return from Tante Mahalt's. Had she expected her mother would breathe flame? Take a sword and smite her?

Perhaps she had assumed a punishment that existed only in her own mind. If her mother had determined to be gracious, Doucette could do no less. She licked dry lips. "What would you like to know?"

"How fares my sister-in-law?"

"Tante Mahalt is well."

Lady Sarpine poked her needle through the silk. "She instructed you in her sorcerous tricks?"

"Yes, Mother."

"Show me, sweetling." The comtesse tucked the needle into the fabric and folded her hands in her lap. "I'd like to see what was so irresistible that you abandoned your rightful place and stole away like a thief to find it."

The knot in Doucette's stomach pulled a little tighter at the request. But her mother's voice didn't sound as angry as Doucette had feared.

Had Jaume failed? Were his trials over? Useless to wonder. Doucette had wanted a chance to prove herself. Here it was, fallen into her lap. She must put her attention on this test and succeed as she had not at Tante Mahalt's.

"As you wish, Mother." She shook the wand from her sleeve and tapped one of the logs piled by the fire.

> Be thou footstool,
> rest for the weary.
> An oakwood base,
> to shine like my mother's hair,
> finished in velvet,
> purple,
> as her noble due.

The log quivered, as if alive, then formed itself into a footstool to match the comtesse's chair.

"A pretty thing," Lady Sarpine admitted grudgingly. One foot prodded the amethyst-colored cushion. "The power's in that stick?"

The truth was more complicated, but Doucette didn't think

her mother wanted a lecture about magical principles. She nodded.

"May I try it?"

Although the request made Doucette uneasy, she couldn't think of a reason to refuse. The de Brochet family's magic ran to weak Divination at best. Her mother had no swan skin, no Transformational magic of her own, to turn Doucette into stone. At most, Lady Sarpine might focus her formidable will to alter the log-stool's spell. She couldn't cast a new one.

Doucette gave her mother the wand.

Lady Sarpine held it between her fingertips and inspected it closely. Then she rapped the tip against the footstool. "Return to log," she commanded.

Nothing happened.

Doucette smothered a gulp of relief.

"Hm." The comtesse sounded disappointed. She toyed with the wand. "And you wore your swan skin? Flew?"

This was going far better than Doucette had dared to dream. "Yes, Mother."

"Show me."

"Very well." Doucette shrugged the swan skin from her back. In the firelight, the gray-tipped white feathers shimmered with the promise of sky and water, flight and safe rest.

She peeled her dress and shift from her body and stepped out of her shoes and hose. Calming herself with a deep breath, Doucette drew the swan skin over her shoulders.

Magic sparked.

The swan skin Transformed her. Webbed feet slapped the

stone floor for balance; broad wings arched, fanning the fire so that sparks shot into the air. Swan-Doucette craned her neck to make sure none had landed on her plumage, then folded the gray-tipped feathers neatly and eyed her mother.

"No! Turn back!" The comtesse shrank against her chair with the first emotion she had displayed during their interview. "Doucette! It's unnatural, monstrous—I can't bear it, child. Turn back!" she said in a shrill voice.

Doucette pumped her neck up and down in wordless assent. She pressed her beak down her body and opened the swan skin.

The world spun, her form changed. The tide of magic sizzled through her blood and receded again, leaving her gasping on the floor.

In the instant when Doucette lay helpless, her mother struck. With a grunt of disgust, Lady Sarpine seized the discarded coat and tossed it on the fire.

"No!" Doucette threw herself at the flames. Not her swan skin! Her magic, her birthright. Her freedom.

"It's done!" Her mother yanked her away but not before the flames had engulfed Doucette's hands to the wrist. She writhed in her mother's grip, screaming with pain and choking on the stench of burned feathers.

How could disaster strike so horribly fast?

Her expression wild, Lady Sarpine pushed Doucette to the floor. "I told Pascau we should have burned it the day you were born, but he swore you'd never wear the cursed thing. Going to Mahalt's behind my back—did you mean to break your mother's heart?" She jabbed the smoking swan skin with the wand before feeding it, too, to the greedy flames.

"No!" Doucette wailed again. She lifted her blistered hands in entreaty.

The fire defied her. It soared to the height of a man, roared like a lion, and hissed like a serpent. Flames flared green and blue and crimson as they raced over the swan skin and wand.

Doucette cried in impotent fury, feeling the heat rage both without and within her body as the fire devoured her coat of feathers. Like her hair and skin, blood and bone, the precious thing was part of her. More—it held the key to her magic.

She couldn't fight the flames' blazing, insatiable appetite, and it was too late to run. Cackling over its prize, the fire took what it wanted.

Like a trail of spilled lamp oil sputters across the floor from its source, magic flared and died inside her. Despite the pain, Doucette would have shielded those last pitiful flutters with her two scorched hands to taste—for just a little longer—the sorcery she would never more command.

An instant later, enchantment had withered to dry flakes of ash. Like the former glory of her swan skin, now a blackened wreck on the coals, her magic was gone.

"You tricked me!" Doucette screamed.

"I saved you, my sweet."

"You had no right!"

The comtesse reared back in her chair, as if Doucette had slapped her. "No right to protect my child?"

"To destroy what I loved!" Doucette sobbed, but Lady Sarpine seemed willfully blind and deaf to the anguish she had caused.

Realization broke over Doucette in a cold wave, drowning her in sorrow. Never again, she mourned, would magic pour over her skin. Gone forever, the rush of wind under her wings, the brief fellowship she had enjoyed with Azelais and Cecilia, the pride at mastering Transformation and Animation, Tante Mahalt's encouragement. The losses struck like poisoned shafts, curling her body over her knees in defeat. She wept, and knew the pain would break her. Such a grievous loss could not be endured.

And yet, Doucette's traitor heart continued to beat. Her lungs forced out the tortured breaths. Her burned hands throbbed and her body shivered, reminding her that she crouched naked on a stone floor.

Stepping carefully around her prostrate daughter, Lady Sarpine unlatched the shutters to let out the smoke. She returned to the fire and prodded it with a poker until no traces remained of the wand or coat of feathers. "You will not defy me again," she said. "Dabbling in sorcery. I won't have it."

Doucette raised her head. Without her magic, what was left? A bag of bones held together by skin and memory. She could hardly speak through her tears and horror. "But—"

Her mother interrupted. "Your father insisted that Azelais and Cecilia become sorceresses. Why shouldn't I guide one of you, at least, to a virtuous life? My last, my dearest girl!" Her mouth twisted. The look in her blue eyes, of anger and yearning mingled, made Doucette drop her own face to the floor while the torrent of explanations poured over her head.

"We had such plans for you!" The comtesse paced to the window and gazed out at the sheets of falling rain. "With Azelais and Cecilia away in Luzerna, even your modest looks might have caught the prince's attention. You're a prize, sweetling, a noblewoman with the knowledge to run a castle and the dowry to furnish it. But, no, you flew away.

"Flew away!" Lady Sarpine repeated with loathing. "We put the visit off a year, and soon his Highness will be snowbound at the winter court with those other girls and their scheming mamas. And then you encouraged that peasant's attentions! I couldn't believe it, at first." Her voice turned cold. "Mahalt's influence, no doubt. A wicked, wicked woman. But I didn't raise you to be a wanton sorceress. We'll risk no further taint from that filthy magic."

"Filthy? No!" Doucette protested. "You could have seen for yourself how beautiful it is—*was*—" she choked on the truth, hating it, "to fly as a swan, an owl, or a falcon. Cecilia or Azelais would have Transformed you. I would have, myself, if you had trusted one of us enough to ask."

"Lady of the Seas! The corruption spreads faster than even I thought possible," Lady Sarpine said. "Be grateful one of us understands the danger to your soul."

Doucette wasn't fooled by her mother's attempt to cover ambition with a cloak of piety. "Did you tell Father you were going to ruin my swan skin?"

Her mother avoided her eyes. "Pascau will not gainsay me."

Doucette's head dropped to the floor again. It didn't matter. The foul deed was done. Whatever he thought of it, her father couldn't undo it. No one could.

"Truly, it's for the best." Lady Sarpine's voice softened. She could afford to be gentle, once she had achieved her aim. "Those burns will fester if not treated straightaway. Ask in the kitchen. Na Patris will have an ointment." She stooped and touched the top of Doucette's head. "Don't be so downcast, my treasure. With that awful peasant gone, we'll make you a good match yet."

Her mother's intended reassurance had the opposite effect. "Gone?" Doucette gasped. She felt as though she had been kicked in the ribs. "Jaume failed?"

"He'll fail tomorrow," Lady Sarpine snapped, "wishing he had never insulted one of my daughters with his rude attentions. The fool thought to steal our treasure? He'll die pursuing it, alone in the dark, in the cavern's depths. Your father has assured me the wretch won't escape the spirit's wrath."

The comtesse's vengeful tone turned peevish. "Do stop sulking in this vulgar fashion, Doucette. Have your hands seen to and eat in the kitchen if you're not fit for company. Someday, when you're a queen, you'll thank me." In a flurry of swishing skirts, Lady Sarpine took her leave.

Alone, Doucette wept against the cold stone floor.

Her tears seemed inexhaustible, as if their source went deep as the caverns below the castle, past Lavena's domain and into the profound reaches of the earth. The hot flood scalded her eyes, an angry counterpoint to the pain that throbbed in her hands, the misery that stabbed at her.

Before Doucette had discovered her swan skin, envy of Azelais and Cecilia's freedom had gnawed a hollow place inside her. The joy of flight, of Transformation, had filled that emptiness with hope and turned useless wishes to purposeful action. Doucette knew she didn't share her sisters' beauty, their grace or confidence, but she'd hoped that with practice she could match their skill. A sorceress could make a new place in the world. Her own place.

That dream lay in ashes.

How could her mother be so cruel? And not only to her daughter. With every breath, Doucette smelled the charred, stinking remains of her swan skin and realized that she had managed to poison Jaume's future as well.

Her dear shepherd had proved the most unlikely of champions: a man whose affection did not depend on Doucette's wealth, her position, or her power. He had cared for Doucette when she was the comte's unmagical—and unattainable—daughter. Out of kindness and honor, he had even refused to take advantage of a swan maiden's vulnerability.

How had Doucette repaid his devotion? By agreeing to marry him. And in so doing, she had exposed him to her parents' retribution. They might not have minded a swan maiden's dalliance with a commoner, as long as she kept it discreet. But marriage meant a permanent connection between two families. Doucette should have known that the comtesse, at least, would never accept an alliance with shepherds.

From the venom in her mother's remarks, Jaume must have dug the pond, completing the second task. But if Lady Sarpine's prediction was correct, Jaume would die attempting the third trial, and that, too, would be Doucette's fault. The caves' guardian spirit permitted no outsiders within reach of the Aigleron, the magical bird that had given her family its name.

Even if Jaume succeeded in finding the fabled treasure, he would never return without Doucette's help.

Divorced from her magic, Doucette was just as lost. Though she'd had had so little time to enjoy it, sorcery had marked her, as Tante Mahalt had promised. She had tasted a sorceress's freedom, daring to claim love on her own terms. After having lost her swan skin and wand, she would never fly again, nor possess the means to call her life her own.

Doucette sobbed in renewed anguish.

Her aunt had warned them. A sorceress had enemies, she had said. Blinded by love, Doucette had never suspected her own mother would lead the attack.

Choking on the bitter taste of betrayal, Doucette shook tear-wet hair from her face. She had to get out of this chamber before some gossiping attendant found her.

Her hands were too blistered to use, so she shrugged awkwardly into her shift. The effort made her light-headed with pain. When she couldn't manage the gown's sleeves or lacing unaided, she draped it over her shoulders in a makeshift cloak and shuffled off to the kitchen, her burned hands extended like a ghost's. She had given Jaume's pot of salve to Na Patris; perhaps a little remained.

After all, Doucette thought dully, a shepherd's healing magic was the best she could hope for, since the High Arts were barred to her forever.

Chapter Twenty-one

———————❧———————

Distantly aware of the laughter and music drifting from the feast hall, Doucette huddled in a corner of the busy kitchen. Her burned hands ached; her throat felt raw from crying. But within her pain and confusion, a dreadful resolve was forming.

"Stew, little lady?" Na Patris set a bowl on Doucette's bench, next to other dishes full of untouched food.

"Thank you," Doucette said, as she had before. She made no move to pick up the spoon.

The baker's freckled face clouded with concern. "Eat," she urged, before the sound of raised voices called her away.

Doucette's thoughts turned inward once more. All evening, she had tried to think of a different way out. For herself, and for Jaume. However much it frightened her, she had seen but one possibility.

The Rassemblement.

If the ritual succeeded, Doucette would gain a new source of magic, as Tante Mahalt had done. Otherwise . . .

Nausea rose in a sour wave.

Doucette swallowed hard. Even if her beloved agreed to help, she might not survive the attempt. A thousand ways to fail, Tante Mahalt had said. The one consolation was that she and Jaume had a better chance together than either had alone.

"Tea?" Na Patris knelt beside her. "Drink, Lady Doucette. I'll hold the cup."

Doucette obediently sipped the steaming liquid, then spoke softly to the baker. "Jaume's staying at your house in town, Na Patris?"

The baker lowered the cup and glanced around the kitchen. Servers rushed in and out with their laden trays; Anfos whistled cheerfully over the soup pots. Nobody was paying attention to their quiet conversation. "Yes."

"Will you give him a message? He must meet me late tonight, outside the caves."

"No, no. Whatever are you thinking?"

With a touch of her bandaged hand, Doucette stilled the woman's protest. "His life is in danger."

Na Patris hesitated. "You'll keep him safe?"

"I'll try," Doucette answered. "Please, will you tell him?"

"Spirit business, is it?" When Doucette didn't reply, the baker frowned. "I will," she said at last. "But if you intend to tramp around in nasty damp caves, you'll have some stew first, so help me. And a bite of bread with Toumas's good honey, to keep your strength up."

"Thank you, Na Patris."

The baker sighed. "You're welcome, little lady."

Under a sliver of moon, the wind whispered through the olive trees and tossed the lavender's purple caps. Behind the terrace wall, the hole in the hillside made a dark, still place in the night's restless shadows.

Crouching on the damp ground, Doucette pulled the cloak over her shoulders with the tips of her bandaged fingers. Frightened thoughts chased themselves like rats trapped in the castle's deepest cellar.

She could still change her mind.

All she had to do was retrace her steps back through the orchard, run across the gardens, and steal up the tower steps to her room. Na Patris would keep silent about the message she had been asked to give her husband's cousin.

Who would know? Not Doucette's parents. Not Azelais or Cecilia, sleeping soundly in the tower chamber.

Jaume might wonder, but he would never reproach her.

The thought was what kept her there, waiting. Only Doucette would know she had missed her best chance—her only chance— to regain the magic her mother had stolen. If the Rassemblement succeeded, she could help Jaume accomplish the comte's third task. Once victorious, they could leave Beloc for good.

The breeze played through Doucette's hair, bringing her the smell of Jaume before the sight of him. The familiar combination of wool and wood smoke, tinged with the sharp scent of bramble sap and rich wet earth, comforted her.

She mustn't think about what would happen to him, to both of them, if she failed. She must remember her training and fix her attention on the task at hand.

Jaume sheltered a small oil lamp with his hat. The wide brim directed light into his face, illuminating the concern in his dark eyes. "Doucette?"

Doucette made her voice strong and welcoming. "Na Patris said you made a lovely pond!"

"Oh, aye," he said. "Built a wall, then changed the spade's spell, like you showed me. It dug in a soggy spot and found a spring, quick as quick. Lord Pascau took it fine, but Lady Sarpine didn't seem best pleased."

"No." Doucette's confident façade crumbled. "She's furious."

"I'm sorry." He set down the lamp and took her wrist gently, mindful of the bandages. "What happened?"

"Yours are worse." She turned his hand to the lamplight, revealing cracked and bloody nails, flaps of skin where blisters had formed and broken.

"Sores will heal, give it a day or two," he said. "What—"

"I must ask you a favor," Doucette interrupted him. "But if you don't want to go on with the last trial, Father said he had offered you a reward."

"To give you up?" Jaume shook his head. "No."

"Good." Doucette took a steadying breath. "I asked you here because I've discovered tomorrow's task. It can't be done without my help. In return, I need yours."

Jaume touched her fingers to his lips. "Command me."

"It will be difficult," she warned.

"I don't mind hard work."

"Not like the others. You'll have to build a ladder of my bones."

"Nay, love." Jaume spun her into his arms. "I'll take no part in such an ill deed."

"You must," Doucette said unhappily, and eased out of his embrace. "From what Mother let slip after she—after we spoke earlier—my father is going to demand you bring him the hidden treasure of Beloc."

He touched her hair, lightly. "You are the hidden treasure of Beloc."

"Please, don't tease me," Doucette said. "The Aigleron is so well guarded that only a family member can find it. I'm sure to be shut in my room again tomorrow. If you're to bring back the treasure, it must be done before dawn."

Jaume rubbed his chin. "We seek a crown, then? A sword? A strongbox?"

"The magical golden bird our family's named for," Doucette said. "I've never seen it, but there are stories. Anyway, the Aigleron's nest sits at the top of a marble pillar, deep underground."

"Doesn't sound too difficult," Jaume said.

Doucette finished. "On the far side of Lavena's Cauldron."

"Lavena's Cauldron?"

"She's a spirit. There's a way we can ask for her help."

Jaume looked skeptical. "Better explain this from the beginning, my heart."

Doucette thought of Tante Mahalt, limping proudly across her courtyard, and chose her words with care. "This ritual—the Rassemblement—may change me. I hope it will change me."

"Change?" Jaume said. "How?"

"Rassemblement means remaking, with magic." In a rush, Doucette explained the ritual.

"What?" Disgust roughened Jaume's voice. "Why would you risk such a thing? What if the spirit takes your eyes or your tongue?"

"Mother burned my swan skin and my wand to punish me, to stop me from helping you, to keep me a prisoner. Only the Rassemblement can return the magic I lost." Doucette held out her bandaged hands. "Please. You promised once that if I were in trouble, I could ask you."

"It's that important? The magic."

"Yes," Doucette said.

After a long silence, Jaume nodded. "Lead on, then. I can't refuse you."

"Thank you," Doucette said quietly. She pointed to the hole in the hillside. "We'll go in here. Mind your head. The entry's low." Gathering all her courage, she pulled her cloak over her hair and crawled into the earthen tunnel. After a short distance traversed on her knees, the rock above her head opened into a high, vaulted space. She stood.

Behind her, Jaume held up the lamp. Though its light made but a small impression on the vast darkness, it showed the cave walls continuing downward, an arm's breadth apart on either side of them. "Can't get lost in this bit," Jaume said. He stamped his feet and coughed at the acrid odor that filled the cool air.

Doucette's eyes filled with tears from the pungent smell left behind by generations of bats. "At least they're out for the night," she said. "By day, we'd have a thousand furry little beasts hanging over our heads."

Jaume held his nose closed. "Lead on."

After twisting downward in a loose spiral, the close-set walls of the cave widened, only to pinch off into two tunnels. Doucette headed for the rightmost one, but stopped at the tunnel's mouth.

While Jaume looked on, she ran her hands along the rock until she found an iron hook set near the ground.

"It's still here," Doucette said in relief.

"You've been to this place before?"

"As a child. Mother forbade it, of course," Doucette admitted, "but that never stopped Azelais and Cecilia. I'd come in after them and have to find my way back alone." Pulling a fat ball of thread from under her cloak, she tied the free end around the hook and started down the tunnel.

It twisted like a snake shedding its skin. A section would curl back in on itself, then split into two, or three, or ten. Though the stone passages took on a dreamy sameness, Doucette was careful to choose always the downward path. She let the thread play out behind her, watching to be sure it didn't snag and break on the uneven floor.

Then the narrow way opened onto a fantastic landscape. Doucette stopped and Jaume let out a low whistle.

Pillars of pale stone rose toward the roof of a huge cavern. More columns hung down without touching the floor.

As a child, the place had reminded her of a giant, fanged mouth. Time had not improved its appearance. She walked more slowly here, warning Jaume of the pits—some filled with water, others deep and empty—waiting between the pillars.

By the time they reached the cavern's far wall, Doucette had come to the end of her thread. She planted it under a loose stone and turned to the rough walls that arched over their heads. "We need to find the entrance. In a crevice, maybe? It may not look like much."

Jaume raised the light and paced in a slow circle around her. He ran his free hand over the stone until a patch of deeper shadow swallowed his arm to the elbow. "Here?" he said.

"Let's try it. Will you fit through?"

"Do my best." Jaume shrugged his broad shoulders and handed her the lamp. "You carry the light."

"I'll go first," Doucette said. "If Lavena's waiting—" She couldn't finish the thought.

Shielding the precious lamp with one hand, she eased sideways into the crevice. The stone caught at her cloak and snagged her hair. Doucette pulled herself free with a jerk. They'd seen nothing living in the caves, but that didn't stop her mind from picturing blind spiders spinning webs to trap them, or many-legged scuttling creatures armed with pincers and teeth, waiting just outside the lamplight's reach.

"Jaume?" Her voice sounded small and frightened.

He grunted. "Coming, love."

Doucette swallowed against the stale dryness in her mouth and forced her legs to keep moving.

They emerged from the narrow cleft to find themselves standing at the bottom of a cylindrical shaft. Like a well, Doucette thought, except that instead of a circle of daylight, darkness pressed on their heads. She concentrated on breathing slowly and steadily. The air had a metallic, musty tang to it.

Jaume sniffed. "Old Lavena's cooking bad eggs down here?"

"Jaume!" Doucette said, half amused, half appalled at his irreverence. "A spirit's home is no place for jokes."

"No?" He stretched his shoulders and settled his hat more securely on his head. "I expected the place to be paved with gold and jewels. It's very plain. And the marble pillar with the nest? Oh. I see it, by the bath."

Doucette's breath caught. "It's not a bath. That's Lavena's Cauldron."

"Looks like a bath," Jaume said. "Right size, right shape, steaming hot. Nice stonework, that."

"Jaume. She might be listening." Doucette's stomach churned with apprehension.

"Your pardon. Whistling against the dark is all." Jaume cupped the side of her face with his hand. "You don't have to go through with this, love. I've swum in scalding springs, climbed a tree or two. I'll manage the Cauldron and the pillar."

Touched by his care, Doucette turned her head so her lips brushed his fingers, then pulled away as a different awareness rippled across her skin. Jaume sensed it, too; she felt his body tense.

A presence. Watching them.

Doucette lifted the lamp high, illuminating steps that led down into the steaming pool. Amber mist rose from its surface. Underneath, the bubbling liquid might be water, or molten stone, or some other substance altogether.

Whatever it was, it looked hot. Dangerously hot. Was she mad, to think of consigning herself to it? Doucette's burned hands throbbed in their bandages. Her body clenched with the will to run, but her mind checked it.

She had spent her childhood fleeing to one hidey-hole or another, smarting from her sisters' tricks. Afraid to confront her parents with her newfound swan skin, she had escaped to her aunt's castle but failed to win the crown. She had even flown from Jaume, due to a misunderstanding as much her fault as his.

This time, she would finish what she had begun. And though Doucette's legs trembled with the urge to run, she didn't. After putting herself and Jaume at Lavena's mercy, she refused to leave without attempting the Rassemblement.

Doucette lowered her head and addressed the unseen depths. "Please, Lavena," she said, her voice quavering more than she liked, "I have come to be remade. By your grace, build of my bones a ladder, so that my companion may reach the top of the pillar and take the bird he finds there."

"A ladder?"

The ancient, husky voice might have condensed from the steam or issued from the rock. Only an aggrieved note hinted at the invisible speaker's lost humanity.

"Young people these days. All they want is ladders and keys, ladders and keys. Why not a nice harp, eh? Delicate bones like yours would make a fine harp, girlie."

Terror chilled Doucette's skin. Her lips felt so numb, she was surprised she could shape the proper words. "A ladder, Lavena, of your kindness."

"Oh, I suppose." The voice took on a wheedling, almost hungry note. "You'll pay for it?"

Doucette spoke quickly, before she could change her mind. "Yes."

"And your companion? He knows what to do?"

Beside her, Jaume stiffened. He could refuse, Doucette knew. She could hardly bear to imagine what the Rassemblement would require of them both. No blame to Jaume if he decided the reward not worth the price.

Light as a bird's wing, Jaume's kiss graced Doucette's cheek. He bowed in the direction of the pool. "Aye, and it please you, Lady."

The hoarse voice cackled. "Nice manners, for a rustic. Well, go on, girlie. We're waiting."

Doucette wanted to cling to Jaume's broad shoulders, longed for him to tell her it was all a mistake. She wished she could wake up safe in her bed and know the rasping voice, the dark cave, for a nightmare vision. But Jaume had not failed her. She would—she must—repay his trust with her own.

She set down the lamp. Somehow, her shaking legs carried her forward, step by slow step. In the expectant silence, she had plenty of time to notice the stonework Jaume had admired. Large blocks fitted seamlessly together and were capped by such an elegantly curved molding that the whole needed no other decoration. In the lamplight, the stone glowed honey-gold, streaked with apricot and ocher. Like the materials that formed the castle walls, town buildings, and fountains above them, these slabs must have been chipped from the quarry across the ridge from the Château de l'Aire.

Doucette spared an instant to wonder about the long-dead mason who had laid these stones so carefully, one on another. A master craftsman, her chastelaine's eye told her. Had he finished his work and lived to see the sky again, smell new grass and wood smoke, walk hand in hand with his sweetheart by the light of a harvest moon? Or had he perished in the endless dark?

Steam curled over the toes of her shoes; she had reached the edge of the pool. She couldn't help looking over her shoulder. If the ritual failed, at least she would carry with her a final memory of Jaume's dear face. His dark eyes held hers.

"Courage, love," he whispered.

She crossed her hands over her heart. Closing her eyes, Doucette started down the stairs. Her left foot found a shallow ledge; her right foot met nothing.

Dragged down by the sudden weight of her sodden clothing, she plunged to the bottom of the pool. The Cauldron's boiling water closed over her head. If it was water, she thought wildly.

Heat engulfed her.

Limitless heat, unlike any she had experienced. Not the oppressive sun of a summer's day, which can be cheated by a patch of shade or a drink of cool water, nor the radiant blast of Na Patris's open oven, grinning with jolly ferocity around a mouthful of loaf-teeth. It was nothing like the fire that had eaten her swan skin and blistered her hands, a swift, voracious blaze that stank of charred feathers and blasted hope.

No, this heat *stripped* her—of clothes, of flesh, of life and will—but Doucette could sense no malice in it. She was simply bathed in currents of elemental magic, which no mortal form could long withstand.

In its way, the experience exalted. Dancing with lightning might feel the same, though no one she knew had survived to tell the tale. Not that she expected to, either. If Doucette had antic-ipated how much the Rassemblement would hurt, she didn't think she could have taken that final step. Ignorance was required. Or faith, perhaps, that this agony served a purpose, that some part of her would remain after the dissolution of all she was and all she knew. But the future was out of her hands. Doucette burned and had no voice to scream.

An eternity later, pain loosened its grip on her mind, though Doucette could make little sense of her surroundings. She could no longer feel her limbs and, again, would have screamed. If she had a mouth. Or breath.

She couldn't move or see, smell or taste.

Alive or dead?

Her senses couldn't tell her. Trapped in a vast black emptiness, a tiny, determined kernel of her self remained. All she could do, it seemed, was listen.

Lavena muttered, "Sweetness, eh? Now, dearie. A sorceress daren't be sweet!" The voice emitted a cackling laugh; invisible lips smacked together.

A faint but steady clicking sound teased the edges of Doucette's awareness.

"Mm, mm. Several fine qualities to choose from," Lavena said. "Kindness, modesty—and what good would that do me, I ask you? Perseverance, perhaps, but—no. You'll need that, and where's your pride? Not enough to speak of, girlie. Not nearly enough, and you an Aigleron!" Lavena sounded affronted. "Too soft by half, but wait—is that jealousy I taste?" Again, the cackle.

"At least you've a young man worth scrapping over. Climbs nimble as a monkey, though he's great big feet that—mind the scapula!" The voice screeched, then subsided into a fretful murmur. "Wait for the leg bones, why don't you? No patience, these young people. What, you've never seen a skull before? Step gently, eh? That's better. Ribs, ribs, ribs. . . ."

Formless, Doucette floated. She couldn't lift a finger to change events, but it appeared from Lavena's mutterings that Jaume had assembled Doucette's bones into a ladder and was busy climbing it.

The grisly idea seemed far removed from her current state. Doucette drifted, lost in a sea of magic, until Lavena's attention captured hers once more.

"Where was I? Oh, yes. Now, girlie," the husky voice said. "What about your memories?"

The eerie tranquility evaporated as ghostly fingers poked and prodded Doucette's mind.

The spirit picked through Doucette's past, shaking out her memories and inspecting them as Lady Sarpine might examine an old gown for flaws. The sensation was horrible, but Doucette could neither avoid it nor protest. She could only endure.

"Pathetic," Lavena said. "Useless. This one's completely threadbare—why'd you keep it? Ah. What about this?"

As a shining bit of thread catches a magpie's attention, the memory of Doucette's first flight as a swan snagged Lavena's interest. Doucette relived the rush of the wind against her skin, the terror of falling, the surge of elation as her wings bore her up.

"Not bad. Not bad at all, but I've others like it. Hm. Your shepherd lad's reached the top." The voice sounded mildly surprised before it turned testy. "Put the bird in your shirt, idiot boy. Don't be climbing down one-handed. Not the jaw, don't hang on the—huh. Stronger than I expected." Again, an almost human amusement touched the inhuman voice.

"Well, dearie, I don't want your virtues, and your past doesn't interest me, so I believe I'll settle for the traditional payment. More than fair. Your young man's putting the ladder down in the—ah! Yes. I'll just take this one. You'll hardly miss it."

Doucette heard a sharp cracking noise. The sound brought on an avalanche of sensation.

Forearm, shin, breastbone, hipbone, backbone, thigh bone— Doucette could feel each one distinctly, tumbling over the others to find its appointed slot. Muscles snapped into place. A lattice of veins wove through her body with dizzying speed. Her heart jumped and then beat strongly within its cage of ribs. Hair sprouted from her scalp, each strand vibrant with life. Slack lungs craved air, but when her mouth opened, a fiery liquid rushed in.

Hot, hot, HOT! Inside and out, Doucette burned.

Arms and legs thrashed, lifting Doucette's head above the surface of the pool. Jaume seized one of her flailing hands and hauled her out of the Cauldron. She sat down and doubled over with pain. Her cloak shimmered.

Her dry cloak.

Whatever boiled in Lavena's Cauldron, it wasn't water.

"Doucette? Are you well? Speak to me!"

Doucette tried to nod reassurance to Jaume's frantic questions. Slowly, the fiery heat receded, leaving her overwhelmed with sensation. Every part of her skin tingled, as if she had been rubbed all over with fresh snow or hot oil. Her right foot, especially, throbbed urgent warning. She looked at her legs, extended in front of her. Her shoes had disappeared; her feet glowed rosy pink in the Cauldron's strange light.

Jaume noticed at the same instant. His face darkened with anger. "Your toe!"

Dimpled skin covered the spot where her smallest toe had been. Doucette's stomach turned over; she turned aside and retched. Mercifully, nothing came up. She wiped her mouth on her sleeve and made herself answer calmly. "Lavena's price," she said. "A toe is minor, compared to what she could have taken."

"What?"

"Truly, Jaume," Doucette insisted, before he could offend the spirit. "It could have been much worse. And you? Did you get the Aigleron?"

"Oh, aye." Visibly, he reined in his anger. He patted his hat. "It's safe."

Doucette bowed over her knees with relief. The Rassemblement had worked! Jaume had the Aigleron, and Doucette hadn't died or lost an arm, her mind, or her memories, only a toe. As for her magic, time would tell. At the moment, she felt alive all over, if rather too exposed, like an earthworm yanked wriggling from its den. "Thank you, Lavena."

A distant, fading cackle answered her.

When Doucette tried to stand, her legs wouldn't hold her. She smiled crookedly at Jaume. "I'm afraid you'll have to carry both me and the lamp."

Willing arms scooped up her limp body. "Gladly," Jaume said.

Chapter Twenty-two

───────────❦───────────

*L*ight speared Doucette's eyes. She closed them tight and burrowed under the bedclothes. Her head felt stuffed with a greasy wool that muffled her very thoughts.

Dark, it had been dark, she remembered, and frightening, but Jaume carried her. In his arms, she was safe. . . .

"Wake up, Doucette," Azelais said. "It's almost dawn."

"Leave her be," Cecilia said. "After what Mother did to her swan skin—"

"Dreadful." Azelais's voice dropped. "But she might as well see the end of this ridiculous business."

"Hush," Cecilia said more sternly.

Azelais hushed. Doucette gave up trying to open her eyes or string two thoughts together and gratefully sank back into sleep.

When she opened her eyes again, Doucette blinked in surprise. She felt so new! Refreshed, restored, no pain anywhere. Even her hair felt alive, swirling over her shoulders like quicksilver. Her bare skin reported smooth sheets that smelled of lavender water under the slight rasp of a wool blanket. She could feel the warmth of individual sunbeams dancing along the foot that stuck out from under the bedclothes. She wiggled her outstretched toes: one, two, three, four.

In an instant, she remembered it all. The cavern, the Cauldron, the spirit.

Four toes.

Doucette pulled her maimed foot inside the covers. It had happened, the Rassemblement. It was real. Lavena had taken her payment. What had she given in return?

Doucette closed her eyes and lay still, exploring the unfamiliar sensations that filled her. Once, when she put on her swan skin, the magic had tingled along her skin. Now it flowed inside her. With every breath, she sensed it surging through her veins, its rhythm as steady as the sea.

With power this strong, she could sculpt mountains, level cities, shift the stars in the heavens. She no longer needed a wand or a swan skin to work the High Arts. Infused with sorcery, her body *was* a wand.

At least that's how it felt. Could she translate this impression into action?

Doucette laid her hand over a bolster.

> *Be thou silk covered,*
> *dappled as my swan feathers,*
> *as crackling frost,*
> *as veined marble.*

Magic rushed through her fingers, draining her strength as it Transformed the pillowcase. With heroic effort, Doucette raised her head. Under her fingers, the plain linen became white silk, shot through with silver threads.

Overcome by weakness, she closed her eyes and surrendered

once more to darkness. When she woke again, the chamber was awash in late afternoon's golden light.

Doucette stroked the Transformed silk bolster, then stared at the backs of her hands. The bandages had disappeared. Doucette turned her hands over. Fresh new skin wrapped her palms where the burned patches had been. She extended her fingers, then let her hands fall on the coverlet.

How strange. Magic roared within her, refreshing her mind and her senses, but it left her body as helpless as an infant. Doucette braced herself against the headboard and struggled to sit up.

Remade.

She could almost hear Lavena clucking. "What did you expect from new bones, muscles, blood, and all? Young people these days! No patience. If I had a lovely new body, I'd give it some time. I would, indeed."

In the end, Doucette was content to sit and follow the spirit's imagined advice. She watched bars of sunlight slant ever more steeply across the walls until hunger forced her out of bed. She could smell the food on the table by the window: a heel of crusty bread and roasted onion salad. Humble fare, but a treat to her heightened senses. The roasted onion tasted delicious mixed with fruity olive oil and tart vinegar. Na Patris had outdone herself, Doucette thought, mopping up the last bit of savory juice with her bread.

After eating, Doucette felt well enough to wash her face. She put on a clean shift and combed her hair, resting between strokes. The effort of moving sapped what little strength she had, though her mind raced, defying her body's weakness.

What had happened to Jaume while she slept the day away?

Her newly keen ears heard the rapid *tap-tap* of feet climbing the stairs long before the bedchamber door burst open and Azelais and Cecilia dashed in, swan skins fluttering.

"Hurry," Cecilia said. "Father wants you."

Azelais's eyebrows were drawn over her brow in a single line. "You're a disgrace to our name."

"Be quiet, Azelais," Cecilia snapped. "Can't you think of anyone but yourself?"

Doucette's pulse drummed in her throat. Her sisters' expressions told her that Jaume had succeeded with the golden bird. If he had been set a different task and failed, Cecilia wouldn't look so concerned, or Azelais so angry. Doucette's fingers lost their grip on the comb, which clattered onto the table. She eyed it and hoped this weakness would pass. "Hand me that pink gown, would you, Cecilia?"

"No time." Cecilia drew her wand from her sleeve. "Everybody's waiting. Father's arranged a final test. If your shepherd wants you so badly, he'll have to choose you."

"What?" Doucette braced her hands flat on the table. "Another test? Unfair!"

"Fair?" Azelais scoffed. "Someone helped him with the first three. Are you afraid that the man can't manage the simplest one on his own?"

"No," Doucette said. "But—"

Cecilia interrupted her. "By your leave, Sister?"

Doucette's hair tumbled over her shoulders as she shook her head, but Cecilia was looking at Azelais.

Azelais shrugged. "Oh, very well."

Cecilia murmured a few words and tapped Azelais with her wand.

Doucette sucked in a breath as the spell took hold. Their oldest sister's face and form wavered, as if seen under water, and then became a mirror image of Cecilia's.

From the tips of their leather shoes to their azure gowns, fair hair, blue eyes, and complacent expressions, the two young women were identical. The second one spoke in Azelais's voice. "You vain thing, Cecilia. However can you breathe with your gown laced so tightly?"

"You next." Cecilia's wand tapped Doucette's shoulder.

The spell sizzled over her skin, but a swift current of Doucette's own magic swept out to repel it. With a loud crackling noise and a shower of sparks, the two spells clashed.

Her sisters jumped back in alarm. A little dizzy herself, Doucette swayed until she could sit upright.

The true Cecilia stared accusingly at an unchanged Doucette and then at her wand. "What happened?"

"You bungled it, Sister. Lost your focus," the other Cecilia said in Azelais's voice. "There's a reason I'm Tante's heir. Strength of mind, remember?"

"No!" The wand tapped Doucette's shoulder again. As before, the spell failed spectacularly.

One Cecilia looked stupefied, the other impatient.

"I told you we should do it my way." Muttering, Cecilia-Azelais took the wand and tapped first her own shoulder, then the real Cecilia's.

Doucette tasted the magic in the air as a cloud of white smoke enveloped her sisters. When it dissipated, Doucette recoiled. Both of her sisters now looked like her! Each one wore her features, her plain shift, bare feet, and trailing hair.

"Not bad, I think."

Hearing Azelais's voice issue from her own face made Doucette feel queasy.

"But look at the hair, Azelais," Doucette-Cecilia said. "Ours isn't nearly as pretty. Really, I don't know how you won that circlet you're so proud of. Heir or no, clarity of vision was ever *your* weakness."

"Mm." Doucette-Azelais tapped her lips just like Tante Mahalt. Gray eyes studied Doucette's head with a disconcerting coolness. "I grant you're right this time, Cecilia." Doucette-Azelais stroked her own head with the wand until her hair gleamed with light and then did the same for Doucette-Cecilia. "What did you do, Sister? It's so shiny, like pearl."

"I combed it," Doucette said blandly, but she was thinking of Tante Mahalt's iridescent hair. Was this, too, an effect of the Rassemblement? Or just Lavena's little joke?

Doucette-Cecilia pouted. "You could give us decent gowns."

Doucette-Azelais sighed with exasperation and raised her wand again.

Before the wand could descend, Doucette stood up, letting the hem of her shift fall over her bare feet. "You said to hurry. We'll go as we are." Their father's game seemed clear enough, but more than one could play it. She walked to the open door and started down the stairs, hoping neither of her sisters would notice how unsteady her steps were.

"I am not facing the court dressed in a shift!" Cecilia's voice rose shrill behind her. "Barefoot, my hair unbound like a child's!"

"Don't worry. They'll think we're her," Doucette-Azelais said.

"Fine," Doucette-Cecilia said. "Then stop dawdling, Doucette. Here, Azelais. You take her other arm."

Doucette's sisters hurried her down the stairs between them, and on through the castle's empty corridors. She was glad of their unwitting support. Without it, she feared her legs might buckle and drop her to the floor.

They stopped before the closed doors of the feast hall. Doucette-Azelais patted her hair, as if she missed the circlet that normally rested there.

"Hide the wand!" Doucette-Cecilia whispered.

Doucette-Azelais glanced down the empty corridor before tucking the wand behind a wall hanging. She beat her fist against one of the doors and returned to Doucette's side.

To Doucette's sensitive ears, the silence had a distinctly menacing quality.

Chapter Twenty-three

The doors swung wide. Inside, courtiers, servants, and townsfolk greeted the trio of barely dressed Doucettes with a collective exhalation of astonishment.

The young women walked through the open doors and straight through the crowded feast hall to the high table.

Doucette's heart leaped to see Jaume standing to one side of the dais, his hat in his hand.

Tucked in the crook of his other arm, a golden bird glowed in the candlelight. About the size of a dove, it had a raptor's beak and crest, though the long, graceful neck curled over a swan's plumage. Doucette thought magic must have made it, for no mortal goldsmith could have worked in such perfect detail. The eyes, two black crystals, glittered.

In contrast to the wonderful bird and the courtiers' habitual finery, the shepherd's stained, ripped clothes bore silent witness to his three days of labor. Despite its tired lines, however, Jaume's handsome face showed no signs of the weakness that had afflicted Doucette since her immersion in Lavena's Cauldron. His eyes narrowed at the sight of three identical girls advancing toward him, but he gave no sign of dismay.

Doucette's heart beat fast. He would know her, wouldn't he? Jaume had seen her as no one else had, down to her very bones. After all they had endured together, she surely had nothing to fear. Pride strengthened her trembling legs and carried her to stand with her sisters before the dais.

Lord Pascau stood, his manner affable. Seated beside him, Lady Sarpine wore no expression whatsoever; she might have turned herself to stone. The castle folk visibly simmered with expectation.

"Jaume of Vent'roux," the comte said, "you have completed your three appointed tasks: clearing the hillside, digging the pond, and finding Beloc's greatest treasure. In so doing, you have won my youngest daughter's hand, and I give it freely."

A low, surprised sound rose from the crowd.

The comte chuckled. "Provided, of course, that you choose the right one."

Jaume bowed. While those assembled held their breath, he regarded first one Doucette, then another. Finally, he walked toward the three identical girls.

Doucette moved her changed foot forward until four toes peeped out from under the hem of her shift. Stopping directly in front of her, Jaume glanced down and smiled as if the sight confirmed what he already knew. "The middle lady, and none other, is Doucette," he said.

Azelais and Cecilia dropped Doucette's arms and stepped away, distancing themselves from their sister and her chosen suitor.

"Yes." Joyfully, Doucette held out her hands to Jaume. He gave her the golden bird, then grasped her wrists, which dipped under the thing's unexpected weight.

Afterward, Doucette wondered whether she had been the tinder or the spark. Had the magic that suffused her flowed out on its own into the golden bird, or had the enchanted thing called it forth?

Whatever the cause, she could feel magic stirring. It passed from her body into feathers that warmed in her hands. Suddenly, the bird shimmered with light. As its glow grew more brilliant, the watching crowd murmured in wonder. Radiance fountained out of the golden bird, washed over Doucette's and Jaume's arms, then pooled around their feet.

Her sisters cried out and shaded their eyes, but neither Doucette nor Jaume could look away.

Between them, the bird awoke into life.

The dazzling feathers shifted. Claws pricked Doucette's fingers. She laughed in surprise and delight as the bird turned its head and brushed her palm with its raptor beak. Bright eyes stared at her, infusing her with their strength.

Onlookers gasped as the Aigleron chirped. It fluttered its wings once, twice, and launched itself from Doucette and Jaume's linked hands. Golden wings cast light, rather than shadow, as the enchanted bird circled over the upturned faces. When it opened its beak again, it trilled notes of a piercing, unearthly sweetness. The Aigleron's legendary song filled the feast hall, and then the bird soared through the open doors and away. It would return to its nest in its own time, by its own way.

Doucette held Jaume and saw her own amazement reflected in his eyes.

The comte groped for his chair and sat down hard next to his wife.

After a long, awed hush, the townsfolk cheered as if to lift the roof from its beams. Servants surged around Doucette and Jaume, offering her their shy best wishes and slapping him heartily on the back.

"My mother's mother saw the Aigleron—never thought it'd fly in my day," the goldsmith said, beaming. "Thank you, little lady."

"Lovely, that was." Na Claro's wrinkled face streamed with tears, but she, too, smiled. "A blessing on your marriage."

Courtiers offered more restrained congratulations. Other eyes besides Doucette's had noticed the stern set of the comte's lips and the comtesse's alabaster face.

Elusive as spring snowflakes, Doucette-Azelais and Doucette-Cecilia melted from the feast hall. When they returned, clad in their own gowns and wearing their own faces, they joined their parents, sitting in unrelieved silence at the high table.

Meanwhile, the castle servants bustled through the crowd, working their own kind of magic. Trestle tables unfolded and were draped in festive cloths. Benches popped up like mushrooms after a rain, their seats dotted with bright cushions.

"This way, little lady, Jaume." A beaming Na Patris escorted them to a table garlanded with wheat stalks and late roses, meadow saffron and purple mallow. The baker bobbed a curtsy to Doucette. "We're so glad, Lady Doucette, that our sweetness has found a husband who will treasure her."

Doucette's eyes filled at the affection in the baker's voice, so lacking in her own parents' reaction.

"No crying, mind!" Na Patris dabbed at her eyes with her apron. "We've a few touches to finish the meal, but first, some gifts for the pair of you."

The wool mistress Na Soufio came up to Doucette. "The weaver's guild offers a gown, which I'll thank you to put on this instant, little lady! Fancy, the bride wearing a shift to her betrothal feast!"

Before Doucette could speak, a bevy of women whisked her from Jaume's side. They bundled her into a wool gown of forest green, with matching hose and a pair of sturdy walking shoes, and crowned her head with a wreath of braided wheat.

As Na Claro slid a stocking over Doucette's changed foot, the old servant drew in a startled breath. She made no comment about the missing toe, however, for which Doucette silently thanked her. When Doucette returned to the table, breathless and smiling, she saw that Jaume, too, had been freshly outfitted in a gold tunic and brown leggings, a wide leather belt, and new boots.

Om Toumas greeted them. "As you see, other folk have been hard at work while some lazed under an oak tree in the park, playing the pipes," he said.

"Did you, Jaume?" Doucette asked. "I slept for ages."

"Oh, aye." Jaume grinned at her. "Rest well earned," he told Om Toumas.

"No doubt. With the gold bird safe under your hat the whole time, eh? Better we not know how you managed that, Cousin." The older man leaned forward to speak to Jaume privately. "If you'd keep your new treasure safe, you'll be gone from Beloc quick as may be." He jerked his chin at the high table. "Not all wish you the same good health and long life as I do, or I misread our comtesse's expression."

Jaume nodded.

Doucette kissed the older man's cheek. "I'll miss you, Om Toumas," she said.

"Long life and happiness to you both." He bowed and left them.

A wide-eyed Anfos came to stand before the table. "They say a bride's kiss is lucky. May I have one, Lady Doucette?"

"Certainly." Doucette planted a kiss on the forehead presented to her, and the boy retreated with a satisfied air.

Gifts were piled on the floor around the table. Doucette was glad for Jaume's solid presence beside her and his arm supporting hers, because it took all her fortitude to receive their well-wishers and bestow the bride's kiss on all who sought it. Mostly the townsfolk and castle servants, she found, with a sprinkling of men-at-arms and courtiers.

The gifts, too, were mainly of a practical nature, unusual for a noblewoman's betrothal. Doucette received a drop-spindle, a sewing case, garden seeds rolled in a cloth, and a warm cloak. Men gave Jaume a pouch of nails, a fire-striking stone, a hand-ax. Others offered crocks of olive oil, sacks of dried peas, millet, and smoked meat. The captain of the comte's armsmen slid two leather travel packs, like those his men carried on long marches, discreetly under the table.

In his serious expression, Doucette read concern for their safety. She pressed his hand. "Thank you, Captain Denis."

"We'll put the packs to good use," Jaume assured him. "Directly."

An unspoken assurance passed between the men. The captain bowed. "Wishing you every joy."

The parade of gifts had barely stopped when the procession

of dishes began. Servers carried each course first to the table on the dais. This was the usual custom, though tonight the comte's family showed so little appetite that plenty of delicacies remained for the humblest pig girl and pot boy to sample.

The variety of dishes astonished Doucette. She counted five kinds of soup, from delicate broths to hearty stews. Grilled eels and roasted meats were served with a variety of sauces: fennel, pomegranate, almond, and olive, while eggs came stuffed, poached, and covered with mustard sauce. Fritters, puddings, and cakes of every variety made up the desserts.

"You prepared this feast in one day?" Doucette asked Na Patris, who had taken it upon herself to supply the betrothed couple with food and drink.

The baker beamed at her. "Why, after Toumas put up the travel pavilion in the new parkland, Lord Pascau and Lady Sarpine convened the court out there. Not a noblewoman underfoot for hours, and we took advantage of it! Maids and washerwomen lent a hand with the cooking, and grooms chopped firewood and turned the spits for the roasts. Town girls picked the flowers and wove the garlands, while their lads found enough tables and benches for all to have a place."

"But how did you know?" Doucette asked.

Na Patris nodded at Jaume. "Heard him playing his pipes, didn't we? Tunes lively enough to make the dead dance. We figured it would come out right."

"It's lovely," Doucette said, touched by the servants' confidence.

Na Patris wound her hands in her apron. "We wanted to give you a proper send-off. Grand fare for a betrothal dinner, maybe,

but with the comte and comtesse feeling the way they do . . .
you'll be married before Jaume's people in Vent'roux town?"

Doucette nodded, too overcome with a rush of emotion to
speak. Soon she would be leaving her home, her family, the only
life she knew.

Sooner than soon.

Tonight.

Om Toumas had suggested it, as had Captain Denis.
Doucette couldn't disagree. Her father hadn't stopped the
impromptu betrothal feast, but her mother would never permit
an actual wedding to occur.

No, they would have to go. She looked around the feast hall,
cherishing the sight and sounds of merriment. The general rev-
elry was broken only by the high table's quiet island of disapproval.

Jaume squeezed her hand. Doucette leaned against him and
was comforted.

When the final plate of fig sweetmeats had been presented to
Lady Sarpine and coldly dismissed, Lord Pascau took his wife's
arm and descended from the dais.

The hall quieted. People gave way to the comte and comtesse
as they passed Doucette and Jaume's table.

"Good night," Lord Pascau said.

Lady Sarpine spared an icy look for Doucette—and for
Jaume, none at all.

Jaume bowed.

Doucette curtsied. "Good night, Father. Good night,
Mother."

Her parents swept away from her, and Doucette felt a sharp

pain at her heart. She knew it might be the last time she saw them. Despite all that had happened, she hated to part on such cold terms. Tears threatened as she turned to her oldest sister. "Good night, Azelais."

Azelais walked away as if she hadn't heard.

Doucette swallowed. "Good night, Cecilia."

Cecilia's lovely face was marked by the sadness they both felt. "Good night," she said quietly. "Go well." She inclined her head to Jaume and followed the others out of the feast hall.

When the door closed behind the noble family, the dancing began. Shortly afterward, Doucette and Jaume slipped away. Jaume carried a pack on each shoulder and supported Doucette by the elbow. Stopping in the shadowed corridor, he searched her eyes. "You're sure?"

"Yes," she said.

The guard at the gate let them pass without challenge, and Doucette and Jaume walked into the night.

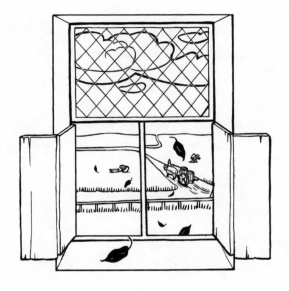

Autumn

Chapter Twenty-four

*D*oucette heard the hoofbeats first. "Father's coming."

Jaume turned and squinted at the distant smudge of dust. "Back on the road a ways?"

"Yes. Not even Cecilia drives her horse so hard." Doucette surveyed their surroundings, hoping for a place to hide.

From the Château de l'Aire, they had descended the ridge and crossed the plain as far as Jaume could go while carrying Doucette and both their packs. They had slept in the shelter of an olive tree and woke to walk again in the misty light before dawn.

The rising sun revealed cultivated areas separated by ditches of muddy water. Harvested wheat fields alternated with those planted in winter rye. Overnight, it seemed, summer had ended and autumn begun. Clouds scudded across the sky, and a mean wind hissed through the fields, picking up wisps of straw and wheat chaff and blowing them into the travelers' faces. But neither the old wheat stubble nor the new rye blades stood tall enough to cover Jaume's boot tops.

"We'll lie down in a dry ditch," Jaume said. "He'll ride right past us."

"Or," Doucette said patiently, "I can Transform us into shapes he won't suspect."

"You're weak as a kitten, love."

Doucette sighed in exasperation. She and Jaume had been arguing about her sorcery since they'd left the Château de l'Aire. Again, she tried to explain. "My magic's on the inside, Jaume. It doesn't rely on the strength of my arms or legs."

His mouth tightened in a stubborn line. "What if it went wrong? Plenty of time to practice your spells when we're safe home."

Under Doucette's feet, the earth quivered in warning.

"If Father catches us, we won't have that time. Please, Jaume. You must trust me."

He fixed her with such unhappy eyes that Doucette almost relented, except that a sorceress kept her attention fixed on her goal. "Please," she repeated.

"If you must."

Doucette ignored his grudging tone. "Put the packs down in the field, off the road," she directed. Eyeing the closest ditch, she wondered whether her legs would carry her over it.

Jaume lifted her easily and set her down on the far side of the ditch. Wheat stubble rustled under her shoes as she walked to the center of the field and pointed. "One pack, here. The other," she walked a few steps, "here."

Jaume glanced back, and Doucette followed his gaze.

The distant smudge was getting larger.

Doucette sank to her knees next to one of the packs and spread her hand over the leather, picturing what she wanted it to become. She summoned the magic within her until her fingers tingled with the pent-up flow, then spoke softly.

> *Be thou a well,*
> *deep-rooted,*
> *stone-rimmed,*
> *water-blessed,*
> *until thy spell, by my name, is undone.*

The pack's edges blurred. With a rumble and a splash, it sank into the ground. The earth where the pack had been foamed up in a circle and hardened into the stone lip of a well.

The force of the magic rushing out of her made Doucette sway a little, but she clapped in satisfaction.

Jaume whistled, long and low. Then he peered over Doucette's shoulder. Picking a small stone out of the dirt, he dropped it into the depths of the well.

They both heard the *plink* as the stone struck the water.

Doucette pulled herself up on Jaume's arm. Though the magic had come easily, she grunted with the effort required to stand. As quickly as she could she walked to the other pack and whispered to it.

> *Be thou fence,*
> *withy-woven,*
> *four-square,*
> *tight and strong,*
> *until thy spell, by my name, is undone.*

Under her hand, the pack shook, flipped itself once, and then tumbled end over end like a ball of wool, unwinding and stretching as it traveled, until a thin brown line edged the field. With a series of loud popping noises, the line stretched upward. Withy shoots snapped over and under one another as they wove themselves into a waist-high fence.

Doucette turned to Jaume. "You see?" she said. "Easy."

He rubbed his chin. "Aye, but it's your body's strength fuels the magic. You're shaking."

Doucette brushed away his concern. "As I get stronger, it won't tire me so much. This way we'll escape Father's notice. We must, Jaume."

"You'll be able to change us back?"

"I promise," Doucette said.

He kissed her, a too-short pressure of lips. "I'm ready."

"Say my name to undo the spell," Doucette reminded him. "And if you have to speak with Father, disguise your voice or he might recognize it."

Jaume nodded, his eyes serious.

She put one hand on his chest and felt his heart beating under her palm. Gathering her magic, she waited for the rhythm of their pulses to mesh. Exultation filled her, drowning out the sound of approaching hoofbeats. "Be thou a garden boy," she said. The moment she felt the spell taking hold, she put her other hand on her own heart and spoke.

> *As I*
> *am thy garden,*
> *fruit and flower,*

husk and seed,
until both spells, by my name, are undone.

It was the most peculiar Transformation Doucette had yet experienced. As had happened in Lavena's Cauldron, Doucette's body dissolved. But it didn't hurt. And this time, instead of hovering outside herself, aware but formless, she sank into the ground and multiplied.

Each speck of her had become a seed. The seeds hurtled forward through their usual growth, absorbing the spring rain's moisture, summer sun's heat, and an early pinch of frost, all in an eye-blink. Innumerable shoots sprouted, rooted, grew tall, flowered, ripened, dropped fruit, and withered, until all that remained was a garden full of dry, spent plants and flowers gone to seed.

Field mice emerged from their holes, their whiskers twitching, to sniff at the sudden bounty. The wind rattled a bean plant's brittle leaves. Doucette heard the *croa-croa* of curious crows and the drone of a bee attracted to a late-blooming aster.

Distracted by the flow of unusual sensations, she tried to sort out the ones that mattered: the thrumming of hooves on the dirt road and, closer, repeated movements in a row of carrot plants.

Jerk—tap, tap. Jerk—tap, tap.

Doucette realized that was Jaume, uprooting the plants and tapping carrot seeds into his sack.

"You, there!"

Her father's voice sounded strange, filtered through her plant senses, but garden-Doucette managed to make out the words.

"Listen, boy," Lord Pascau said. "Have a young man and woman passed you this morn?"

"Carrot seeds, Sieur," a high voice replied. "Get the carrot seeds in before Ma gives me my dinner, what she said."

"The man wears a shepherd's hat," the comte said. "The girl's hair shines like pearl. Have you seen them?"

Jerk—tap, tap.

"Buy my carrot seeds, Sieur. Don't ask for onion. Ma won't grow them, what she said."

The comte's horse stamped. "Enough about the seeds, boy!" Lord Pascau snarled. "Have you seen the man and woman, or not?"

"Eyes on my work, Sieur, what Ma said." The childish voice sounded sulky. "Fine carrots this year. Won't you buy our seed?"

The comte muttered a curse. "They could be anywhere!"

"Sieur?"

"None of your affair, boy."

The horse squealed. Its hooves danced in place and then hit the ground hard and fast, returning the way they had come.

The gentle tapping sound continued. Grasshoppers rasped. Beetles crawled around garden-Doucette's roots, intent on beetle business. Leaves curled and dropped. A gourd's skin split with a sigh.

"Doucette," Jaume said. "He's gone. Come back, love."

Magic shuddered through the field as Doucette's garden self retreated, shedding roots and leaves and stalks like a snake discards its outgrown skin. The well closed with a grinding noise and the fence melted away, leaving their two packs on the ground.

Doucette sat in scratchy wheat stubble, feeling too confined within her own shape.

"That was well done." Jaume knelt beside Doucette and scooped her into his arms. Lifting her clear of the prickly stalks, he cradled her to his chest. "Breathe, Doucette." He wiped dirt from her face. "Sweetheart. Breathe."

Doucette opened her mouth and sucked in air.

"Again." Jaume's hand moved up and down her back. "Breathe, love."

She coughed and choked until her lungs remembered how to push the air in and out. Magic ebbed through her veins with such force that she held out her hands, convinced they must be glowing with the power that had flowed through them.

Her fingers trembled and dirt smudged her skin. Otherwise, her hands appeared as usual: a chastelaine's hands, capable enough, but giving no hint of the uncanny work they could do. She rested them on her knees and breathed.

"My mistake," she said, when she could speak again. She raised a frightened face to Jaume. "I wasn't thinking. What if Father had said my name? The spell would have come undone before his eyes."

"But he didn't," Jaume said.

"I was clumsy. Careless."

"Shh. You saved us, but we have to move on," Jaume said. "Hard to hide in the lowlands. We'll find better cover in the orchards and woodland ahead."

"He'll keep after us." Doucette knew it with a chill certainty. "Mother will insist."

Jaume squeezed her hand. "Once we cross the river into Donsatrelle, we're out of their power. Can you stand?"

"I don't know." Doucette lurched upright; her legs wobbled and she sat as quickly. "No."

"Best eat, then," Jaume said. "Build your strength."

"I'm sorry," she said.

Jaume shook his head. "Sorry? If I had my way, you'd sleep for a week after such a piece of sorcery." He opened his pack. "Instead, we have smoked beef, fruit, and Na Patris's oat bread before we must be off again."

Doucette's mouth was too dry to swallow, so Jaume dribbled water down her throat. He fed her, too, in little bites, as if she were a baby bird in the nest.

"It's odd," she said. "I feel like—like a cask of fermenting apple cider. Fizzy inside, if you could see through the barrel." She laughed, breathless. "All magic and hardly the strength to use it."

"Think you can walk?"

"I'll try." With Jaume's help, Doucette stood and took a tentative step. Her legs didn't crumple, so she took another.

"That's the spirit." Jaume shouldered their packs and tucked her arm in his.

Doucette clasped him tightly. "Lead on," she said.

All that day, they walked and rested, ate, walked, and rested. Though she and Jaume met few people going in either direction, Doucette couldn't ignore the itch that had settled between her shoulder blades, as if an archer's target had been painted there.

Hurry! the feeling said, but her feeble legs kept them to a slow pace.

The sun was well along its downward journey when the road climbed out of the lowlands and into hills dressed with vineyards and orchards of apple, apricot, and pear trees.

Jaume caught Doucette when she fell. Her arms around his neck, Doucette watched over his shoulder for signs of pursuit.

She didn't mean to fall asleep.

Chapter Twenty-five

She woke to a confusion of movement and sound. Jaume was hoisting her over a stone wall, into a pear orchard. From down the road sounded the clatter of horses about to overtake them.

"Jaume!" Doucette whispered. "Who is it?"

"Don't know," he said. "We'll hide, in case."

Doucette didn't wait. As her feet found the ground, she reached for her magic. Squeezing Jaume's shoulder, she spread her hands over his sleeves and the two leather pack straps.

> *Be thou pear tree*
> *and pear fruit,*
> *alone unharvested,*
> *until I release thee*
> *from these unaccustomed shapes.*

The two packs twined together and pushed upward. Jaume shouted as he was carried into the air.

"Don't worry!" Doucette called. Her betrothed disappeared into a tangle of bare branches. Good! The spell had performed exactly as she intended. At the top of the tree, dangling from a twig, hung a single unblemished fruit.

Doucette closed her eyes and hugged her elbows to her sides, relishing the power that slid under her skin. This was what she had been born to do. She spoke deliberately.

I'll be filthy,
diseased,
as ragged a crone
as ever breathed.

Her limbs twitched; her spine curved at an awkward angle. Pearly hair darkened and fell out in clumps, while smooth skin erupted in angry boils. When Doucette opened her eyes again, the world had changed to an indistinct place. She blinked, but her vision didn't clear, showing patches of dark and light for the rows of trees that divided the sky. Above her head the single pear glinted, a spark of gold against brown and gray.

Doucette took a step forward. Her hip twisted, and she fell, landing on her knees. Huffing painful breaths, Doucette scrabbled through the crackling leaf litter to find a dead branch. Next time she disguised herself as a crippled old woman, she'd remember to imagine a cane. And warmer underclothes. The wind's chilly fingers poked her, finding every hole in her threadbare tunic and rag of a skirt.

The group of riders swept up the hill and would have passed her in a twinkling if one of them hadn't pulled up her horse.

"Halloo!" Cecilia's voice called out.

Crone-Doucette's cloudy eyes couldn't distinguish the riders accompanying her sister. She could identify them, however, by the jingle of chain mail, the familiar rattle and clank of mounted armsmen. Still, Cecilia presented the greatest danger, though she carried no weapon but her keen blue eyes. And her wand.

Doucette pushed herself to her feet with the stick. She poked it gingerly at the tree.

"You, there! Have you seen a young couple on the road?" Cecilia said over the sound of horses blowing and stamping. "A reward's waiting for your help."

Doucette's neck was canted stiffly. She braced herself on her stick and shuffled her feet sideways until she could look over her shoulder at the riders.

"What a loathsome creature!" Azelais's disgusted voice cut across Cecilia's gurgle of surprise.

Doucette blinked and felt the scabs crack on her skin. "Eh?" she said in a gruff voice. "Who's there?"

"She can't help us, Cecilia," Azelais said. "The hag's blind, so you can stop waving your purse at her. Come—we'll ask in the town ahead."

Reins slapped a horse's neck. Several sets of hooves pounded up the road.

"I was sure I smelled magic," Cecilia said.

"Smelled it, my lady?" a man's voice asked respectfully.

Doucette realized that at least one of the armsmen had stayed with Cecilia.

"Or tasted. . . ." Cecilia said.

Muttering under her breath, Doucette swung back to take another stab at the tree. She felt her sister's stare boring into her deformed shoulders.

"We seek a young woman," Cecilia said loudly. "Her family will pay for news of her."

Doucette spat on the ground and shook her stick at the tree. "A rotten pear don't fall till winter."

Cecilia made a sudden movement; her horse danced backward.

"Wait, Lady Cecilia, your sister forbid—"

Doucette didn't understand the man's protest until she heard the jingle of coin. A purse flew through the air and landed with a thump at her feet.

Doucette twisted her body toward her sister.

"Azelais is hard-hearted enough for the two of us," Cecilia said to the armsman, her voice pitched to reach Doucette's ears. "This poor soul may as well have the reward as anyone. We're not going to find them, Renod."

"But Lady Sarpine vowed—"

Cecilia's tinkling laugh hung in the air. "Mother can't enforce her will outside Beloc county. If my sister is wise, she'll make haste to cross the Turance into Donsatrelle."

Doucette bent her knees and reached awkwardly for the purse. Velvet, her fingers told her, and heavy. She clutched it to her dirty tunic. "For me, Lady?"

"May it bring you good fortune," Cecilia said. Without waiting for thanks, she challenged the armsman. "Race you, Renod. Best we catch up to Azelais and the others."

"Yes, Lady Cecilia."

The man didn't sound happy about leaving the purse, but Cecilia didn't give him a choice. "Go, *chère*." She chirped to her mare and rode off, the armsman close behind her.

When the vibration of their horses' hooves had faded into the distance, Doucette returned herself, Jaume, and the packs to their own shapes.

As the tingling rush of magic subsided, she stretched her neck, turning it from side to side like an owl. "Oof, that's better," she said, before her legs folded and she had to sit down. She poked at the velvet bag in her lap. "Did you see them, Jaume? Azelais and Cecilia and the rest?"

"No," Jaume said curtly. "Pears don't have eyes."

Doucette giggled, then wheezed, catching her breath. "My eyes didn't work very well either. I could hear them, though. Cecilia may have suspected. She threw me this bag, and—what is it, Jaume? What's wrong?"

Jaume shook his head. "You have to ask?"

Doucette bristled at the note in his voice. "About what?"

"You just—*changed* me!"

"So? You didn't mind before."

"You consulted me the first time. I agreed to it."

"They almost caught us!" Doucette said, stung. "I had to act."

"If that were all, I wouldn't mind. But this magic you work. It's like a fever, burning you up." Heavily, he dropped to sit beside her. "It frightens me."

"But, Jaume, I'm getting stronger as we go. Didn't I walk quite far today before you had to carry me?"

"My heart." He cupped her cheek in one callused hand. "There's no point escaping from your family only to die of exhaustion on the road." His hand dropped, made a fist on his knee. "I won't be changed into a stupid pear with magic that wears you into a shadow!"

Doucette's lower lip quivered. "I protected us."

"And I'm grateful," Jaume said. "Truly. But won't you ask before you start enchanting things? Rather find a way that doesn't eat you from inside."

Reluctantly, Doucette nodded. Why didn't he understand? She was a sorceress. Things could be so much easier if he let her cast a spell or two. Why, the night they left, she could have turned them both into birds. They could have crossed the Turance already! But something in Jaume's expression kept her from pointing out the obvious.

Again.

"I'm hungry," she said instead.

"Aye," Jaume agreed.

They leaned against the orchard wall and finished the oat bread. Silence stretched out between them while twilight darkened the sky. "It was kind of your sister to give you the purse," Jaume said at last.

"How kind? I wonder." Doucette untied the knot that was holding the bag closed. She poured the contents into her lap. "Ooh, very generous! Some silvers and coppers, but mostly gold."

"*Aigleron* gold?"

"What do you mean?"

"Will it still be gold if you melt it?" Jaume asked mildly. "Or only twigs and leaves?"

"Cecilia wouldn't cheat me."

"I hope not," Jaume said.

Doucette didn't feel strong enough to argue with him, especially if he was right. Were her proud sisters counterfeiters in their father's service? Had the luxuries she grew up enjoying at the Château de l'Aire been bought with lies?

Jaume stirred the money with a finger and came up with a wrinkled nutshell. He held it out to Doucette. "And a walnut?"

Doucette pried the nutshell open. A pair of earrings had been wrapped in a scrap of cloth and hidden inside the walnut. "My pearls! Cecilia knew it was me."

"So why the tears?"

Doucette wiped her eyes, laughing and crying at the same time. The exultation of magic-working was fading, leaving her empty as a husk. "They don't all hate me."

"Sweetheart!" Jaume held her close and kissed her. "No one hates you. They hate me, if anyone, for stealing you away."

Doucette put the money and nutshell back in the bag and tucked it into her pack. "Whoever I married would have taken me from home."

"You don't think Lady Sarpine and Lord Pascau would have picked a shepherd?" Jaume waggled his eyebrows in mock surprise. "Afraid I'd drag you off to my hut and feed you millet porridge for every meal?"

Doucette flushed at how close Jaume had come to her father's prediction. "Father named the tests," she said. "He could have chosen different ones."

"Proof of a noble lineage, grant to a castle, and a treasury full of gold and jewels?"

"If that's what he wanted," Doucette replied.

"He meant to mock me," Jaume said. "It was only through your grace that the tasks were accomplished."

"And then Father cheated by adding the extra one at the end, telling you to choose me from my sisters." Doucette brushed the crumbs from her lap. "It's not your fault my mother's too angry to let us go. She already punished my disobedience once, by burning my wand and swan skin. If she catches us, I'm afraid she'll have you killed."

"Your family won't find us. They've tried and failed twice, already."

Doucette stood up. "How far are we from Donsatrelle county?"

"A few days." Jaume shouldered the packs and glanced around. "We can go a little farther. I'd be away from this place before we seek out shelter." He lifted her over the orchard wall and Doucette took his arm.

"What of your family, Jaume? What do your parents think about you asking for my hand?"

Jaume watched the road. "They don't know," he said.

"What?"

"Doucette—it sounded so foolish. What was I to tell them? 'Farewell, all. I'm off to Beloc, see if Lady Doucette will have me, now she's a swan maiden.'" Jaume winced. "If you'd refused, do you think my brothers would have let me forget it?"

"You mean you left home without any explanation?"

"Fall is the quiet season in Vent'roux. We've sold all but the beasts we can afford to overwinter, the breeding ewes, and a ram or two, the old ones who lead the rest. Once the flocks are snug in winter quarters, my brothers and I take turns hiring out to help farmers with the harvest. We pick apples, walnuts, field crops."

"So your parents think you're earning some extra coin, and instead you'll ask them to host your wedding?"

"Oh, aye."

"To an evil sorceress, a disinherited noblewoman who doesn't know the first thing about tending sheep?"

Jaume stopped in surprise.

Doucette, too, was shocked to hear her father's vicious words spill from her own mouth. They burned her tongue as she spit them out, and she averted her eyes in shame.

"Doucette. Love." Jaume tugged teasingly on a loose strand of her hair. "Have I asked you to do anything you wouldn't or couldn't manage?"

"No."

"Why would I start, once we were married?"

"Husbands do," Doucette said. "Tante Mahalt warned us."

Jaume snorted. "Do noblemen and sorceresses live in such different worlds? Where I'm from, folk try to treat each other decently, married or no."

"Your family won't mind me being a sorceress?" Doucette persisted.

Jaume scratched his neck. "They'll get used to it."

"Like you are?" she said, acidly.

"I'm trying," Jaume said. "Harder than I thought, seeing how it wastes you."

"It doesn't," Doucette began, but she could see he wasn't convinced. "Never mind."

From nowhere, her aunt's voice echoed in Doucette's mind.

"Beware of men," Tante Mahalt had said. "Their promises are not to be trusted."

Chapter Twenty-six

After several days of travel, they had left behind the lowland fields and hill villages near the Château de l'Aire. The road narrowed as it wound toward the river Turance, which divided Beloc from Donsatrelle. This was a wilder and less settled country, with stands of pine, cedar, and juniper bushes dotting a rocky plateau.

Jaume helped Doucette step over a fallen tree. Intent on her recitation, she hardly noticed the obstacle. "Your house in Vent'roux has a blue door and stands on rue Droite, three fountains from the market square, where your mother, Na Eleno, sells wool from a stand. Your father is called Om Bernat, and your family owns one of the county's larger flocks. All your brothers live at home."

"Oh, aye. You've met them," Jaume said. "Two years apart, like stair steps. Tinou after me—he's eighteen—then Vitor and Eri."

"Yes." Doucette tugged on her pack straps, proud that she had regained strength enough to carry it herself. "Eri's only interested in music, but Vitor's sweetheart is Suriette, the blacksmith's daughter, and Tinou's sweetheart is Mireyo, the miller's daughter."

A shadow crossed Jaume's face.

"Did I mix them up again?" Doucette asked. She had spent much of the past few days peppering Jaume with questions about his home and family. She wanted to know, and it kept the two of them from arguing about magic.

"Well," he said, after a long pause. "Tinou loves Mireyo, sure enough, but Widow Jonselet doesn't favor her only child marrying a second son." He shifted under his pack and eyed the sky. "Our families' grazing lands adjoin, see. Our parents have talked about bringing them together."

The reserve in his manner alerted her. "You're the oldest; you'll inherit the property," Doucette said, working it out. "The mother wants Mireyo to marry you, doesn't she?"

"Aye. But I never agreed," Jaume said quickly. "Since we were children, Mireyo and Tinou have only had eyes for each other."

The anticipation Doucette had been cultivating soured a little. If Jaume's parents were anything like her own, they wouldn't welcome a stranger meddling in the future they had planned for him.

"They'll love you like I do," Jaume said, as if he could read her thoughts.

Doucette wished her answering smile held more confidence, but she had lost the urge to ask Jaume any more questions about his family. She concentrated instead on keeping up with his easy stride, and they walked on without speaking.

Though they had passed few dwellings, the countryside was hardly empty. Rabbits startled from cover, and birds twittered in the bushes. Doucette listened to the distant cries of hawks wheeling overhead, the closer buzzing of bees that foraged among blue stars of late-blooming gentian. As autumn advanced, each dawn seemed colder and wetter than the one before. But every morning, Doucette warmed up with walking, and at night she slept soundly in the circle of Jaume's arms. During two days of heavy rain, they had taken shelter in a cave and waited for the weather to improve.

The weakness that plagued Doucette after she cast a spell still troubled Jaume greatly. Over and over, Doucette had assured him that it soon left her. Finally, out of respect for her betrothed's sensibilities, Doucette had taken to practicing sorcery in the early evening, when Jaume left their camp to gather firewood. The resulting fatigue was nothing more than he seemed to expect of her after their long days of walking.

Even had she wanted to, Doucette couldn't have kept from using the magic that pulsed inside her, demanding to be expressed. As Tante Mahalt had said, it was delicious. Even small Transformations delighted her. Mostly, Doucette contented herself with turning rocks to twigs, and weeds to pinecones— nothing that didn't belong in their humble campsites.

Within days, Doucette could summon the magic to her fingertips and loose it with a breath. She disliked deceiving Jaume by casting spells in secret, but she knew she must hold herself ready in case they were surprised.

Her family's pursuit had not been dropped.

She hadn't seen them since Cecilia and Azelais's party met the "old woman" by the pear tree, but the invisible thread that bound Doucette to her home wasn't slackening with distance as she had expected. She tried to cast her thoughts forward, toward her new family and her new life. Yet at times, a noose of worry looped so tightly around her throat that she strained to breathe.

"There!" Jaume stopped and pointed. "The bell tower ahead? That's Saint-Trophime. From the abbey garden you can see the bridge into Donsatrelle. We could cross the Turance tonight."

Doucette nodded and saved her breath for climbing, as the road had taken a steep upward slant. Ahead, tall stone walls loomed over the road.

Apprehension wound its coils around her. By the time they reached the shelter of the abbey walls, she was gasping. Jaume looked at her with concern.

"Thirsty," she said.

Jaume lifted the pack off Doucette's shoulders and sat her down on a stone bench while he went to fill their water skins at the abbey well. He returned with a brown-robed woman, who offered Doucette a hot infusion flavored with herbs and honey.

"Drink, child."

"Thank you, Sister." Doucette sipped it slowly. "Juniper honey?" she asked, and was rewarded with a grave smile. The tea slipped down her throat and warmed her stomach, but she couldn't sit still. Unease prickled her skin, as if eyes watched her from the undergrowth.

"Can you go on?" Jaume asked. "We're a few hours, no more, from the crossing place."

Doucette swallowed. "Where's the bridge?"

"It's visible from the bell tower." The woman pointed to a narrow door in the wall.

Jaume and Doucette left their packs by the bench and climbed the stairs. They eased around the large iron bell and peered through the slits in the wall.

The sun hung like a pale gold fruit in the western sky. Below the tower, a tree-covered hillside dropped steeply to the water. Doucette searched for a break in the cliffs that contained the river.

By his indrawn breath, Doucette knew that Jaume saw what she did. The river, a narrow thread. Beyond tall, jagged rocks, the stone arches of the bridge. And before them, a white square, harmless at this distance.

Doucette squinted to make out more detail. It was a travel pavilion, flying the blue and gold flag of Beloc.

"Mother." Doucette knew it with a dread that snapped the noose tight again. She rubbed her throat. "She must have circled around us. She's at the bridge, waiting."

Jaume put his arm around Doucette's waist. "Then we'll out-wait her," he said. "Or cross farther up."

"You don't understand," Doucette said into his chest. "She won't give up. If we delay, the others may join her. The longer we stay on this side of the river, the worse our chances of escaping. We have to cross, soon. And we can't go undisguised."

Jaume rubbed the base of her spine, smoothing the tight muscles. "You want to Transform us again."

"Yes. I know you don't like it." Doucette tipped her head against Jaume's shoulder. In the pit of her stomach, tendrils of fear seethed like a mass of serpents, but excitement pushed them back. He'd learn what her power could do. They all would.

"We must change," Doucette insisted. "No pears, I promise."

Jaume kissed her, and Doucette felt herself melting into a soft lump of girl. Or widow, she warned herself, if she let him distract her. Reluctantly, she ended the kiss. "Trust me," she whispered.

"Oh, aye." His answering smile went crooked. "I'll be a pear again if it gets us over the river. But let's walk a little farther. No need to offend the good sisters with sorcery on the abbey grounds."

Silently, they collected their packs and bowed their heads for a blessing. The woman laid soft hands on their shoulders and bent her head. "Walk safe in the light to your journey's end."

Doucette heard both benediction and warning in the words.

Once the road curved and the trees hid them from sight, Doucette turned eagerly to Jaume. "Shall we?"

"I trust you," Jaume said, as if he needed to remind himself. He set down his pack and stood motionless.

Doucette dropped her pack beside his and twined the straps together. "Combine to make a bee skep," she commanded, before resting her hands against Jaume's chest.

> *And, thou, be old man,*
> *sturdy-legged,*
> *blue-eyed,*
> *gray-haired,*
> *gap-toothed.*
> *Wear thy years lightly,*

until the Turance is crossed
and a place of safety gained.

As the magic flowed over him, Jaume's body changed, becoming thicker and more compact. Wrinkles carved deep lines in his face. His brown curls turned light and wispy; his dark eyes faded to a pale blue. Most of his teeth disappeared, leaving a gummy grin on his old-man face.

The packs at his feet melded into a tall, domed basket with a wooden base. A leather strap looped across the sides of it. Jaume studied his wrinkled hands, then lifted the basket. "Empty," he said. "What's—oh. It's a beehive."

"Yes." Doucette closed her eyes, crossed her arms across her chest, and surrendered to enchantment.

Bees.
I will be
bees,
until my love, Jaume,
summons me.

The magic washed through her, and she exploded into a swarm of tiny flying bodies. Like drops from a windblown fountain, bees danced in the air.

As in the garden Transformation, Doucette's attention splintered. Through faceted bee eyes, she saw a hundred old-man Jaumes, the concern in his eyes multiplied with every glance. She might have stopped to reassure him, but caught between the delirium of flight and the power that flooded her many selves, she forgot.

Jaume held out the basket. The queen bee flew inside the hive. The rest followed her, a cone of purposefully moving bodies that funneled through the small opening.

Jaume stood calmly as the bees buzzed around him. When they were all inside the hive, he lifted the humming basket against his back. He put the strap over his forehead and settled his burden, then walked down to the river on sturdy, if bowed, legs. A handful of Doucette's bee selves crept through the opening and happily circled his head, then landed on his sleeves and clung there, elegant as gold-and-black buttons, to stand sentinel for the rest.

Wreathed in thin gray clouds, the sun made a crimson disk on the horizon when Jaume reached the approach to the bridge.

"You, old man." An armsman blocked his way. "Halt."

Several bees detached themselves to investigate the nearby campsite. Men dressed in chain mail and leather sat by a cook fire, warming their hands and eyeing the progress of their meal. Om Toumas laid a string of trout on the fire. When a bee alit and danced on his nose, he scolded gently. "You're out late, little sister. Best get along home."

Behind the fire, the white pavilion's canvas sides were closed. The smell of horses not far away and grilled fish, closer, drifted into the chilly air.

"We seek a shepherd without a flock," the armsman said to Jaume. "And a young woman with light hair. Have you seen such a couple?"

"Me, Sieur?" Jaume's toothless gums slurred the words.

The tent flap lifted and Lady Sarpine emerged. The comtesse's cloak and riding skirts were creased, her white coif smudged. In her hard, pale face, her blue eyes burned as fiercely as the fire. "Who is it, Renod, travels at the cusp of dark?"

"An oldster. Harmless." The armsman's voice sharpened. "But the lady asked you a question, man. What rogue's business brings you here at this hour?"

Jaume turned so the man could see the straw hive on his back. "Can't travel before the bees are abed."

"Shall he pass, Lady?" Renod asked.

"Bees!" Lady Sarpine drew her cloak close to her and retreated partway into her tent. "Send him along."

Jaume touched his fist to his breast. "Aye, Lady," he quavered. "Be kind to the bees that you find on your way."

The armsman waved him on. A commotion at the fire had attracted his attention. "What's amiss there?"

Jaume walked toward the bridge.

"Om Toumas dropped the biggest trout in the fire!" an aggrieved voice was saying. "Clumsy fool!"

"Your pardon." The servant turned his face from the firelight.

"What about my dinner? It's cinders!"

The servant wiped his hands on his leather apron. "I'll cook you another," he said, fumbling as he turned the fish. The whole string fell into the coals, raising a shower of sparks. Men sprang back, swearing.

"Hellfire." One armsman's irritation turned to disgust. "What's the matter with you, Toumas?"

Lady Sarpine paused with her hand on the tent flap. She stared at Om Toumas, then hissed under her breath. "The cousin." Long skirts flapping, Doucette's mother ran after the old man. "Wait, you!" she shouted. "Renod! Fools! To me!"

The armsmen ran after the comtesse.

The old man kept walking. Five steps to the bridge. Four. Three.

Lady Sarpine reached Jaume first and spun him around by the elbow. "Steal my daughter, would you, knave? Your wretched life is forfeit," she panted. "She'll be longer a widow than a wife."

A bee lifted from the old man's sleeve and hummed in warning. Jaume was hers. How dare her mother threaten him?

Jaume turned, his toothless mouth turned down in a sorrowful expression. "Doucette's her own woman, not your property to dispose, Lady," he said. "That was ever your mistake."

"Insolence!" As the comtesse's free hand clawed for his face, bees boiled out of the hive and swarmed around her head. She screamed but kept her grip on Jaume's arm.

Insects landed on her eyelids and loosed their stings.

"Help!" Lady Sarpine swatted at her face. "I can't see!"

Doucette wondered whether Jaume could feel the magic crackling in the air around him. As some of her bee selves stung and died, the rest flew more swiftly, thrummed more loudly, attacked more viciously. She felt like a cloud of sparks, or a host of tiny, vengeful lightning bolts. The sensation frightened and exhilarated, both at once.

Jaume had spoken the truth. Doucette's mother could no longer order her daughter to do her bidding. No one commanded a sorceress.

When her mother fell back, tears of pain and rage squeezing out from under her swollen eyelids, Doucette attacked the armsmen.

They tried to protect their faces and catch hold of the old beekeeper at the same time, but the bees crawled inside their helmets and stung the exposed skin around eyes and noses. The men had to retreat, shouting and cursing, as their faces swelled grotesquely.

Haloed in bees, Jaume set foot on the bridge. Once he had crossed to the Donsatrelle side, he whispered Doucette's name.

This time, Doucette's dizziness passed quickly. She seized her pack and was on her feet and waving to Om Toumas while Jaume still sat on the ground collecting his wits.

"That will teach them to interfere with a sorceress," Doucette said. Relief and glee bubbled up in equal measure, spilling out of her mouth in giddy laughter. "Did you see their faces? We're safe, Jaume!" She spun in a tight circle. "I can't imagine why I was so worried. If they come after us again, they'll not get off so easy!"

"No?" Jaume said in a low voice. "The armsmen looked bad, and your mother—"

"They deserved it for trying to stop us," Doucette said. Her chastelaine's training surfaced, and she continued in a more reasonable tone. "If Om Toumas packs mud around their stings, the swelling will go down overnight. What do you care?" She tugged Jaume to his feet, tossed him his pack. "Let's go."

He caught it, barely.

She grinned at his expression. "That spell didn't leave me a bit tired, you know. I could walk all night! We could fly!"

He opened his mouth, closed it, and slung the pack over his shoulder. "Rather walk."

Doucette charged forward. Why had it taken her so long to claim her freedom? Only a few steps separated Beloc from Donsatrelle, after all.

"Are you sure?" With a wave of her hand, Doucette Transformed herself into a bat and swooped playfully over Jaume. She tugged on his hair, then, swift and silent, landed behind him and reclaimed her girl shape.

He made such a comical sight, standing with his elbows over his head and staring wildly around, that Doucette laughed out loud. "Let's fly to your home, Jaume. We'd get there in no time," she coaxed.

"Doucette. It's not like you to tease me."

"Oh, very well." As she marched down the road, her lips turned down in a Cecilia-like pout. What had happened to his sense of adventure? She loved night flying!

When the river fell away into darkness, Jaume insisted they stop and rest. He dropped his pack in a sheltered spot, under a pine tree. "I am tired, even if you are not," he said when Doucette complained.

They made camp in silence.

Jaume slept beside her, while Doucette lay awake for a long while, staring at the stars and thinking.

When she arose in the morning, she had reached a decision.

Chapter Twenty-seven

———— ❦ ————

After she and Jaume had broken their fast, Doucette sat on a rock and teased pine needles out of her hair. If she turned her head, she could just see Vent'roux town in the distance, tucked under a giant crag. "You should go first and tell them," she said.

Jaume spooned millet gruel from the little pot. "Why?"

Doucette jerked on the comb. "My hair's sticky, and my clothes are filthy. I want to wash."

"We've a big tub at home. Flower soap, all that."

"It would be more polite to give your family some warning."

Jaume licked the spoon. "Why the delay, when we're so close? It's silly."

"Silly or not, you can't make me go." Doucette's voice faltered. Couldn't the man understand that a person might want to be clean on such an occasion?

Abandoning the millet, Jaume squatted next to her. He tugged a lock of her hair and wound it around his finger. "You look beautiful, as always. What's the matter, love?"

"I don't know," Doucette lied. "Go on and tell them. When you return, I'll be ready." One way or another. What had seemed so clear under the distant stars was less so in the morning light.

Especially when Jaume studied her like she was a present he couldn't wait to unwrap.

He released her hair and watched it coil against her cheek. "If that's what you want. I hate to leave you alone."

"I'll be fine." Now that Doucette had persuaded him to leave, she found herself reluctant to say good-bye. This journey had proved such a magical interlude between the hostility of her family and the unknown quantity of his. Just the two of them walking hand in hand through wild country, speaking or silent, content together. To ease his worried look, Doucette wagged her finger. "And don't go kissing all the pretty girls of Vent'roux town, or you'll forget about me."

"Never."

As she had intended, he reached for her. Doucette dropped feather-light kisses on Jaume's nose, his eyebrows, his chin, then met his seeking lips with her own.

"No town girls for me." His arms tightened around her. "You're the only one I'm kissing."

"Promise?" She said it teasingly, then buried her face in his shoulder, afraid he would see the tears that had sprung to her eyes. Silly to be crying *before* she had lost him.

Whether it came from the new closeness between them or the kindness he had always shown her, Jaume seemed to understand that she needed a serious answer. He took her hand and put it over his heart. "I swear it."

Doucette made herself wave cheerfully as Jaume left the hollow where they had spent the night. But her pretense faded as she tended the fire and boiled water in the little pot, then stripped and bathed. After heating more water, she washed her hair and her clothes, then fanned them dry by the fire. She completed each action from force of habit, her head too full of conflicting thoughts to pay much attention to the work of her hands.

Once clean and dressed, Doucette tidied up: dousing the fire, putting the empty pot into her pack, braiding her hair. A bird drilled its beak against a cedar branch. The rapid tapping sounded like a summons.

Which call would she heed? Marriage or freedom? Jaume or magic? The choice might tear her in two, but it had to be made.

Doucette retied the leather strap that closed her pack and reminded her aching heart of the reasons she must go on alone. She loved Jaume. Sending him away was one of the most difficult things she had ever done. Even now, she felt the increasing distance between them like a physical wound, draining her strength.

Her sorceress self stirred. Wasn't that very pain a sign she had made the right decision? If love required she give up her magic, what would remain? An exiled chastelaine, a powerless girl with dove-colored hair and no fear of bees.

The girl Jaume loved, her heart mourned. *The girl who loved him in return.*

Of course she did, the sorceress responded impatiently. Jaume had helped her complete the Rassemblement and escape her family's control, and for that she would always be grateful. But she was just coming into her powers, and she refused to be ashamed of them. Would she let passion blind her to the fact that throughout their journey, Jaume had fussed over her casting the tiniest spell?

Oh, he had said what she wanted to hear, promised he wouldn't be afraid. But his resistance the previous afternoon, when it was clear that only her magic would get them past her mother's guards . . . it showed how little he understood.

He was afraid for you, Doucette's heart told her.

Afraid *of* you, her head replied. Afraid of magic—he had admitted it! What if she hadn't been secretly practicing? What if she hadn't known how to wield her new powers and win their freedom? He would have been killed, and she dragged home like a runaway heifer, bawling and struggling to no purpose. Instead of a powerful sorceress, Jaume was treating Doucette like one of his flock, to be herded here and there, and then safely penned. He meant to be kind, but a shepherd didn't appreciate sorcery's demands. He couldn't comprehend that the magic running through her had to be expressed.

You don't know that, her heart countered. *Why don't you trust him?*

Trust. Who could she trust, if not herself? All her life, other people had decided what was best for her. Unless she seized this chance to explore her gift, she would never know what she might have accomplished.

"Enough!" Doucette said aloud. She clapped her hands to her buzzing head, as if that would still the arguing voices within.

At least she wasn't married, her mind contributed, slyly. Betrothals had been broken for less cause. And in this case, a clean break was best. No ugly confrontation, no recriminations. If she could, she would take the pain upon herself rather than hurt Jaume for an instant. But as Cecilia had once warned her, a sorceress did what she must to keep her freedom. As much as she loved Jaume—*because* she loved him—Doucette shouldn't bind him to a woman who didn't really know who she was.

The time had come to find out.

Magic thrummed through her, its siren call muting the grief that hollowed her chest. Relieved of the burden of decision, Doucette focused her mind on the complicated spell. She rested her hand on the pack.

> *Be thou a golden chain,*
> *slight as fairy silk,*
> *strong as dwarven steel,*
> *thy links endowed with further charm,*
> *thus:*
> *while clasped around my neck,*
> *lend me crow form:*
> *black-winged,*
> *hoarse-voiced,*
> *impertinent.*

With a shiver of anticipation, she fastened the necklace around her neck.

The Transformation into bird shape felt smoothly, perfectly familiar. Magic surged over her skin and left glossy feathers in its wake. Her legs shrank, her arms lengthened, and she reached for the heavens with a crow's black wings.

Croa! She opened her beak and croaked a laugh, then soared away from the campsite and over the treetops. With every wing beat, she thrilled to the freedom of the sky. Enchantment sang through her body, from strong claws to ebony feather tips, and pushed aside all doubt.

She had made the right choice.

Flying east, she studied the landscape below her. The rough gorge that contained the Turance gave way to a flatter, flinty pastureland dotted with sheep. Dry-stone walls and huts marked one holding from another. Jaume had said his people lived in town and that during the winter and early spring the brothers would take turns staying in the huts to protect the flocks from wolves and bears. In the spring, the shepherds and their dogs drove the sheep west through Beloc for the shearing, then on to the mountain pastures.

At a place where several roads met, a steady stream of ox-drawn carts and riders converged on Vent'roux. Market day?

From the shadow of a giant granite crag, the town beckoned. Curiosity sent Doucette flying closer.

Vent'roux's winding streets were lined with rows of stone houses capped with red tile roofs. Behind each house, gardens contained rows of vegetables or well-tended fruit trees. Fountains graced many of the town's small squares, which would be shaded in summer by large plane trees. Bare, spiky branches now admitted the autumn sunlight, which warmed the stone facades of the surrounding houses and brightened the colorful skirts and kerchiefs of girls fetching water.

A sturdy wall circled the town on three sides; the granite crag protected the fourth. Once past the town's main gate, Doucette swooped lower. Following the flow of people, she found a tree-lined market square next to an imposing guild hall. Behind tables heaped with harvest bounty, vendors cried their wares.

"Sound and round, cabbages! Fresh cabbages!"

"HO-la-la! White turnips and fine carrots!"

Crow-Doucette perched on the knobby limb of a plane tree and searched the busy square for a tall man in a shepherd's hat.

"Knives to grind, bring your knives to grind."

"Millet here, buy your millet."

"Wool for your spindles, good wives. Clean spinning wool!"

An eddy in the bustling crowd, then the sound of voices raised in shouts of welcome caught her attention. She flapped toward the disturbance and landed on the back of a cart piled with tanned leather.

Doucette recognized the stocky young man slapping Jaume's back. His brother Tinou.

"We expected you weeks ago! Where have you been?"

"Beloc." Jaume pushed his hat back on his head and surveyed the market with visible pleasure. Other people clustered around him, blocking the aisles between the tables.

"You went to Beloc?" A bronze-skinned young woman with sparkling black eyes elbowed her way through the crowd. "What did you want with those sorcerous folk?"

"Too bad he didn't get turned into a frog," Tinou said. "Improve his looks, wouldn't it?"

The girl wrinkled her nose. "He's fine as he is." She held up her cheek to Jaume. "Give us a kiss, then, and welcome!"

Ready to peck, Crow-Doucette croaked and sidled along the cart-bed.

Jaume patted the woman's cheek. "The summer hasn't changed you, Mireyo," he said. "I'm hardly home, and you're getting me in trouble with Tinou already?"

Mireyo flashed a warning glance at Jaume's brother. "Some people need a little encouragement."

Tinou sounded harassed. "I've told you and told you—"

Jaume interrupted his brother. "Mother's at the stand?"

"Oh, aye," Tinou said. "Father and Vitor are meeting a farmer about a grain purchase. Eri said he'd help her, though you know what that promise is worth."

"It'll hold until the first minstrel comes along with a song to share." Jaume chuckled and settled his hat on his head. "Come with me, you two. I've news." He strode forward, returning the greetings called out from all sides.

Crow-Doucette couldn't help herself. She flew in his wake, her reluctant body pulled along by a heart desperate to be near her beloved.

The townsfolk seemed glad of Jaume's return. The friendly shouts and good-natured teasing made quite a contrast with the scornful welcome her family had extended. Despite her resolution to leave him, Doucette was touched by the effort Jaume made to keep his promise. Without causing offense, he managed to ease away before kissing any of the women—and there were many, she observed—who came up to him with an inviting smile.

"Cousin Jaume! Cousin Jaume!" A tiny girl broke loose from her mother's grip and hurled herself at Jaume, lips puckered for a smacking kiss.

"Beatris!" Jaume caught the girl by the arms and swung her in a wide circle.

She shrieked with laughter. He put her down and pretended to stagger, then wiped his brow with exaggerated relief. "What a great girl you are! How's the orphaned lamb coming along?"

"She's this big!" The girl spread her arms wide. "She can skip! Won't you come see?"

"Soon, Beatris." Jaume touched the tip of the girl's nose with his finger. "I'm glad you're taking good care of her. I knew you would." He turned the little girl toward her mother, who flourished a bouquet of leeks and parsley at him.

Inside her coat of black feathers, Doucette squirmed. She hadn't meant Jaume couldn't kiss a small child who obviously adored him! Had she? Was she so petty?

"Jaume! Son!" An angular woman dropped the skeins of white, gray, and brown wool she was arranging on a table.

Jaume held out his arms. His mother rushed into them, then coughed in surprise to be neatly set aside before she could kiss his face. He squeezed her waist. "I have good news."

"About time you came home," Na Eleno said. "Om Sergi's finally ready to part with that western field. With what you've brought . . ." Her voice trailed off as Jaume shook his head.

"We'll have to lease the field for another year," he said. "I wasn't working. I went to Beloc and came back with a bride."

"A bride?" His mother looked over Jaume's shoulder, at a well-dressed older woman who had come up behind pretty Mireyo. "From Beloc? What's wrong with Donsatrelle girls?"

"Nothing's wrong with them," Jaume said.

"What possessed you?" Tinou punched his brother's shoulder. "Fall under a sorceress's spell?"

"Doucette's a swan maiden, aye, but also the bravest, dearest, most beautiful—"

"Lady Doucette?" Tinou sounded shocked. "That sweet girl, a sorceress? You're thinking of her sisters, surely?"

Na Eleno's hand flew to cover her lips. "Not Doucette Aigleron!"

Jaume nodded.

His mother sagged against the table. "You'd wed a witch girl?"

Doucette croaked in affront.

Mireyo rested her hands on her hips. "Are you mad, Jaume? The false gold their father spreads has ruined half of Donsatrelle's traders."

"Doucette isn't responsible for Lord Pascau's actions," Jaume said sternly. "You, of all people, should understand that, Mireyo. Did Vent'roux blame you for your father's rigged weights?"

"Jaume!" His mother voiced the disapproval that spread through the ring of surrounding faces.

Mireyo's black eyes filled with tears.

Tinou put his arm around her. "Listen, Jaume. If you weren't under a spell, I'd thrash you myself for saying such a cruel thing."

Jaume bent his head. "Your pardon, Mireyo. Na Jonselet."

Mireyo nodded. Her mother sniffed, unappeased.

"So where is she, this lord's daughter?" Jaume's mother asked. "Too good to walk into town on her own two feet? Sent you to fetch a carriage, so she could make a grand entrance?"

"No," Jaume said. "We would have come together, but she wanted me to tell you first. I'm sorry to see she had the right of it. I hoped you'd welcome the woman I love."

His mother sighed. "Loving a sorceress and marrying her aren't the same thing, Son."

Widow Jonselet's voice was cool. "Really, Jaume. A noble-woman? And an Aigleron!"

Doucette ruffled her feathers. Clearly the townspeople didn't hold a very high opinion of Beloc folk, and her family in particular. Their insulting attitude bolstered her determination.

She wasn't a bit like her sisters, as they would know if they had troubled to find out. How could she have been happy living with people who despised her before they'd met her?

"Jaume!" A glad shout and a frenzy of barking broke the silence that had fallen over the knot of people at the wool stand. A gangly boy loped down the street past the guild hall, then wove his way between the shoppers and the market tables. As he got closer, a small brown-and-white shape streaked from his heels and leaped into the air.

Doucette hopped in surprised alarm, but she was not the dog's intended target. Four flying paws struck Jaume square in the chest, while a pink tongue swept out and licked him across the lips.

Aha! Her sorceress self crowed in triumph. Jaume had broken his promise not to kiss anyone but her. He had let his dog kiss him. When he found Doucette gone, he would know it was his own fault.

"Fidele! Down, girl!" Jaume laughed and held the ecstatically wriggling body away from his face. "Missed me, did you?" The dog barked and snuffled and licked him again with such fervor that Jaume's family laughed at the sight.

Doucette's heart made a final effort. *You could join that laughing, loving family.*

Not on their terms, her head insisted. Not before you know what you'd be giving up.

With a resigned squawk, crow-Doucette took wing and flew away from the market square, the town, her beloved, and his family. She didn't see Jaume's head turn to follow her flight, or his face sober as he took a hasty leave of his brothers, dropped his pack, and ran back the way he had come.

Keeping her face resolutely forward, she skimmed over the granite crag and flew east, toward the deep forest. In time, Jaume would forget her. She'd seen plenty of women who might be persuaded to take her place by his side.

And she? Doucette might miss his kisses, but it didn't matter if she forgot him or not. Her magic would console her.

She flew for several hours, veering away from roads as she skimmed over the thickest forest, not knowing what she sought until she found it.

A break in the trees revealed a spring-fed pond and a cleared patch of land hidden in a fold of the hills. She circled it twice before her keen crow eyes picked out the building at the eastern edge of the pond. After dipping closer to see who might be occupying such a remote place, she cawed in relief. Long abandoned, by the look of it.

This far from any road, it must have been a hermitage, or perhaps another sorceress's retreat. Doors and shutters had rotted in place, and brambles grew over the tumbledown walls between the untended orchard and vegetable garden. Missing tiles gave the roof a gap-toothed appearance, but with proper care, it could be a sturdy refuge. Given a little attention, the fruit trees and garden, too, could flourish again.

Doucette landed by the pond. Then she put her head down and twitched her neck until the gold chain came free of her feathers and landed on the ground. Magic flowed, smoothing the black feathers into paler skin, elongating her body and reshaping her arms and legs until Doucette crouched next to her pack, her feet crunching dried reeds.

She stood and twitched her skirts into place. She felt fine. Better than fine; magic and possibility filled her to overflowing. Every bit of her newfound strength would be needed, she thought, to make this remote place comfortable before the winter winds howled through the trees.

Tante Mahalt had built a great estate from wild lands once upon a time. Doucette would, too.

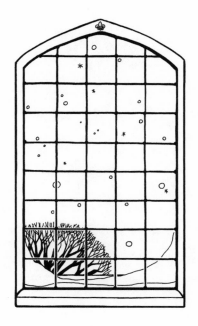

Winter

Chapter Twenty-eight

*C*hill autumn days gave way to frost-spangled nights as Doucette repaired the ruined dwelling. She didn't mind the worsening weather. When night fell, she had only to Transform herself into a mouflon and sleep warm in the mountain sheep's thick wool.

Between her training as a chastelaine and the tools she had found in a corner of the abandoned building, the work went swiftly. Doucette knew how roof tiles should be laid, edges over-lapping, to shed the rain. She had supervised carpenters replacing doors, masons laying stone, laborers building fences. Now she had only to picture the task in her mind and Animate ax, saw, hammer, and chisel to their tasks.

Doucette lavished magic on her tools and materials, her power spilling into them as a pitcher pours water, but she felt no ill effects. Instead, it seemed the magic ran more easily through her body, as if her previous days of secret practice had opened new channels through which it could flow. Wherever she laid her hands, wonders appeared. The rush of power intoxicated her, and delight left little room for melancholy.

At first she caught herself wishing she could show Jaume her achievements or imagined she heard a shepherd's pipes playing on the wind. But the instant a wistful thought intruded, Doucette pushed herself harder. Magic, she found, cleansed her mind of useless memories, her heart of unwanted emotion.

Once Doucette had made the building's structure sound, she played with its form, sculpting the stone as a potter sculpts clay until the previous long, low shape stretched into towers and walls. When she finished, a small, elegant castle perched at the edge of the pond, its two wings curving out from the center hall like a swan protecting her nest.

Next, Doucette paced around the outside, dragging her feet through the leaf litter. Behind her, the ground sank into a steep-sided moat. A stroke of her hand made a drawbridge from a downed tree; a length of twisted cord changed into an iron chain so perfectly balanced on its wheel that a child could have raised and lowered the bridge.

Finally, she turned her attention to the garden and orchard. Over years of neglect, carrots and turnips, bean and onion and garlic plants had escaped from their rows and wandered as they pleased, multiplying within the crumbling walls. Several trees were heavy with walnuts. On others, the last apples clung stubbornly to their twigs, though plum and cherry trees were long bare, their dropped fruit eaten by forest creatures.

At Doucette's command, spade, mattock, and rake worked the earth. The wild-grown vegetables rolled into tubs and casks while nuts pattered down into waiting baskets. Stones leaped into place on the garden and orchard walls. The ground shook as rocks and roots and twigs tumbled out of the soil and into the forest, leaving the earth seamed with furrows and ready to be planted in the spring.

When the winter rains arrived in earnest, Doucette went inside. She pulled up the drawbridge, took stock of the bare rooms, and summoned her power. In the great hall, the roof arched its back like a cat; tiles clattered back into place as if a soothing hand had petted them down. Columns sprouted like lilies, nodded gracefully, and wove their tips together over her head. Gray-veined marble replaced mossy paving stones. Painted scenes livened the bare walls.

From a few chests of moth-eaten linens and ragged furs, Doucette furnished her castle with every luxury her mind and magic could conjure up: warm fur robes, sumptuous table coverings and cushions, soft linen sheets for her canopied bed, hangings like carpets of spring flowers.

She couldn't conjure food, of course, so she flew into town and bought supplies with the gold Cecilia had given her, then enchanted a cartload into a nutshell and carried it home.

As winter storms broke harmlessly over the roof, Doucette let a sense of whimsy guide her work. She made a fire-bellows shaped like a dragon, with wings to pump air from its wide-open mouth. A bent iron poker took on the head of a crane and a three-toed foot. Doucette fashioned mirrors with jeweled frames, copper lamps shaped like flowers, crystal goblets, silver utensils, and plates of hammered gold.

And then came the morning Doucette woke up inside her grand bed with her throat raw from screaming. She clawed the sweat-plastered hair from her face and pushed aside the smothering curtains, breathing in gulps as she remembered the nightmare.

Falling.

As in her dreams at the Château de l'Île, Doucette had been falling. But in those dreams, Jaume had caught her. This time she had screamed and plunged into an endless void. Moonless, starless, dark, and cold, the air was too thin to hold her, the night empty of all but her cry of despair.

Doucette scrubbed her face with her hands and jumped out of bed. Barefoot, she ran up cold stone stairs and pushed open the door to the flight court.

In the next breath, she beat a pair of white wings and slapped two webbed feet over the frosted stone of the tower balcony. As Doucette had hoped, magic dispelled the strange fear that had possessed her. With a defiant honk, she leaped into the gray sky.

Beat after steady wing beat reassured her; the night's terror ebbed with her mastery of wind and sky. Below spread the silent forest, above, heavy clouds, and yet she passed between them, unharmed. A spiteful wet snow irritated but did not stop her. When it thickened to heavy flakes, she turned homeward once more to wait out the storm.

She was a sorceress and a swan maiden. She flew where she willed. She would not fall. The certainty sustained Doucette through the next day and into the evening, when the bell across the moat surprised her by ringing.

A visitor?

Curiosity ruffled the peace she had achieved. Doucette pushed her soup pot back over the fire and went up to the flight court. Deep snow had altered the landscape. White drifts coated the base of the castle walls and twisted low walls and trees into sinister shapes. A trail of pocked snow led from the woods to the drawbridge and gate.

As tall as Jaume, but older and broader, almost bearlike, the fur-clad figure standing on the far side of the moat gave a last convulsive tug on the rope. As the bell's clamor subsided into a murmur, then died on the quiet air, her visitor stared at Doucette with his mouth open so wide that she could have counted the blackened stumps of his teeth. He must have been out in the elements for some time. Ice edged his fur garments, and his face was red and chapped-looking over a bristle of black beard.

"Yes?" Doucette called.

"My lady!" The man thumped his chest with his fist. "Shelter, I beg." His teeth chattered, breaking up the words so that Doucette could hardly understand him. But it was clear enough what he wanted, and she felt a sudden urge to hear news of the wider world.

She went down to lower the bridge and open the door for him, though she stepped back a pace at the rank smell of his garments. A trapper, judging by the bundle of bloody pelts he left in the courtyard.

The man headed straight for the fire in a small chamber off the vaulted hall. For a while, there was nothing but the sound of his rough breathing, the crackling logs, and the hiss of ice sliding from his clothes and hitting the hot stone.

Doucette stirred the soup and ladled the man a bowl, then picked up her needlework and sat on a bench. She kept her eyes demurely on her work, enjoying the trapper's amazed expression as he turned in a slow circle, taking in his surroundings.

Well he might stare, she thought with satisfaction. It would be hard to imagine a warmer, more luxurious room than the one she had created. Copper lamps cast a ruddy glow over cushions and tapestries woven in the rich hues of autumn leaves. It even smelled good. In addition to the bubbling soup, dried herbs strewn on the stone floor gave off a pleasantly spicy aroma.

When the awe in his eyes changed to fear, the sight unsettled her, but only for a moment. Though Donsatrelle folk might be ignorant of magic, this rough-looking fellow must understand that a castle's sudden appearance in the wilderness smacked of sorcery.

Her guest didn't say much as he plowed through three bowls of soup. Doucette was pleased at her guest's appreciation of her cooking, even if he didn't offer much conversation.

The quality of the silence changed as the fire died down. Noticing the man peering furtively in her direction, Doucette's skin prickled with warning. She sidled to the fire and picked up the crane poker, then whispered to it, just in case.

> *Poker, fine poker,*
> *stick fast to his hand.*
> *Cover and uncover*
> *ashes with coals,*
> *till I bid thee loose.*

When the trapper lunged, Doucette was ready. She shoved the poker into his hand and slipped neatly out of his reach. "Cover the fire," she said, stern as Tante Mahalt.

Reflexively, the man obeyed her command. Once the coals were blanketed with ashes, he spun to face her. A growl of surprise turned to alarm as the poker forced him back to the fire.

He tried to drop the fire tool, but the enchanted poker held him tightly. It darted back and forth over the fire, pulling his unwilling body with it.

Doucette watched him struggle against the poker as it covered and uncovered the glowing embers.

"Witch!" He cursed her, viciously at first, then in a weakened voice as the poker beat the fight out of him.

When he fell silent at last, lunging helplessly with the poker, Doucette spoke. "It's time for you to go."

Red-faced and sweating, the man grunted agreement.

"Release, good poker," Doucette whispered.

It fell from his hand and the crane beak pecked the floor. Eyes averted, the trapper seized his coat, retrieved his bundle of furs, and ran from the castle. As if Saint Hubert's hounds nipped at his heels, the man galloped through the drifts of snow and vanished into the forest.

Glad to be rid of him, Doucette raised the drawbridge and closed the door. If this was how men usually treated a woman they found alone, it was no wonder sorceresses preferred their own company.

Spring

Chapter Twenty-nine

—————— ❦ ——————

Perhaps the trapper spread word of the forest's dangerous new resident; perhaps later snowstorms discouraged travelers. Whatever the reason, Doucette's solitude remained undisturbed for many weeks.

Snug in her refuge, she entertained herself with needlework, baking, spellcraft. And when indoor pursuits palled or nightmares troubled her, she took wing and flew from them.

As crow or swan by day, owl by night, Doucette discovered the secrets of the winter forest. She learned where bears denned and mice foraged, heard the slow, sighing song of ice-covered pines, read the signs of cruel death from blood spots in the snow. After a time, it seemed that wildness had penetrated her bones. Restless and impatient in her girl form, which persisted in wondering how Jaume fared, Doucette wore it less and less.

And if her flights took her over Vent'roux town, over the house with the blue door or the wool stand in the market square, she told herself those places had little meaning to a sorceress.

The wheel of seasons turned.

One soft spring morning, Doucette woke and stretched. Before her eyes were quite open, she craved the crisp green taste of peas.

Turning the idea over in her mind, she remembered a cloth roll of seeds, given to a girl long ago at her betrothal feast. Dressing hurriedly, Doucette found the cloth roll still tucked in her pack. She carried it outside in triumph.

From the air, she had watched farmers working their fields. It was time she planted her own garden. The furrows had been prepared after the previous autumn's harvest and been waiting under the snow for the sun to warm the ground.

Humming to herself, Doucette moved along the rows, planting peas and beans, gourds and carrots and lettuce as the gardeners did in Beloc.

The sun played "hide the princess" with a scattering of clouds; the breeze toyed with Doucette's unbound hair. She savored the smell of moist earth crumbled between her fingers. Birds darted overhead, caroling the joys of spring. Beetles and ants trundled over the ground, and once she spied a fox trotting past before his russet shadow faded into the trees.

The whole world seemed alive. As though she, too, were waking from a long sleep, Doucette savored it all. She patted soil over her seeds, then squinted up at the thickening clouds. Standing and stretching, Doucette scratched at the dirt under her fingernails, then took an empty pail down to the pond.

The man came up behind her so quietly that Doucette squawked in surprise when he twitched the pail out of her hand.

"Allow me, Lady." He dipped the pail in the water and carried it to the garden.

"If you like." The words tasted odd in her mouth. She had grown unused to speaking.

Without asking, her visitor splashed water over a newly planted row of peas. After emptying the pail, he followed the path from the garden back to the pond, stepping politely around Doucette.

Her visitor acted so pleased with himself that she decided against telling him his labor was unnecessary. It would rain within hours, from the look of the clouds. The water had been meant for washing, not to water her garden. Silently, she waded into the pond and scrubbed her hands while he labored.

The man must have been observing her from behind the trees for some time. He watered every row she had planted.

Like a farmer, he handled the pail with ease, but he was dressed too well for a common laborer, in a knee-length tunic and cape, woolen hose, and good leather shoes. He wore his fair hair long, like a courtier, but he couldn't be a noble—he didn't carry a sword. The big leather gloves and bag he had dropped by the garden wall made Doucette suspect a falconer hunting for nesting pairs, or perhaps a nobleman's servant, traveling between estates on his master's business.

As if he had heard her unvoiced question, the man set the empty pail at Doucette's feet and struck his chest with his fist. "Messenger Garmel, Lady. Bound for Vent'roux with a commission for my patron."

"Your patron?" Doucette asked at his expectant pause.

"Sieur Nicolau," he said, with such a self-important air that Doucette bit back a smile.

She had never heard of Sieur Nicolau—a Donsatrelle lordling, apparently. His lands must lie within a day's journey of her castle, as his servant traveled lightly. "Indeed," she said. At least this servant seemed well-spoken. Perhaps his conversation would prove more amusing than the trapper's. "Will you join me for dinner, Om Garmel?"

"With pleasure, Lady," he said. Gesturing for her to precede him, Om Garmel picked up his gloves and bag and followed her into the castle.

By the time Om Garmel served the meal, Doucette was remembering why she lived alone.

Not that her guest acted surly or threatening, like her first visitor. No, Om Garmel's manners were perfectly respectful, and he had been eager to help.

Too eager.

The man had hovered at her elbow the entire afternoon, begging to finish every task she began. And however he served Sieur Nicolau, Doucette did not think the servant's duties included handling food before it was cooked, as his enthusiasm far outpaced his skill in the kitchen. She had assigned him simple tasks: picking the greens that grew wild by the pond's margins, sorting lentils, and chopping vegetables, while she stuffed a squash and rolled out pastries.

Alas, the dinner he served with such a courtly flourish was almost inedible.

Bitter weeds studded the field greens, the lentils tasted gritty, and the stew (which he never stirred) had cooked unevenly. One mouthful might hold scorched bits of meat, the next, chunks of undercooked turnip.

Doucette ate little, though she had to constantly decline Om Garmel's offers of the choicest morsels from his own plate. As rain pattered onto the roof, they talked about the changeable weather. When that topic flagged, Om Garmel described Sieur Nicolau's estate, situated on the eastern flank of the forest, in glowing terms. He seemed ignorant or uncaring of the world beyond, and never asked Doucette about her own history.

She didn't volunteer it.

Still, she was aware of his eyes following her every move while he ate, and ate, and ate. Doucette toyed with a pastry and listened to the wind whipping the branches of the trees and moaning around the windows. With relief, she noticed her guest scraping the last spoonful of lentils out of the pot.

The interminable dinner had drawn to a close.

Before Doucette could move, Om Garmel jumped up to clear the table. With fawning haste, he stacked the gold dishes so high that they tipped over and crashed to the floor.

"A thousand apologies!" he said, scrambling to collect the fallen plates and carry them off to the scullery.

Doucette picked up a bowl that had rolled to a stop beside her foot. A dent marred the bowl's rim. She scowled at it, then tossed the damaged thing onto the table, amused by her own pique at the man's incompetence. She had created the dishes out of fallen leaves and magic. She could make more of them easily.

Thank fortune. Judging by the clatter and smash Om Garmel was raising, all her dishes would need to be renewed on the morrow.

Doucette pushed away from the table, crossed to the window, and leaned out. The air smelled clean and soft, of wet leaves and earth. Raindrops spattered her face. She pulled one shutter toward her and reached for the other, then turned, her hand still on the latch.

Evidently, Om Garmel felt no need to ask her permission to spend the night. He was busy pulling cushions from benches and setting them by the hearth for a bed.

He was making very free with her hospitality. Who did he think was going to clean the ashes off those cushions? Doucette suspected she had been too gracious a host. If the man decided her home would make a good way station on his errands for his master, he would return again and again to vex her.

Except that a sorceress needn't tolerate any man's arrogance. Doucette murmured to the shutter.

> *Latch, good latch,*
> *stick fast to his fingers,*
> *then open and close*
> *through the dark night*
> *till daylight comes.*

Om Garmel looked up at the sound of her voice. "Please, allow me, Lady," he said, and hurried to pull the shutter closed. In his haste to reach her side, he kicked a cushion into the fire. It crackled and vanished in a shower of sparks.

Doucette released the shutter and moved to stamp on the sparks before the makeshift bed caught fire. "Good night," she said.

"Good ni-eeeeooow!"

The window shutter swung wide, pulling the man halfway out the window before he succeeded in slamming it closed.

The shutter opened again.

Closed again.

Opened.

Ignoring the tiresome fellow's cries for help, Doucette retired to her bedchamber. From time to time in the night, a distant knocking sound roused her from evil dreams. The next morning, her head ached and her eyes felt full of sand. It seemed her visitor had spent an equally unpleasant time.

When she freed him from the window latch at dawn, Om Garmel cradled his arm to his chest. "Lady, how did I offend?"

"Men often sleep ill in a sorceress's house," Doucette answered austerely. She handed him his gloves and bag and showed him to the door. "Good-bye."

"Good-bye." Head low, Om Garmel trudged away.

Doucette pulled up the drawbridge and secured its chain before returning inside to Transform the broken plates and soiled velvet cushions her uninvited guest had left behind.

Chapter Thirty

As the days lengthened, Doucette's garden flourished. Seeds sprouted and bright green leaves unfurled into the welcome banners of spring. She carefully tended the young plants, thinning the carrots, staking the peas and beans, watering and weeding and fussing over the seedlings.

Inside the castle, she prowled her silent rooms like a caged beast, picking up her needlework and dropping it again. She stroked a fur robe, turning it from winter white to summer brown. As always, the magic came easily, bubbling out of her like an inexhaustible spring. She changed her golden plates to blue-and-white porcelain, pictured different scenes for all her wall paintings. When she Transformed her bed hangings to summer silks, she remembered the fateful day of spring cleaning in her parents' bedchamber and how she had found her swan skin.

A year later, nobody kept her from flying where she willed.

On the thought, Doucette strode out to the courtyard and changed into a hawk. As so often when she took bird shape and flew over the woods, she turned west, as if pulled by an invisible string. Soon she glimpsed familiar tile rooftops and swept in a wide circle around Vent'roux.

She was done with Jaume, she reminded herself. That part of her life was finished.

Still, when she soared over pastureland flecked with sheep, her hawk's eyes tracked the shepherds, alike in their broad hats and simple clothes, watching their wooly charges. The flocks were gathering, it seemed, making ready for their annual journey to the mountain pastures.

As the breeze stirred the grass below, memories ruffled Doucette's serenity. Perhaps she had followed these same sheep in the exhilarating flight to Tante Mahalt's. Doucette thought of bathing in the hot pools, of Jaume walking toward her hiding place with his little dog capering beside him.

How innocent her younger self had been! Keenly eager to discover her sorcery, unaware of the treachery and triumph succeeding days would bring. She had been so frightened, then, and now . . . Doucette was mistress of her own domain, independent and powerful beyond her dreams.

So why did the memory tug at her? Why did she envy that foolish girl, succumbing to the promise in two merry brown eyes?

A group of men caught Doucette's attention. Their easy stances, their lanky bodies. The resemblance between them was so strong she didn't need to see the curly brown hair under their broad-brimmed hats to recognize Jaume and two of his brothers.

Curiosity sent hawk-Doucette a little lower. She circled lazily over their heads, until the brown-and-white dog sitting by Jaume jumped up and yipped with excitement. The men looked around, then up, shading their eyes with their hands. Doucette veered away, but not before Eri shouted and pointed. She glanced back and saw Jaume staring after her, hands at his sides while Fidele barked and pranced.

Stupid, Doucette scolded herself. What purpose was there in raising the ghost of a love she had left behind?

But Jaume was well, her heart sang. A little thin, but healthy, his skin browned by the sun. Perhaps he, too, had forgotten what had passed between them, and was making a new life without her.

The thought brought no pleasure.

Doucette flew back to her castle and resumed her human form. Driven by an upwelling of restless energy, she kneaded dough for bread, chopped vegetables for stew, and baked a cake. In the garden, she picked the first tender lettuce leaves. Disdaining the Animated hoe, she sank to her knees and yanked weeds up by their roots, wishing her tumultuous emotions could be as easily subdued.

The sight of Jaume had reawakened an undeniable, seemingly unquenchable longing. Doucette was a little frightened by the strength of her desire to drop out of the sky and speak with him. More than speak, if she were honest with herself. She had wanted to taste his kisses again, to feel those strong arms close around her.

Given her stained skirts and the lank state of her hair, it was fortunate that she had resisted the temptation, Doucette told herself sternly. For a powerful sorceress, she was a rather dirty example. A bath and fresh clothing would restore her spirits. And if she chanced to see Jaume again, her appearance wouldn't disgust him.

Luxuriating in hot water, Doucette considered the gown she would make. She was in the mood for something special.

Violet-colored, she decided, trimmed with lace as creamy as her pearl earrings. A stroke of her hand, a whispered word, and it was done. The purple silk rustled over her skin. She hummed as she braided her hair and clipped on the pearls.

Steaming with yeasty promise, the bread came out of the oven. Doucette put it aside to cool, then set the table with her new blue porcelain and floated water lilies in a silver bowl.

Before she could admire the effect, the gate bell rang.

Doucette laughed out loud. When she wanted company, it seemed, she had only to dress for it. And if she *had* conjured a gown to please one curly-haired, dark-eyed Vent'roux man in particular, why shouldn't her desire bring him to her door?

She had left the drawbridge down after picking the water lilies. On the far side of the moat, the bell-ringer waited courteously.

Her pulse quickened with expectation, but upon seeing the elegant person who stood there, Doucette was hard-pressed to hide her disappointment.

No lost servant or woodsman, this young man's black eyes and pointed features were attractive in a foxlike way, framed by shoulder-length red-brown hair. A wide embroidered band bordered the neck of his blue tunic, and his shoes curled up into fashionable points. A sword in a tooled leather scabbard hung from his belt.

Doucette's polite invitation sounded flat to her own ears. "Come in and be welcome, traveler."

"Thank you, Lady." The man walked across the drawbridge and bowed. "Sieur Nicolau de Valescure Saint-Senlis, yours to command."

Om Garmel must have reported Doucette's presence to his employer. Doucette wondered whether the servant's story had included the hours he had spent banging to and fro with the Animated shutter.

Sieur Nicolau's serene expression showed little fear of suffering a similar fate. Unlike her previous two visitors, the nobleman surveyed Doucette's luxurious appointments with calm approval.

"Exquisite. A fit setting for your beauty, Lady——?" His voice rose on a note of inquiry.

"Doucette," she said, and belatedly curtsied. "Doucette Aigleron, Sieur."

"Of the Beloc Aiglerons? Why, I've had the honor of meeting your parents." Sieur Nicolau kissed the tips of his fingers. "Lady Sarpine, what a treasure."

Doucette thought of her last sight of her mother, shrieking threats at Jaume from a swollen, bee-stung face. She shrugged away the unpleasant memory. "We didn't part on cordial terms."

"Ah," Sieur Nicolau said. Tactfully, he changed the subject. "What a marvelous residence, and constructed in a season! I understand you're a practitioner of the High Arts?"

"Yes," Doucette said.

Sieur Nicolau favored her with a warm smile. "Beloc's loss is Donsatrelle's gain, that such a great sorceress would make our humble county her home."

Deciding to be amused by his flattery, Doucette invited the nobleman to share her meal.

Each dish was met with fulsome praise. He pronounced the stew "superb," the bread "excellent," the greens "delightful."

After the cake had been sampled and likewise approved ("divine"), Doucette offered to show her guest the rest of the castle. With impeccable courtesy, the nobleman extended an arm.

For a moment Doucette had the strange sensation that she had been transported back to the Château de l'Aire, to a court she had never imagined. There she, not Azelais or Cecilia, was considered the fairest, and knights vied to serve her, and paid her compliments, and asked her opinion about their verses.

The only thing that tempered her enjoyment was the calculation in Sieur Nicolau's eyes as he praised her handiwork. But it was only natural, she thought, that he should be curious about an enchanted castle springing up in the forest where a ruined hermitage had been.

They strolled outside to admire the glow of sunset on the pond and returned to sit by the fire, where Sieur Nicolau recounted amusing stories about Donsatrelle's noble families. "Though none of our county's beauties," he said suavely, "could hope to outshine a lady of your refinement."

"You're very kind," Doucette said.

"In truth, I am overcome." Sieur Nicolau's expression turned serious as he took Doucette's hand. "I had meant to wait, to make your acquaintance properly, but my dear, dear Lady Doucette—if I may make so bold as to style you after a single delightful evening—I believe we might make a mutually advantageous alliance."

Doucette drew back. "How so, Sieur Nicolau?"

Still holding her hand, the nobleman sank gracefully to one knee. "Lady Doucette, will you do me the honor of becoming my wife?"

"What?" Doucette stared at him.

"No, don't answer immediately. I've startled you, I see. Only consider, dear lady, what we might accomplish, between my connections and your Arts. Why should you languish in the wilderness, when you could ornament the entire realm as comtesse or duchess—nay, as a queen!"

"But, Sieur Nicolau, I don't trust—I don't *know* you," Doucette stammered, surprised into speaking the awkward truth.

"Know me? Trust me?" He laughed gently. "Your pardon, Lady Doucette. Such charming frankness deserves an honest response. You may trust me to further both our interests, far better than, shall we say, a shepherd ever could?" He winked at her alarm.

"Your little adventure is the talk of Donsatrelle. But now that your former swain is to marry a Vent'roux girl—"

"What?" Doucette said again, even more stupidly than she had the first time.

"I thought," Sieur Nicolau squeezed her palm, "that you might welcome a suitor who could restore you to the world's admiration and your family's esteem."

Though Sieur Nicolau blathered on, Doucette didn't hear the rest of it.

Jaume was to wed?

A cold fog filled her chest; she couldn't breathe. Her hands tightened over Sieur Nicolau's until he winced. She wrenched away from him and jumped up from her bench to pace back and forth between the fire and the door. She hoped the motion would hide the trembling that had started in her stomach and spread to her arms and legs.

After the shock, anger swelled inside her. Potent as magic, it coursed through her body and stopped the shaking.

The spirit Lavena had said that Doucette lacked pride, but she could summon enough to hide her true feelings from this titled opportunist, this—this—velvet vulture who hovered at her hearth. If Sieur Nicolau thought to wound her with his sly announcement and then sway her will with his fine manners and easy compliments, he was mistaken.

"You have me at a disadvantage, Sieur Nicolau," Doucette said. Her voice sounded calm, as if it came from a woman standing outside the inferno of Doucette's heart and mind, speaking the words good manners required. "As you say, your suit is unexpected. Perhaps we could talk more in the morning?"

"Certainly." Sieur Nicolau's smirk broadened, fanning the flames of Doucette's silent rage.

He dared imagine he could twist her to his will, but he would repent his presumption! A sorceress was nobody's toy, least of all this pompous courtier's, with his pretty clothes and his silky condescension.

Doucette paused, her hand by the door, and bent her head.

Bolt, strong bolt,
stick fast to his hand,
lock and unlock
until I release thee.

The surge of magic made her clutch the doorframe for balance, but Doucette felt a savage delight in the strength of the spell streaming through her.

Haughty Sieur Nicolau might not enjoy experiencing a sorceress's true power as much as he imagined.

"Your pardon, Lady Doucette?"

"This bolt is stuck," she said. "Would you be so kind as to pull it closed?"

"As you wish, dear lady," he answered.

But the moment he shot the bolt home, the iron bar reversed course. Sieur Nicolau closed it. Again it opened, dragging his arm to one side. He chuckled uneasily. "Ahem. This bolt seems to possess a mind of its own."

"As do I," Doucette purred.

The nobleman's face changed as he realized that he could neither remove his hand from the bolt, nor still its motion. He tried, but the bolt jerked his unwilling arm from side to side. "Lady Doucette," he said sternly, "it is ill done, to tease me."

The hauteur that glazed Sieur Nicolau's features would have been more convincing, Doucette thought, without the sweat beads dotting his brow. The pompous lordling imagined it his duty to instruct her in manners?

She curtsied with an elaborate flourish. "Good night," she replied, and left him before a worse punishment occurred to her.

The tide of anger and magic swept her down the corridor to her bedchamber. Blinded by the tears that burned her lashes, Doucette didn't see candles slumping into wax puddles as she brushed past the wall sconces.

Her head was ringing with remembered voices. Na Claro's quavered with emotion. "Our sweetness has found a husband to treasure her."

"Their promises are not to be trusted," Tante Mahalt said, low and urgent, while Jaume's voice held tender laughter.

"You're the only one I'm kissing."

The only one. *The only one.* The lie echoed behind her eyes.

"No!" Doucette said aloud and pushed aside the bed curtains. At her touch, a silk panel smoldered, then sparked like the green branch of feather-pine it had once been.

Doucette threw up her hands in surprise.

Overhead, the bed's canopy rippled into a sheet of fire. Doucette jumped back to avoid the burning clumps of blackened needles that dropped to the coverlet. In an instant, the rest of the linens, too, were burning.

Entranced, Doucette watched the flames consume her bed.

She spun to the left and her hand stabbed out, dashing scent bottles and jeweled gloves and colored ribbons to the floor. Flames leaped, emerald and apricot at their heart. The ghostly fragrance of lilies touched the air before it was suffocated by the scent of burning cedar.

Doucette sobbed a laugh, partly in surprise, but more with a kind of angry satisfaction.

Why not let it burn?

Let it all burn!

From the ashes of her swan skin, she had found the courage to dare the Rassemblement. What phoenix might arise out of the destruction of everything her magic had wrought since then?

Deliberately, Doucette gestured at the chests, the benches, the lovely rugs and gowns and hangings her imagination had called forth. Spells hissed over her tongue and set the furnishings alight.

When the quick, bright crackle of twigs and grass failed to satisfy, Doucette turned her attention to the wooden shutters. A stroke of her hand, and they flared into blue flames. She basked in the glow, though the smoke made her retreat into the corridor. Wind sighed through the window and stirred ash into a glittering cloud.

Doucette craved more.

One man had betrayed her; another sought to use her. Hurt and outrage demanded release. Like a moth pushing free of its cocoon, Doucette stretched her arms over her head. Power burst from her hands as she chanted destruction into the thick air.

The roof exploded outward in a clap of heat and light. It sucked Doucette's hair straight up from her head and then knocked her flat onto her back. She shrieked, clapping her hands over her ears in a vain attempt to shut out the thundering roar.

When she brought her hands down, the sight of the blood trickling over her fingers shocked Doucette out of the mindless passion that had possessed her. But it was too late to call back the magic she had unleashed.

Majestic as a summer sunset, molten radiance washed down the walls. Unlike wood and straw, the stone was slow to react. It groaned and sagged, crumbling away from her like a wall of wet sand.

Doucette realized her own danger at the same time she heard a loud yell.

Sieur Nicolau!

She pushed herself to her feet and ran to the front of the castle.

"Help!" The nobleman stood at the door, his face contorted in the fire's glow. Soot from the burning shutters dusted his shoulders, and his hand jerked back and forth as the enchanted bolt continued to close and open, dragging him with it. "Please," he choked, "help me!"

With a muttered word, Doucette released him. The two of them stumbled across the drawbridge and chased their shadows down to the pond. As Doucette beat out the sparks that had fallen onto Sieur Nicolau's tunic, he coughed smoke from his lungs. Behind them, the castle burned like a beacon in the night.

Doucette splashed water over her face and arms until the front of her amethyst gown was sopping. She glanced up and met Sieur Nicolau's frightened gaze.

The nobleman scuttled away from her, as if he would throw himself into the pond to escape her clutches. "Your pardon, Lady Doucette," he rasped. "No wish to offend. I'll be off with the dawn and trouble you no more."

"It's I who must beg your forgiveness, Sieur Nicolau," Doucette said, but he did not stay to hear her apology. Bowing and gabbling in a frenzy of politeness, the scorched nobleman pushed his way through the reeds toward the far side of the pond and was soon lost in misty darkness.

Heavy as a fur robe, exhaustion dropped over Doucette's shoulders. Shivering in her wet, queenly dress and pearl earrings, she sat on the muddy bank and watched the pool of glowing stone, once her home, subside into the earth. It reminded her a little of the night of the Rassemblement, when she had bathed in liquid magic and floated alone in the dark.

But unlike that time, when her body and mind had been strangely divorced, now she felt her various pains far too acutely. The palms of her hands throbbed from the magic that had ripped through them, uncontrolled. Her chin and arms smarted from the touch of flying embers. One ankle ached—she had twisted it hurrying over the rough ground.

Also unlike her time at Lavena's Cauldron, in this dreadful hour no spirit but Doucette's own rifled through her memories, judging action and intention, reason and result. Fatigue formed a thin crust over darker, bleaker emotions.

She had been selfish, she realized.

The desire to work magic had pushed aside both her good judgment and her love. She had taken such of Tante Mahalt's advice as suited her—beware of men—and ignored the remainder: that her gift could be corrupted. Lady Sarpine had said so, too, though it hardly excused her cruelty.

When the thrill of practicing magic had consumed her, Doucette had not sought to curb it. Her single-mindedness had led to the mistreatment of others and the destruction of her castle.

She didn't regret beating back her mother and the armsmen, or defending herself against the trapper, but Om Garmel . . . Doucette's lips tightened in shame. Even Sieur Nicolau, scheming busily for his own gain, had offered her no real harm. She could have sent him on his way without injury.

Little wonder Jaume's countrymen distrusted the High Arts.

When Doucette considered the ruin her magic had caused, she understood in her bones why it had worried Jaume. After the Rassemblement, the pleasure of each Transformation had fed into the next. The more spells she had cast, the more she wanted to do, to the exclusion of all else. Since she had completed her castle, Doucette realized, she hadn't gone a day without changing into bird or beast. Like a drunkard swilling wine, a miser counting coins, she had lost herself in magic.

Eyeing the smoking remains of her home, she kneaded her sore hands together. What would Jaume say if he knew?

As if her thought had shaped it, an eddy shifted the drifting smoke into a well-remembered likeness. Wrapped in a sheepskin, Jaume sat by the embers of a dying campfire. A brown-and-white shape stirred at his side. Fidele's ears pricked, her head turned.

Doucette ached anew to see the sadness in Jaume's dark eyes. Her hand lifted as if to smooth the weary lines that marked his face.

He looked up, surprised, then intent. His lips rounded in her name, and his hand rose to meet hers. But before their seeking hands could touch, a breeze disturbed the smoke. The shepherd's likeness shredded into wisps of mist.

Doucette curled over her knees and cried.

If the strength of her previous anger was any measure, she had never really stopped loving Jaume. Too much bound them together for the tie to be lightly broken. During the Rassemblement, she had trusted him with her life, as he had placed his faith in her through the magic-working of the comte's three trials and then the perilous flight from Beloc. Even Jaume's caution about her sorcery had stemmed from his urge to protect her.

So why hadn't she discussed it with him like the loving partner she claimed to be? As Azelais and Cecilia toyed with, then discarded, their many suitors, Doucette had repaid Jaume's devotion with indifference. Then, like Tante Mahalt, she had fled the company of men, only to enclose herself in a prison of her own making.

Why had she cast his love aside? Why had she closed off her own heart? Woman or swan, wife or witch—was there no other way a sorceress could live? The question tormented her, until Doucette wiped her eyes and turned her face to the sky.

Why not both? Who had decreed she must lose her love to magic or deny her magic for love?

"Other people aren't us," Jaume had said.

If Doucette believed him, she could learn from her mistakes, work to balance the two sides of her nature. How would she know, unless she tried? Didn't she owe Jaume—didn't she owe *herself*—a second chance?

In word and deed, Jaume had demonstrated his devotion. If Doucette was to have any hope of reclaiming him, she must do likewise.

But no one else need know. Perhaps it was her Aigleron pride, but Doucette didn't want his family's pity. She would find some way only Jaume would understand to convey that she had changed. If Jaume truly loved her, he would accept her apology and take her hand again. Doucette would have to show him that she had stopped running. That she, too, was bold enough, honorable enough, to claim the one she loved.

Alone in the smoky night, Doucette hoped she hadn't waited too long.

Chapter Thirty-one

With a sweep of gray-tipped wings, a swan landed in the back garden of the house with the blue door.

Drawn by the unexpected noise, a curly-haired man opened an upstairs window. "Jaume, come here," Eri called over his shoulder. "It's the strangest thing."

"What's that?" Another dark head joined the first.

In the far corner of the garden, swan-Doucette seized a bramble cane in her beak and pulled until the branch came free. Lifting her neck high, she dragged her prize to the garden's waste pile.

She waddled back to the bramble bush, caught another branch, and tugged.

"A swan's clearing our garden," Eri said.

Jaume said nothing.

Eri frowned. "Have you ever seen the like?"

Doucette deposited another branch on the growing waste pile. She arched her neck, fanned her wings, and gave a plaintive, barking honk.

Do you remember? She pleaded silently with the tall figure at the window.

Do you remember how you once cleared brambles for my sake?

"No," Jaume said, and disappeared from view. Eri lingered at the window while the swan dismantled the bush, branch by thorny branch.

Inside the house, voices called. Footsteps pounded up and down the stairs. As the morning advanced, other faces watched from other windows, but none of Jaume's brothers interrupted the strange gardener's labor.

When Doucette finished her task, she preened her feathers. Thorns had pierced her skin and stung like dots of fire. As patiently as she had pulled apart and finally uprooted the bramble, she cleared her gray-tipped feathers of the prickly stems, blood, and dirt.

No one ventured into the garden.

Neck arched, she paraded around the chestnut tree, past the tall blue irises, the fragrant lilies. Jaume had recognized her. She knew it, though the set of his face had told her he was angry and hurt. She didn't blame him, nor did that change what she needed to do.

The garden door remained closed.

Then Doucette heard the tramp of many feet in the street outside. A horn sounded a flurry of silver notes: a wedding march. Fists pounded on the front door.

Had the groom's party come to collect him? If so, she had less time than she thought.

Shaded by a chestnut tree, Doucette changed. The familiar intoxication flooded her, tempting her to fly high and far. She resisted. If a sorceress needed her mind on her spells, a courting woman had better keep her eyes on her beloved.

In duck form, she flapped out of the garden to catch the procession. The man with the horn went first, flanked by a smiling

Na Eleno and an older man Doucette thought must be Jaume's father, Om Bernat. Dressed in fine wool tunics, Jaume and his brothers followed.

Duck-Doucette peered down at them. Jaume walked at a measured pace. Next to him, Tinou carried his shoulders stiffly. A group of boisterous young men, including Vitor, ranged around them, but the joking and laughter didn't touch either Jaume or Tinou. Both seemed lost in their own thoughts.

Eri, the youngest, lagged behind the rest. He craned his neck to follow the whistling noise of Doucette's wings.

She spied their destination. In the square by the guild hall, the trestle tables that vendors used on market day had been set end to end and decorated with flowers. Approaching from another direction, a line of festively dressed women sang as they walked.

Doucette folded her wings and plummeted into the middle of the street, fifty paces from the head of Jaume's procession. She scraped at the dirt with one webbed foot and jabbed her beak into the ground. Again and again, she dug, though to no great effect. The street had been packed hard by generations of feet and cart wheels. A metal blade would have had difficulty cutting through it; a duck's beak was completely unsuited to the task. She ignored the pain and worked harder.

The leader pointed his horn at Doucette. "Hey there," he said. "A digging duck!"

"Go back to your pond, silly thing." Na Eleno flapped her skirts.

Doucette held her ground.

"The bird's crazed." Tinou would have kicked her aside, but Jaume held him back.

"No. Not crazed."

"Then what?"

Jaume shook his head.

"An ill omen for your wedding day, Brother," Tinou said, his voice bitter.

Doucette fixed Jaume with her round duck eyes. *Do you remember?* she asked without words. *Do you remember how you dug a pond for my sake?*

"No," Jaume said, but his brows knitted together and his footsteps slowed.

Doucette quacked forlornly. So close. He had almost softened. He had almost stopped.

The rest of Jaume's party gave Doucette a wide berth, except for one young man who bent down to catch her. She flapped her wings and snapped her beak in his face. To the taunts of the others, the man yelped and jumped back as if she had taken off his nose.

Eri shooed the rest of the men forward. Several times, he turned to watch the duck until the street curved around the side of the guild hall and he, too, disappeared.

Doucette folded her wings and changed again. Once more she would remind Jaume of his promise, and then she would abide by his decision.

The groom's procession met the bride's in the square. Little Beatris threw flower petals as a group of smiling girls pushed a veiled maiden from within their ranks. The horn sounded, but Jaume stayed where he was, his face thoughtful.

"Son." His mother tapped her foot.

"Three trials," Jaume said to no one. "First was clearing brambles, then digging the pond. Last, finding the golden bird, so . . ." He looked up, searching the sky. When he spotted the gold-winged hawk circling overhead, his expression cleared. He nodded once and stepped away from his parents. Instead of taking the veiled woman's hand, he lifted his arms to the sky.

"Doucette," he called. "Love, return to me."

The hawk screamed in answer. Then, like a star falling from the heavens, the golden shape hurtled toward Jaume.

"Help!" Na Eleno shrieked.

Flinching, the bride covered her head.

"Mireyo!" Tinou ran to stand guard over the veiled woman.

Before the hawk's talons touched Jaume's fist, the air shimmered. In her own form, Doucette alit to stand beside him. She paid no attention to the shouting men and crying girls. "Marrying the wrong woman, aren't you?" she asked Jaume.

"Me? You're the one who left." His voice challenged her, but the light in his eyes gave her the courage to go on.

Doucette lifted her chin and spoke in a carrying voice, so the people gathered around them could hear. "Do you remember, Jaume of Vent'roux, how you suffered many trials and enchantments for my sake, and vowed you would love only me?"

"I remember, well enough," Jaume said. "All this winter, I thought you had forgotten."

He deserved an explanation. Doucette blushed, admitting her fault. "I shouldn't have asked for the last."

"What?"

Doucette was taken aback to see Jaume's joyful expression sag into despair. "No, no, you mistake me," she said. Stepping forward, she rested her hands on his chest, over his heart. "I was wrong to envy your affection for your family, and theirs for you. It's their care made you the man you are, the man who loved me better than my own kin. I was also wrong, my love, to count my magic more important than our promises. Will you forgive me?"

Jaume's beautiful smile spread across his face. His arms wrapped around Doucette, keeping her where she most wanted to be. "Oh, aye," he said. "If you'll forgive my mistrusting that same sorcery as saved both our lives."

"I will," Doucette said. "I've learned to take care, great care, with my spells." Her lip curled in the tiniest pout. "Now, if Fidele has not stolen all the kisses meant for me, I'd like to remind you of your last promise."

Jaume laughed and obliged her, taking his time. Doucette kissed him back with a will. The young men in the crowd were hooting and stamping when the two parted. Doucette could feel herself blushing again, but she didn't care who saw it.

"Three cheers for the—" Eri's shout ended raggedly when a well-dressed matron marched out from behind the now-giggling girls. Na Jonselet seized the veiled woman's arm and dragged her next to Jaume. "What of your promises to my daughter Mireyo?" she said in a hard voice.

"Ask Tinou," Jaume said. "I think he will honor them in my stead."

"Gladly." Tinou stepped up to Mireyo's other side. The young woman's hand reached out from under the veil and clasped Tinou's.

Na Jonselet snorted. "A second son? No offense intended to you, Om Bernat, Na Eleno, but that was not our agreement."

"Beware, Na Jonselet," Eri said. "If Jaume's pretty sorceress turns you into a crow, what will you care about inheritances?"

Doucette was briefly tempted by the woman's gasp of fright. But after another look at Mireyo's hand holding Tinou's so tightly, Doucette remembered that even the humorless Na Jonselet would be part of her new family. Besides, today was a good day—the best day—to be done with misusing her power out of temper.

"Be easy, Na Jonselet," she said. "I have no desire to steal Mireyo's future, nor she mine."

Mireyo's veiled head nodded vigorously.

"I won't see my daughter cheated," Na Jonselet insisted.

Slowly, Doucette unclasped her pearl earrings, the only token that remained of her home. She hesitated, then leaned forward and tucked them into Mireyo's free hand.

If Doucette wanted to adorn herself with pearls, she could make them. "No artifice, these, but true jewels, Na Jonselet. Will such a bride-gift settle your mind?"

Na Jonselet's eyes widened as she calculated the pearls' worth. "Aye," she said. "The match has my blessing."

Mireyo lifted the corner of her veil to smile shyly at Doucette. "Thank you."

"A hundred thanks." Tinou bowed to Doucette and winked at his brother. "Jaume has found a great sorceress, indeed, to make all our wishes come true at once. Shall we have a double wedding?"

"Oh, aye." Doucette and Jaume spoke as one.

This time, Eri led the others in a cheer that went on and on until Om Bernat raised his hand for silence. Jaume tucked Doucette's arm in his, and they faced his parents together.

"You see how it is, Mother, Father," Jaume said. "Like the old riddle. If I had lost the key to the salt box and ordered a new one but then found the first again, which one would you have me keep? The old key or the new?"

Na Eleno and Om Bernat exchanged a long, silent look. Om Bernat nodded at his wife.

Na Eleno's shoulders drooped. "The first one, Son," Jaume's mother said in a low voice. She bowed, a little stiffly, in Doucette's direction. "It was made for the lock."

"So will I keep Doucette," Jaume said. "I lost her once, but now she is returned to me. I will not be so careless again."

Doucette's heart sang at the love that shone in Jaume's dark eyes. She nestled close to him. "Whatever form I take," she promised, "I'll always come home to you, beloved."